Holy Boy

Holy Boy

Lee Heejoo

*Translated from Korean
by Joheun Lee*

PICADOR

First published 2026 by Picador
an imprint of Pan Macmillan
The Smithson, 6 Briset Street, London EC1M 5NR
EU representative: Macmillan Publishers Ireland Ltd, 1st Floor,
The Liffey Trust Centre, 117–126 Sheriff Street Upper,
Dublin 1 D01 YC43
Associated companies throughout the world

ISBN 978-1-0350-7643-7 TPB
ISBN 978-1-0350-9327-4 HB

Copyright © Lee Heejoo 2021
Translation copyright © Joheun Lee 2026

Originally published in South Korea as 성소년
by Munhakdonge in 2021

The right of Lee Heejoo to be identified as the
author of this work has been asserted in accordance with
the Copyright, Designs and Patents Act 1988.

All rights reserved. No part of this publication may be reproduced,
stored in a retrieval system, or transmitted, in any form, or by any means
(including, without limitation, electronic, mechanical, photocopying, recording
or otherwise) without the prior written permission of the publisher.

This book is published with the support of the Literature Translation Institute of Korea (LTI Korea).

Pan Macmillan does not have any control over, or any responsibility for,
any author or third-party websites (including, without limitation, URLs,
emails and QR codes) referred to in or on this book.

9 8 7 6 5 4 3 2

A CIP catalogue record for this book is available from the British Library.

Typeset by Palimpsest Book Production Limited, Falkirk, Stirlingshire
Printed and bound in the UK using 100% Renewable Electricity by CPI Group (UK) Ltd

This book is sold subject to the condition that it shall not, by way of
trade or otherwise, be lent, hired out, or otherwise circulated without
the publisher's prior consent in any form of binding or cover other than
that in which it is published and without a similar condition including this
condition being imposed on the subsequent purchaser. The publisher does not
authorize the use or reproduction of any part of this book in any manner
for the purpose of training artificial intelligence technologies or systems.
The publisher expressly reserves this book from the Text and Data Mining
exception in accordance with Article 4(3) of the European Union
Digital Single Market Directive 2019/790.

Visit **www.picador.com** to read more about
all our books and to buy them.

Holy Boy

TWO DEAD BODIES FOUND IN AN EUNGRANG MANSION

The police have found two dead bodies while investigating a hostage situation that took place earlier this month in Eungrang, Gangwon-do. The victims were identified as Mr. Shin, 20-year-old grandson of the late Mr. Gyeongseop Choi—former Narae Children's Foundation Chairman and the mansion's owner—and Officer Seo, a 26-year-old junior officer of Seomyeon Precinct Police Station.

Further developments have added a third fatality to the Eungrang mansion hostage crisis: the now-deceased suspect, Ms. Lee, aged 40. There is also one missing person connected to the case.

'Are we good? Am I not too late? . . . Oh, no, I'm fine for coffee. I'm sweating buckets from rushing over here . . . . Haha, it's because I'm young? Thank you. It's my birthday tomorrow, actually. I should be celebrating, but, I don't know. I also feel a bit sad, to be honest. No, not because I'm afraid of getting older . . . But because it feels like I'm drifting away bit by bit from that crucial point in time. He was gone a year before I was born, and to think that over twenty years have passed since then . . . even as flames flicker on top of my velvety birthday cake, I can't quite force myself to smile.

That doesn't mean I'm always in mourning. I may have been a mere lump of cells back then, but I'm proud to have shared a moment in time with him, no matter how brief. You see, some people fall in love with a figure in an old painting while strolling through an art gallery . . . Compared to them, I would say I'm lucky. I dipped my feet in the same water as him, if only for a moment. Even if the history of humankind inevitably repeats itself, he is *the one* who'll remain unprecedented and irreplaceable. Well, how should I put this? Should I call it a blessing? Fate, perhaps?

You all think so too, don't you? You do still . . . love him, right? Him, the one and only? . . . How incredible. You, me. And him, too. I always thought wealth was the greatest inheritance the dead could leave behind. But the moment I stepped through that door, with your sparkling eyes gazing at me, I realized something. Wealth can't create or sustain the energy necessary to constantly look back on someone who has left this world. As old-fashioned as it may sound, love remains the only power that conquers death.

Oh, you're saying I shouldn't use *that* word . . . I'm sorry. No, you're right. Not knowing where his body is doesn't indicate that he's dead. I'm really sorry. Let's change the subject—what were you doing? You were looking at his photos. Your favorite photos. Which ones did you pick? May I look at them? Oh, I love this one, too. He was only eighteen, right? He still had his plump cheeks. His face looks a bit puffy with all the baby fat. And his front tooth is slightly too big, which makes him look even younger. His body is scrawny, flailing. He doesn't seem to know how to use his arms and legs yet. He was like that when he danced, too. He tried hard, but he still looked unsure, ridiculous, yet adorable.

Ah, that photo there is immaculate, too. It's late spring, after he turned nineteen, right? The flash went off because it was taken at night. His dry, pale face. That slight frown. With eyes sunken from fatigue, he is wading through the crowd, deep in thought. The trees are bent toward the vanishing point on the right, into the darkness, and strands of his hair are swept across his forehead in the same direction. His loose T-shirt reveals his slender waist. Whenever I look at this photo, I can really smell the era. The air of a late spring night in the '90s, an era I never actually experienced. The smell of something damp and cold. Of exhaust fumes left behind by cars and urban noise lingering like hallucinations. Of wet soil. Of chestnut flowers moist with dew. The acrid smell of fallen, decaying fruit. The sweet, heavy scent of chestnuts starting to rot. Now, close your eyes. And put your hand on the photo. You can really feel the wind blowing from behind him, standing there as pale as a ghost. Right? You can feel it, too, can't you?

But I must say, this is my favorite. The one taken when he was twenty years old. With his chin slightly pulled down toward his chest, his pale face is floating against the dark background as if he's half-submerged in black water. You can see his thick hair, seemingly planted by a skillful royal seamstress at his fairy godmother's request. His eyes, as cold and dark as the depths of the ocean, are looking straight at us. He was pretty skinny around this time, so his cheekbones stand out as if a potter's thumb has smoothed out his cheeks. His chin is also sharp like a cat's. A brown mark on his tender skin stretches from under his ear to his chin. The one as light-colored as a freckle . . . Yes, he had quite a lot of beauty marks. All over his face and body, as if someone had splattered him with ink. He said his moles made the makeup sessions longer and more exhausting, but I never considered them to be defects. They were more like flaws in Persian rugs, so to speak. Persians believe perfection belongs only to the gods, so they intentionally leave out a thread. That missing thread is what completes a genuine beauty.

Let's go back to the photo. There's his nose, tipped up like the toe of a beoseon sock, and below it are his lips, slightly parted as if about to say something. His lower teeth are as pearly as the whites of his eyes. Those eyes, wet and slimy like fresh sea-turtle eggs. Eyes that could easily be scooped up with a pointed golden spoon without leaving a trace. Eyes like pure white eggs laid by a blue hen. And his teeth are the exact same color. There are one, two, three, four teeth, as even and straight as fairies' gravestones. If the gods could grant me a wish before I die, I would ask for one of those teeth. Then I'd cover it in dried violet petals and put it in a locket to wear around my neck before I finally closed my eyes. Or I'd hold it in my mouth like an imperishable candy when I drew my last breath on earth.

But all praise is rendered meaningless next to his lips. The arched upper lip, and the plump lower lip. Softer than a fish's organs, those lips are smeared with ignorance. An ignorance oblivious of the cowardice that eventually curls an old man's lips. Ignorance is a privilege shared by all youth. Time, as impatient as it is, takes away their right to remain unknowing. But even as everyone else grows older and understands many more things like gloomy scholars, he remains forever a fool. That genuine ignorance is what brings me sweet sadness . . .

We're back to talking about his death. I'm sorry. I know you don't like discussing it. But it's also time to face the truth. I understand, you don't want us to sound like we're gossiping. But let's face it, who else would talk about him but us? Those who have absolutely no interest in him?

Those who pity him solely because he's dead? No. Let *us* talk about him, just between us. We're all dying to know, aren't we? Because there's so much that remains untold about those women and him. Or we could at least try to imagine. Imagining isn't a sin. We can invent a story amongst ourselves without telling anyone else. In the order that the gods created this world, let's set the stage and begin our story there. From the mansion deep in the rainy forest. Yes, right in front of the door of the small guest room where he stayed . . .'

Chapter 1

The wooden floor inside the guest room always buckled. Rusty nails barely kept the planks from falling apart, and the squeaking was ceaseless, day and night. The mansion was old, so it was natural for it to signal its age here and there, but that spot was particularly obnoxious. Even the temporary measure of an old rug was of no use, and the floor groaned in the slightest wind. Not even a ghost could get past it quietly.

Nami was the only exception. Her body, as thin as a twig, maneuvered around it like a well-trained snake. Her nimble hands were precise, and her expression remained unchanged even when cleaning up the patient's excrements. She never sweated, wore wrinkled clothes, or let even a single strand of hair escape from her short ponytail. Above all, her hands were always clean. With neatly pared nails, her hands bore no scar nor smell, as if they were self-purifying. No matter how nasty the filth on them, all it took was a gentle wash to restore them to the immaculateness of a newborn's. No smell ever lingered on those hands, which meant those under her care were spared from thinking about the biological tragedy that had just happened between their legs, distracted by the pair of soap-scented hands feeding them. Like her hands, Nami was a person of neither smell nor color. She came across as brusque, but any sensible person would know to covet her as an asset to the care for their gradually collapsing bodies. After observing Nami for ten minutes, even a child would think, *Ah, that's what they call innate talent—so there is such a thing as a natural-born nurse.*

However, the imagination of the restricted is bound to race toward negativity. The young man in the bed—or the boy, as the women called him—was no exception, so he interpreted her impassive face as a marker of apathy rather than consideration. He often imagined Nami as a machine, and wondered what might happen if her circuits went awry. As soon as the switches were flipped, he feared her cold, callous hands might pull out his guts as nonchalantly as they spoon-fed him soup. His delusion ballooned day by day, and the boy trembled in fear rather than in shame when he lay there face down with his buttocks exposed. Sometimes, he fought the urge to cling to Nami before she left with a basket full of soiled laundry. That way, he wouldn't have to dread her return.

The sharp shrieking of the kettle stopped, and for a moment the entire house fell shockingly silent. To shatter the stillness, the boy cleared his throat and deliberately shifted under the blanket. He could sense a peculiar presence outside the door. A pressing silence. The pressure, pushing its way in slowly like a tide, soaked his forehead with sweat—until a knock came at the door. Through the door on the wall crammed with hunting trophies entered Nami, as expected, carrying a new set of clothes for him.

"You should have called for me," she said.

"I thought you might be busy . . ."

He cooed instinctively, but Nami displayed no reaction as usual. With her unique gait that barely swayed her upper body, she approached the dispirited boy on the bed and laid her hand on his forehead.

"It looks like your fever's gone, at least. Is anywhere causing you discomfort?"

"No."

"Any headache? Dizzy at all?"

"Not really."

"You're not quite recovering. We should take better care of you. How about the toilet?"

This was a subject that the boy didn't want to talk about.

"You must have to go by now," pressed Nami.

He closed his eyes without saying a word. He imagined being at the beach for a summertime swim and relaxed himself. Even when she knew he had, Nami muttered in a monotone voice as if reciting a Buddhist prayer, "Now, relax . . . I'm going to pull down your pants . . ."

After she was finished, the room reeked of alcohol. Regardless of what had just happened, leaning against a pile of pillows in clean underwear appeased the boy. He felt an impulse to look outside. It would be nice to let out the headache-inducing smell of alcohol and inhale the fresh air from the forest. After some hesitation, he asked Nami to open the window.

"It's raining outside," she objected.

"It's okay. Just for a bit."

Without further comment, Nami unlocked the swinging window. When she put her entire weight on it, the window swung open all the way, instantly pelting the boy's bed with rain. The violent wind hummed loudly.

Flustered, the boy blurted out, "Wait, wait a second."

But Nami seemed not to have heard him as she tried to tame the window swinging in the wind. After struggling with the stubborn stopper for a while, she finally managed to fasten the window in place and straighten up. At that point, both she and the boy were soaking wet as though they had braved a storm. But unlike the boy, who was writhing on his bed, Nami just stood there upright, facing the forest like a robot awaiting its next command. The sight made the boy let out a weak moan. Fighting against the lump in his throat, he forced out his voice.

"Excuse me."

Nami didn't respond.

"Excuse me, Nami."

Only when he called out her name did she slowly turn her head around. The boy nearly yelped at Nami's bizarre movement, which made her head seem separate from the rest of her body. Nonetheless he managed to smile.

"Thank you, you can close it now."

At his command, Nami bent over again and pulled on the window with all her might to lock it. She seemed to have realized she was soaked only after hearing raindrops dripping on the floor in the room's stillness. After a long stare down at her own chest, Nami began to speak.

"It's raining hard," she observed. She paused briefly and then continued. "It must be stifling."

Only after a few seconds did the boy realize her concern was for him. Startled, he forged a smile with his trembling lips.

"I'm okay. I can't move by myself anyway. I'm sorry for causing you this much trouble."

Then he added under his breath, "If only I could go to the toilet by myself." He stole glances at Nami, but she showed no reaction. The boy plucked up some more courage and asked, "It's a nasty job . . . Aren't you tired of it?"

Still she remained silent, only shooting him an emotionless stare. Their gazes intertwined midair. The boy closed his eyes to sever the connection. The sensation of Nami touching him with her stare lingered on his cheek. He diverted his attention elsewhere. He focused on the rustling bedsheet, the mushy old mattress against his spine, and the soggy touch of his clothes sticking to his skin. Nami's gaze didn't vanish, but rather, became palpable. His soft hair felt ticklish on his cheek. He couldn't bear it any longer and half-opened his eyes. At that moment, something white flashed before his eyes, and when he opened them completely, he could see Nami had brought herself just inches away from his face.

"I should go."

The boy was at a loss for words.

"It's late."

Nami left him with that, taking an armful of dirty laundry with her. Only after she locked the door behind her could the boy be at ease. With a flushed face, he mused, *What did she do just now? Did she touch my cheek?* Even if she did, it was probably because an error occurred in her movements, not because she harbored any feelings for him. Did Nami even have emotions? He relaxed his cheeks, which had grown stiff from unconsciously clenching his teeth. With his eyes fixed on the closed door, it occurred to him that steel bars in zoos not only lock up animals but, perhaps, sometimes, protect the animals from humans, too.

Left alone, the boy wiped his face with his unbandaged left hand. He thought the room would have turned into a total mess, but only the floor had gotten wet, and the candlestick had toppled over. A relief, he supposed, but he didn't quite feel relieved. As he stared at the candle lying on the floor, he reflected upon his situation. He couldn't even set that small thing upright by himself. His current lifestyle wasn't so bad if his only goals were to eat and excrete, but he needed a higher sense of accomplishment than that. His rib cage was wrapped in bandages and his legs were tightly splinted like a toy soldier, but still. He was a human, after all, not a doll.

He had been sighing at the candlestick when the door opened and the floor squeaked. It was Mihee. She noticed the wet floor and gave him a puzzled look.

"I forgot to give you your painkillers . . . what happened to the floor?"

"I asked Nami to open the window," the boy replied.

"In this rain?"

He smiled silently, and Mihee let out a breathy chuckle. "How silly of you. You must be cold."

"I'm okay."

"What do you mean, you're okay? Were you going to spend the night like that? Summer colds can be harder to shake off, you know."

She approached his bed and pinched off the strands of hair stuck to his cheek, whispering, "We'd better . . . change you, don't you think?"

The boy gulped and agreed to the suggestion, and Mihee's hand began its work. The buttons coming undone one by one, and the feel of thin, wet cloth sliding over him like the peel of overripe fruit made his skin crawl. When her hand lightly grazed his nipple, Mihee blushed.

"Oh my, I'm sorry."

She seldom reacted so shyly, which gave the boy a thrill. His bony chest puffed out, signaling she could go on. But instead of drying his naked body, Mihee handed him a towel. Her gaze was provoking. Couldn't he do this much by himself? Mihee had never wiped or cleaned him before. But the boy still wished she would this time, as he rubbed his wet body vehemently to feign indifference. As he did, Mihee wiped the floor and windowsill. She straightened the fallen candlestick and drew open the curtains slightly so he had a view. Beyond the window was dim, and the boy couldn't tell whether it was day or night. He didn't really want to see outside, anyway. His gaze drifted to Mihee standing before the window. His bad eyesight allowed him to see only her soft, fleshly silhouette, but that was enough.

How beautiful. Staring at Mihee's long, lustrous dark hair, he thought of a fairy tale about an accident-stricken traveler marrying the daughter of a family who looks after him. If he were the traveler, Mihee would be his betrothed. She wasn't the only young woman in this house, but only a beauty could take on the leading role.

"Are you finished?" Mihee asked, turning around.

"Yes."

She dragged the chair closer to him and buttoned him up in his new clothes.

"She usually isn't, but Nami can be absent-minded sometimes," she smiled. "Please try to be understanding. She's still better than me, isn't she?"

"No."

"You don't need to flatter me. I don't think I'm cut out for caregiving. I always make a mess."

"I really don't think that way," the boy said in earnest. Really, he preferred Mihee over the other two women, who looked after him in silence. Mihee wasn't a skilled caregiver, to say the least. She would drop hot soup on his tender chest and spill water all the time, so whenever it was just the two of them, he would have to feed himself with his trembling left hand. Even though it wasn't easy to use his left hand, the boy felt most at ease with Mihee. It wasn't merely because he liked her. To do things on his own— Mihee seemed to understand that was what he needed more than freshly ironed pajamas and crisp bedsheets. As if to prove the point, Mihee missed a button on his shirt before she straightened his collar and handed him his medicine.

"It all feels like too much sometimes, doesn't it?" she asked.

The boy remained silent.

"But Nami is doing the best she can. Auntie and me, too. I know you must feel suffocated sometimes, but hold on a bit longer, okay?"

He gulped down the white pill and muttered, "No, I'm just grateful for you helping me when you don't even know who I am . . ."

"We're more grateful for you," Mihee said, enunciating each word. "We can't even go outside in this rain . . . We would suffer if we didn't have you. Looking after you is our pleasure."

Her face was almost comically serious. Her piercing gaze, slightly flared nostrils, and quivering lips were as delicate and beautiful as a small bird's skull. She was indeed different from the other two. She was incomparably lovely. As the boy thought so, he blurted out a question.

"You said the three of you are related, right?"

That was all he said, but Mihee seemed to know what he really wanted to ask.

"Yes. Don't we look like complete strangers, though?" She smiled. "It's because we all take after our respective fathers' families. It's almost uncanny how little we resemble one another when we're actually related on our mothers' side."

"Your father must be the most handsome among your fathers, then."

Haha. His compliment made Mihee laugh, which sounded like a tuberculosis patient squeezing a breath out of her lungs. A short silence followed. *I screwed up,* the boy thought, but his joke hadn't totally bombed—a hint of shyness lingered on Mihee's face as she pursed her lips to wipe the smile off her face. His blood boiled from deep inside as a masculine bravado shot upward. *Take her hand.* But the moment his instincts kicked in, Mihee sprang to her feet, swiftly, as if she had predicted his next move.

"Get some rest," she told the bewildered boy.

"Oh, okay."

He managed to raise his left hand like a gentleman. Mihee reciprocated with a smile and left the room with an empty water glass and the wet clothes in her hands. The boy lay down in his bed, the last sight of her leaving flickering before his eyes. The sweet sorrow of waiting for the next time seeped into his heart. He sniffed as he rebuttoned his shirt. Though everyone must use the same soap, Mihee's scent was special. It was nostalgic somehow. His heart always raced when he was with her, in a very good way. Surrounded by Mihee's aroma, he blinked his leaden eyelids and immersed himself in thought. A beauty and the two kind women who saved his life. Aside from the fact that he was injured and had lost his memory, he was one lucky dude. He knew this better than anyone. It was only because of his lack of freedom that he had nightmares of someone standing by his pillow . . .

How long was he asleep? The floor creaking woke him, and he could barely open his eyes due to the splitting headache. He spotted Ahnna, thin as a twig, walking toward him with an ingenuous smile.

"Are you awake?" she asked.

"Yes . . . How long was I asleep?"

"Well, for quite a while . . . You were so fast asleep that I couldn't wake you."

Ahnna stuck her tongue out. Awkwardly forming a smile at her childish behavior, the boy tried his best to ignore the strange ray of hope he saw on her face. He was afraid to admit it, but Ahnna was probably in love with him. Her gleaming eyes, hissing breaths, and cheeks sweaty from passion were the proof, and her thick makeup highlighted rather than hid the fact.

As usual, Ahnna set a steaming basin down on the bedside table and began to wet a towel. The water was scalding hot, and even a drop or two of it accidentally splashing on the boy would make him jump, but Ahnna was calm, as if she were gauging the warmth of a baby's bathwater. He stared at her in awe, only to be startled and quickly look away when he noticed her eyes were welling with tears.

"Open up," she said, her shrill voice making its way between the boy's alarmed heartbeats.

The boy unbuttoned and pulled his shirt aside, and Ahnna thrust the wet towel at him, her head hung low. She looked like a nauseated novice nurse on a battlefield, all too aware of the situation she was in. Her clumsy touch dampened his clothes, but the boy didn't complain. She would try to change him if he did, and he didn't want to show her his flesh. He was also afraid of how she would react to his completely naked body when she couldn't even hide her excitement at wiping his chest while he was still clothed.

The basic wash was over. Ahnna pulled the chair near and sat facing the window. The two silently watched the forest drenched in rain. Actually, only the boy was watching, but Ahnna was imitating him, acting as his shadow. She had been stealing glances at him, and at some point he realized her face had become completely fixed on him. He could see drool forming in her gaping mouth. Unable to stand the sight of water filling its small cave or her intense gaze any longer, the boy spat out the first thing that came to mind.

"It was an accident, wasn't it?"

"Sorry? What—"

"You said I was in some kind of an accident."

Ahh. Ahnna tilted her head at a vague angle, in neither a nod nor a shake. The day must have remained an unpleasant memory for her as well, judging from how the very mention of the accident turned her gloomy and reticent.

"Yes," she answered slowly. "I suppose you could call it an accident. Although I don't know too much about it."

The boy felt strangely reassured at the sight of her swallowing.

"How did you say I was found again?" he asked.

"You had been abandoned . . . abandoned in the bushes. It was in the middle of the night . . . It had been raining a lot then, too, and me, and my family . . . we carried you together."

"Was it a car accident? Or a fall?"

"I'm not sure . . . Car accident . . . Or was it a fall? It could have been both . . ." Ahnna trailed off before she asked, "Why are you asking that all of a sudden?"

"Nothing, just because." The boy hesitated before adding, "It's just . . . I'm curious how serious my injuries are, and when I can start moving again."

"It's better to stay put until your bones are completely healed. You're still having headaches, too . . . Is something bothering you?"

"No, not at all. Not at all . . ."

A scene of someone staring down at him by the bedside flashed through his mind, but he shook his head.

"I'm okay, really. Everything is just fine."

Ahnna nodded. "You should be patient. The most important thing is to regain your health. Everything else comes later . . ." Then she muttered, "The soup must be done."

She left and came back with a tray. The menu was the same as usual: white rice in a bowl, soup in a mug, and a glass of water. The boy was growing tired of it, but in his situation he couldn't grumble. He changed his mind and sat up straight, waiting for Ahnna to feed him. But Ahnna didn't budge. He looked at her curiously and found her staring down at the spoon with a serious look. Was something wrong? Just as he was about to ask, Ahnna sucked on the spoon as if it was smeared with honey.

"Mihee must have done a sloppy job at washing it," she said, laughing.

Then she spooned some soup and shoved it in the boy's mouth. His front teeth rang from bumping into the metal. His tongue pushed away the lukewarm spoon in reflex, but the soup had already trickled down his throat. He choked and coughed, and Ahnna quickly handed him the water glass.

"Are you okay?"

At the sound of her concerned voice the boy raised his wet eyes. The moment Ahnna's bashful smile filled his cloudy vision, he swung his hand, unable to contain his disgust, pity, and fiery rage. *Smack.* The water glass fell onto the floor. The boy was shocked by his actions and stiffened up. The sound of water droplets falling from the wet sheets to the floor was as clear and loud as an axe hacking at his forehead. Still in her chair, Ahnna bent over and picked up the glass. Fighting off the strange sensation of a caterpillar crawling up his spine, the boy started to stammer.

"I-I'm sorry, I just—"

Just what? Just thought that you were disgusting? That I wish you'd disappear? As the boy dithered, the spoon approached him once more.

"*Ahh,*" Ahnna made a sound, opening her mouth. She urged him, "*Ahh . . .*"

She had already cleaned up the mess and was spooning the soup for him again. She wore a composed smile as if nothing had happened. The boy was horrified, but reminded himself that he still needed these women's care. Ignoring the long, high-pitched ringing in his ears like a warning, he meekly opened his mouth. For a moment, he imagined Ahnna reaching in and gouging out his uvula, but the spoon only grazed against his tongue. He gulped the sense of relief down with the soup.

Once she saw his Adam's apple jolted, Ahnna asked, "Is it good?"

"Sorry?"

"The look on your face says it is. You're enjoying it."

"I think you're an excellent cook."

At that moment, a peculiar expression flashed across Ahnna's face. The boy felt his chest tighten, but she continued spoon-feeding him rice as usual. Next, water. Then soup again. Following the sequence of fluid hand movements, he diligently chewed and swallowed. The food quickly disappeared, and his nervousness began to wane. Ahnna finally put down the spoon. The empty bowl was clean, without a single grain of rice left. Lastly, she held out her hand, a white pill resting in her palm.

"Here, take this."

The boy contemplated the pill for a moment before bending over, like a bird pecking its feed, to swallow it. Ahnna's palm smelled of an egg boiled in hot spring water. It tasted salty and felt lukewarm, like a shallow, mossy creek in midsummer. He pretended not to see that she hid her hand behind her back, clenching it where his tongue had lightly touched it. He permitted her to feign checking if he had swallowed the pill, her finger exploring the inside of his mouth as if it was a remote coastal cave, trawling past his cnidaria-like tongue, teeth that resembled wave-weathered pebbles, and scarlet palate.

Only after hearing the lock click could the boy let out a long sigh. This tense atmosphere, this air, that resembled a recurring nightmare, always came with Ahnna. Did that mean it wasn't a dream? Did she really visit him during the night? If he stayed up all night, he could know for certain. He wanted to try, but lying on his back all day made him sleepy after eating. Whenever he tried to think about something, his head ached, and sleep as heavy as a sandstorm swept over him. The boy quit fighting to stay awake and immersed himself in the darkness and in his own thoughts. No, this could all be a dream. The mounted animal heads in the room were to blame. Having so many eyes, even if fake, surrounding him was bound to cause bad dreams. To have so, so many eyes staring down at him . . .

"It's because you feel stifled. You stay in the room all day long, indisposed," said Mihee, standing by the window.

It would have been nice to have some sunlight pour in, but the rainy scenery was hopelessly unchanging. Mihee stared at a pine tree with broken branches before she approached the boy and sat down by the bed.

"You haven't seen sunlight for a long time, that's why. Don't worry about it too much."

"But I've had a similar dream before," the boy objected.

"When?"

Every night, he nearly said, but he kept his mouth shut. He didn't want Mihee to see him as weak. But Mihee empathetically nodded as if she knew what he was trying to say.

"It's okay. Illness takes a toll on everyone. You've gone through a serious accident, too. Maybe having those kinds of dreams is good for your health. It means your anxiety has an outlet." She held onto his hand hanging outside the blanket, and added, "Don't worry. You're healing well."

A lot had happened between them, but she had never

held his hand before. At once surprised and delighted, the boy felt his heart stop for a moment. Pure love washed over his young cheeks like a warm breeze, but just as he began to savor her soft touch, Mihee squeezed his hand once and swiftly took hers away. Before he could stop himself, the loneliness of his empty hand made him blurt out:

"But—"

"Yes?"

But he didn't know what to say.

"Is there anything else you need?" Mihee smiled.

"No." The boy was about to shake his head, but then said, "I've just been wondering if someone is coming into the room while I'm sleeping."

"No way," Mihee replied flatly. "The door is always locked. And you know the bridge is cut off so no one can enter or leave."

"Yes, that's true, but . . ."

When his voice trailed off, Mihee frowned slightly.

"Are you saying that one of us is sneaking in?" she snapped, in a tone the boy had never heard before.

"No, not at all." He backed off. "I don't think that at all. I think I'm just a bit anxious. I'm sick, and it's rainy. There's a lot of taxidermy in here, too."

Only then did Mihee look around the room and realize what he meant.

"The interior design could be more soothing," she admitted.

"Right. I'm not saying it's messy or anything, but . . ."

"They're all nailed onto the wall, though, so we can't

take them off. We also can't risk moving you to a different room when you're recovering."

Mihee began a staring contest with a stag's head with giant antlers for a while, then muttered to herself flirtatiously, "It's kind of cute if you keep looking at it."

The boy couldn't even pretend to agree.

"Maybe it's just me," shrugged Mihee eventually. "Do you want me to hide its eyes, at least?"

She got up and pressed a towel folded lengthwise against the deer's eyes. A brief silence fell over the room. Neither of them wanted to say it, but the blindfolded head reminded them of a convict on death row.

"This won't work," Mihee sighed. "I suppose we have no other choice."

"I agree."

"Why don't you just deal with it for a while and we'll move you to a different room once you're better, hmm? And have your meal now before it goes cold?"

She returned and coquettishly moved the tray from the bedside table to the boy's lap. The distance between them was so small that the action could hardly be called "moving", but her rushing caused the water glass to rock back and forth. Startled, she tried to grab the glass with her hand that had been supporting the tray, causing the soup mug to slip. The boiling broth touched Mihee's hand, she screamed and waved her hand around. The cup and mug were flung off the tray with a loud crash. While the boy couldn't blame her for her reflexes, his blanket was soaked as if a water bomb had dropped. The soup shot up to the ceiling like an eruption, leaving sticky yellow spots all over the room.

Mihee turned to the boy. "What should I do?"

Did she just ask him what she should do? Her naive yet expected reaction calmed the boy down.

"Shouldn't you wipe it first?" he asked.

"Oh, yes. You're right."

Mihee rubbed at the blanket with a towel. The boy advised her to gently dab the smudge since she was only making it spread, but even as she nodded, she cluelessly flailed about without making much progress.

She soon put down the towel and sighed, "It's going to take forever to get this out."

Mihee's calves dancing in white soapsuds suddenly flashed across the boy's mind. While the images of her doing laundry delighted him, the boy decided to do her a favor. As he slowly flipped over the blanket with his left hand, Mihee gave a puzzled look.

"What are you doing?" she asked.

"I'm just going to turn it over."

"Why?"

"That way you won't need to wash it. I'll just pretend that I made a mistake and ask someone else to take care of it."

"Are you sure? It's going to smell . . ."

"I'll be fine."

"Gosh . . . Thank you, I don't know what to say . . ."

Mihee squirmed a little. She stared into the boy's face before leaping out of the room like a doe, bringing back with her a bowl of rice mixed with soybean paste soup.

"We made this for ourselves, but please enjoy some."

The boy had lost his appetite but still picked up his spoon. He wanted to put on a smile for Mihee, show that he was okay. But as soon as he put a spoonful of food in his mouth, his plan went awry. The soup was salty. So salty that it tasted bitter. His expression contorted as if he were in pain.

"What's wrong? Does it taste weird?" Mihee asked.

The boy gulped down the unchewed rice grains and lied, "No, it's so good. It must be because you brought it for me."

As if she found what he had said funny, Mihee laughed out loud with her snaggletooth showing.

"I must have acted too sad after making a fool of myself. You don't need to flatter me."

"No, I'm serious."

"Don't lie. It's a bit salty, isn't it?" she asked, then added, "Auntie tends to use a lot of salt. What about your usual soup? It's not *that* salty, is it?"

"No, it's fine."

"I thought so. I heard that patients need a bland diet. I gotta give it to Auntie, though. One time, I told her I'd rather cook myself, and she yelled at me for meddling with her kitchen. I've been putting up with her food ever since . . . But everything she cooks tastes so bitter, it spoils my appetite. And Auntie herself eats so little she doesn't even realize it . . . You could probably tell just from looking at her, but she has such a small appetite . . ."

The boy finished his food while listening to Mihee complain about her meals. She sloppily wiped the soup spatters from the floor and left, vaguely promising to finish cleaning later. Now alone, the boy leaned against the soup-scented pillow. The more he thought about Mihee, the more thankful he felt toward her. While she could be frustrating sometimes, he actually liked that she was frustrating. Mihee was a dimwit—the girl had the bedridden boy beat in that regard. She was beautiful, though not the kind of a beauty so cold that she wouldn't shed even a drop of blood when pricked. Rather, she was a fool with a voluptuous bosom and fleshy arms. As he daydreamed about his nebulous future with her, the boy concluded that humans gave birth to babies because they wanted to feel omnipotent over an inferior being. The soiled blanket and pillow bothered him, but he had gained a precious peace of mind, which lulled him into the most comfortable sleep he'd had in the past few days.

At first, he thought it was a cloudy morning, but it turned out he was wrong. Lying awake in the middle of the night, the boy kept still to adjust the time difference in his head. He mulled over why something felt off, only to realize that there was no sign of the dizzying headache he always felt when he woke up. Was he still dreaming? But the shadow that had been lurking above his head was gone. He was in a lucid state of mind, as if he had made it back into his own backyard after wandering in the foggy woods. He blinked. Had he woken up from a coma? Terrified, he wanted to check the date and time, but the room had neither a calendar nor a clock.

His thirst was so severe that it felt like someone had shoved sand down his throat. He was fumbling for water on the nearby table when he heard sobs. That in itself was bizarre, but the source of the sound was even more so. Unless he had gone mad, the sound seemed to be coming from the floor.

The boy calmly pulled back his left arm that he had stretched toward the table and tucked it back underneath his blanket. Then he closed his eyes, trying to shake off visions of monsters wearing the women's skin crawling out from under the bed and looming over his head. He didn't want to hear anything. All he wanted was dreamless sleep. But the more he tried to sleep, the louder the sobbing grew, and the more tense he became. Heat surged from his body. Sweat beaded on his nose. His tightly sealed lips felt like they would part at any moment to let out a yelp, his cheek trembled in spasm, and a huge drop of sweat rolled off his temple into his ear. He couldn't endure it any longer. He was going to burst soon. Like a heart after a race, like a balloon blown up with air, his entire body expanded, just about to explode, and then—

The weeping suddenly stopped. A cold and futile sense of freedom swept through every erect hair and open pore. The boy suppressed his sigh and waited until his body cooled down before slowly opening his eyes. Thankfully, it was just him in the room. No monsters under the bed. He thought he might have glimpsed a thin sliver of light under the corner of the rug in front of the door, but even that disappeared the moment he squinted for a closer look. Like an abandoned child, the boy blinked vacantly. What could that noise have been? What about the light? Was it all just a dream? Was he dreaming right now?

Deep in thought, he didn't get a wink of sleep until dawn.

Or rather, to be more accurate, he couldn't. While his mind was in a bit of a daze, his body felt like a canoe floating on the ocean of slumber. Gravity usually won over buoyancy, grounding his body in place, but not last night. Under the mounted animal heads' unclosing eyes, he drifted through the long and frightening night. Time crept above his skin. Writhing in peculiar anguish, the boy realized it was morning only after hearing someone descending the stairs. After a couple of knocks, Ahnna entered the room with a bright smile.

"You're up."

Her girlish voice dispelled last night's nightmare. For the first time, the boy felt grateful for his repulsive daily routine. Perhaps sensing his fragility, Ahnna seemed more cheerful than usual. The boy obediently entrusted his body to her hands to be washed and fed. Everything was back to normal. Really, everything was fine until he licked up the painkiller from her palm and realized that he hadn't taken his pill last night.

—

"Were you sleeping?" Nami asked.

"Just for a bit . . ." answered the boy.

Even a lie as tiny as that made him sweat nervously. He examined Nami's face. She wore no expression as she prepared his meal, so he couldn't tell what she was thinking. But the same was true for himself, he thought. If he didn't express them, Nami also wouldn't know his thoughts. The door to this room was locked on the inside and unlocked from the outside, but his mind could only be locked and unlocked by himself. It was a safer and stricter cage than anything else.

Nami was probably fresh out of the shower; her short hair was still wet. Droplets of water had left grayish stains on the shoulder of her white T-shirt. Below, she wore a pair of elastic-waisted pants. Her uncharacteristically relaxed demeanor intrigued the boy, but he quickly shifted his gaze down to his hands. Was it because of the bleak, rainy weather, or because she had showered in cold water, or—and this was unlikely—because she was aroused? Nami's nipples, which had hardened like a pair of red beans, kept tugging at his attention. Was she trying to seduce him? He wondered but soon expelled the thought. It was ridiculous to imagine such a thing. She was probably wearing comfortable clothes because she'd stayed home all day. Sometimes her indifference terrified him more than anything else.

The boy carefully opened his mouth to drink the soup Nami spoon-fed him. Stealing glances at her, he gulped it down much more slowly than usual. He had to avoid taking the pill one way or the other. But how? He racked his brain but failed to come up with a good gameplan. To buy time, he nibbled on the freeze-dried vegetables with his front teeth, soaking them in saliva, but the bowl kept emptying. Nami tilted the bowl to reveal its bottom and scooped the last spoonful.

"Here," she offered.

The boy wetted his lips and opened wide. He couldn't hold out any longer. With the pill in hand, Nami was waiting for him to gulp down the last of the soup. While her lips were tightly pursed, her eyes were asking, *Why won't you finish it?* In the end, the boy couldn't endure the silence and swallowed the soup. Defeat written across his face, he was lowering his head toward Nami's palm when a noise sounded outside the door. Judging from the hushed voices, Mihee and Ahnna were in the middle of an argument. *Here they go again,* he thought. The boy didn't give it much attention, the two often fought. But Nami's face hardened and quivered. All her attention seemed focused on what was going on outside. An opportunity. The boy quickly pecked the pill with his front teeth and hid it behind his tongue.

"All done."

He opened his mouth wide to show her, but as expected, Nami rose without checking to see if he had actually taken the pill. The door closed behind her, and the boy spat out the medicine and shoved it under his pillow. He thought of it as a kind of experiment. If he didn't fall asleep until the light in the living room went out, his hypothesis that he was being given sleeping pills rather than pain relievers would be proven true. If he fell asleep, then his hypothesis would be null. No matter the result, the boy was ready to accept it. Maybe they were giving him sleeping pills to help him get a good rest. Or they could have mistakenly mixed up the medication. Trying hard to ignore the fact that these very thoughts proved he secretly wished for the experiment to fail, the boy closed his eyes. He wanted to believe that the women who devoted themselves to his care in a secluded mansion weren't lying to him.

Before the boy knew it, the commotion outside had died down. A long time passed but sleep never seized him, and the more time passed, the greater his anguish grew. As he repressed the scream that kept crawling up his throat, he helplessly stroked his chest wrapped in bandages. The fact that he wasn't in physical pain tormented him. If he was free of pain despite not having taken painkillers, what did that imply? Were they really sleeping pills? *No way, they can't be,* the boy persuaded himself. He wasn't in pain because he was almost healed. He'd been here for many days. While he couldn't tell for sure, he had eaten dozens of meals, so it seemed to be a fair estimate. Besides, why would the women lie about his injury when they were going through the trouble of cleaning his urine and feces?

Just at that moment the door opened, and someone entered. The rug-covered floor creaked loudly as footsteps carefully snuck towards the boy's bedside. Seconds later, he heard clattering and scratching. When the sounds stopped, an orange glow came to rest upon his closed eyelids. Someone must have lit the candle to light the room without waking him. Feeling the heat licking his cheek, the boy wondered if that someone was the shadow. *Will I finally find out who it really is?* His stomach boiled with curiosity, but only for a moment. He soon realized that the shadow looming over him every night was different from the person currently staring down at him. The former was much more overbearing. The gaze fixed on him now only lightly caressed his cheeks, whereas the usual stare felt as heavy as someone sitting on his stomach until he couldn't so much as flinch.

Eventually, the shadow cast over the boy disappeared. The footsteps headed to the window, and soon he could hear the sound of scrubbing. The boy hesitantly opened his eyes a slit. A woman, presumably Nami, was crouching down to wipe the floor, but perhaps because of the candlelight, something felt different than usual. The boy quickly closed his eyes again before she turned around. Come to think of it, he had never seen the women cleaning his room. The thought of them sweeping and mopping it while he was fast asleep was oddly moving.

A couple of knocks sounded on the door. The woman rose from wiping the floor to open it, and after a loud creak arrived a short silence, eventually broken by Ahnna's subdued voice.

"Come out for a second. We need to talk."

"Can't it wait?" the woman in the room whispered back.

The boy nearly gasped. That didn't sound like Nami. He was sure he had never heard that hoarse voice before, which cracked on the last syllable. But Ahnna talked to the voice as if she knew it well.

"It won't take long. I just have something to ask you. Besides, now you'll get to see him every day."

The hoarse voice said no more but complied with Ahnna's request. There was a rustling sound as someone rummaged through the dresser, and the candle went out before the door finally closed.

The boy flashed open his eyes. As soon as he took a deep breath, the pungent smell of melted paraffin filled his lungs. He choked, trying to calm his racing heartbeat. He wasn't surprised, but confused. Mihee had said the bridge had been cut off. The rain had flooded the only passage to the village, which left them marooned inside the mansion. But if that was true, how could someone else be here? Had they lied to him? Why? And what for? Question marks hacked away at his head like sickles. A light headache swarmed over him, and clear water streamed down from his eyes.

The boy swallowed hard, consoling himself. He had been harboring so many strange thoughts—he could have just misheard the voice. Now that he thought about it, nothing about the situation was crystal clear. He was basing everything off a single sentence the woman in the room had said, and even then, her voice was so soft that he couldn't hear her properly. She could have sounded a little gruff because she had phlegm in her throat. Yes, that must be it. Her voice had croaked like that because she had a bit of a cold. The mansion in the mountains was cold yet humid. Even in the summer, a cold breeze could seep into the bones and make those with their guards down ill . . .

Having stayed up the entire night, the boy dozed off. When he startled awake, the room was pitch dark, suggesting it was still the middle of the night. At that moment, something caught his eyes like lightning; a crack of light shone below the rug in front of the door. He slowly sat up as if possessed. The taut bandage squeezed his chest, and after lying on his back for so long, even the slightest movement left him breathless. But that didn't deter him; for the first time since he had arrived, the boy sat at the corner of the bed all by himself. Then, as though he were about to dive, he took another deep breath and hurled a pillow onto the floor, flinging himself on top of it. For a moment, his vision flashed pure white, and a powerful pain like a steel straw pierced through the center of his heart. He clenched his teeth to let it pass. Thankfully, the pain quickly subsided. As if he was on a frozen lake, he used both his arms to drag himself to where the light was leaking out.

Even before he flipped over the rug, the boy was convinced. There was a basement under the room, and someone was inside it, right now. The buzz of a conversation came through the basement ceiling. He strained to hear it; two people were talking, but he couldn't make out a single word. Despite his hesitation, the boy lifted the rug slightly. A door connecting to the basement suddenly appeared before his eyes, just as he had anticipated. *Maybe they spread the carpet to hide this*, he thought. He lay flat on the floor and pressed himself close to the door crack.

He could faintly see inside the basement. Two people were hauling something wrapped in white cloth. It seemed quite heavy, since they occasionally paused for breath while exaggeratedly bending forward or resting on their knees. They moved out of the boy's sight, and soon grunted as if they were mustering their strength. Several splats and thuds, a long silence, and a short conversation followed—then the light suddenly shut off.

The boy quickly climbed back into the bed, still confused about what he had just seen. One of his feet peeked out of the blanket, but the tight bandage around his chest prevented him from bending over. Giving up, he closed his eyes and evened his breaths. Just as the sweat that oozed from his armpits came to a stop, someone opened the door and entered the room. She picked up the pillow that had dropped on the floor, and tucked it underneath the boy's head, as all the hair on his body stood on end. She pushed his protruding bare foot back under the blanket and left the room again. Once the boy managed to calm himself, he re-opened his eyes. The light seeping in from the living room had disappeared.

The boy was once again sweating profusely—even the light blanket on top of him felt heavy. His luck had helped him avoid getting caught, but his curiosity had swelled manifold. What in the world was going on? Why did they go down to the basement in the middle of the night? What were they moving? Why did the women go through the trouble of immobilizing him?

The only thing that the boy, who had forgotten even his own name, knew about himself was that he was a coward. *But it is now or never,* his mind cried out. As he went back and forth between hesitation and courage, he counted from one to a hundred and stared down at his feet. According to the women, those were broken feet. Bloodied, splinted feet. The boy hadn't questioned the women. He trusted their words about how hopeless it would be if his bones fractured further or his wound got infected since they couldn't go to the hospital, so he had never tried standing on his own two feet. But things were different now. He carefully placed his feet on the floor as if he were trying to toddle for the first time in his life. They didn't hurt. He rested his weight on them and took one step after another, but his legs and feet weren't painful at all. His right hand would probably be fine as well. His entire body quivered from the betrayal, but he had no time to be angry. *You have no time to waste like that*, the raindrops tapping on the window in a sudden gust seemed to be telling him.

The boy quickly grabbed the matchbox and candle the woman with the unfamiliar voice had left on the bedside table. He crept to the basement doorway and pulled back the rug. He shoved his left hand into the groove on the edge of the secret door and lifted it open—and as he expected, a ladder appeared, stretching down to the basement. He took a deep breath. Then he swallowed his fear and stepped down into the darkness resembling the gaping mouth of a giant beast.

The windowless basement was darker than he had imagined. His room, seen through the square hole above, seemed relatively bright in comparison. A flash of bad feeling that he could never return made him shudder. To shake off the hopeless darkness, he lit the candle and looked around. The first things that caught his attention were the taxidermied animals hanging on the wall, their glass eyes creepily glistening. For the first time since he'd arrived at the mansion, he was grateful to be staying in the guest room with the freakish taste. Otherwise, he surely would have shrieked and dropped on his behind. He didn't scream even at the sight of a corpse sitting on a chair, either. His heart raced madly, and his vision spun round and round. But since he had witnessed two people whimpering while moving something wrapped in white cloth, he suspected it could be a human body, judging from its shape and size. He had now passed the stage where he could appease himself by thinking that it couldn't be, that it was all his delusion. The women were dangerous, he concluded. The only logical response to that conclusion was to escape as soon as possible. However, as his heartbeat returned to normal and his eyes grew used to the darkness, he felt like something was off. He couldn't exactly put his finger on what, but the corpse looked strangely unnatural. Assuaging himself that he had to face the truth now that he had come down all this way, he dragged his feet, heavy with fright, and approached the body. Once his trembling hand brought the candle close to the corpse, he muttered out loud with relief.

"Oh, it's just a mannequin."

But the mannequin, its hands brought together and its head hanging low, was different from the kind seen in clothing stores. It resembled God's original human so much that the correct way to appreciate it seemed not to dress it in clothes but to leave it naked. The dummy looked to be somewhere between a boy and a young man, with pale skin and long arms and legs. Its lean torso revealed every single bone underneath the skin as if only a thin layer of cream was applied to it, but the body didn't look fragile, either. Its pointed kneecaps shone like ivory even in the dark, and its long, slender neck reminded the boy of a deer's. Its hands, on the slightly bigger side compared to the rest of its body, were extremely delicate, proving that the mannequin was a tool integrated with several advanced technologies. Even the finest muscles that would have been omitted in regular dummies were carved in detail, and its silky hair that came down to its cheeks was meticulously planted strand by strand. If the creator aimed to fashion an almost fully mature boy left only with the slightest hint of innocence, they had indeed succeeded—that was the only way to describe what he was seeing.

Before he realized, the boy had lightly placed his hand on the mannequin. The touch, much more slippery than he had imagined, made his skin crawl but enticed him at the same time. For all he could tell, whoever owned this exquisite creation must have paid quite a fortune to acquire it. It was only scaring an uninvited guest in the corner of the basement now, but it would make a flawless exhibit elsewhere. The boy mustered more courage and lifted the dummy's chin slightly. Its face, as expected, was so delicate that it gave him the creeps. Its reflective glass pupils were expressionless, but the thin lines and transparency of the irises were meticulously reproduced. Its slanted eyebrows and countless freckles, resembling sand grains stuck to an ice pop dropped on the beach, added a little bit of humanity to its face, and its left earlobe was marked with a piercing. The boy unconsciously placed his hand on the mannequin's cheek. Slowly, with a movement that verged on instinct, he slid his hand over its ears, neck, and chest, realizing that the dummy had been used to give pleasure to the women. The boy felt a visceral disgust as well as an intense pity. Only women lived in this place. They would have needed something more than a mere tool to devote their love to. Maybe the women knew that his bones were mended already, the boy thought. They must have hidden the fact and put up with the cumbersome nursing because they were too sad to say goodbye. Perhaps they had moved the mannequin to soon reveal to the boy that he was completely healed. They must have brought it here, worried that he would wander around the mansion like a newborn fawn and scare himself at the sight of it.

Staring down at the neat crown of the mannequin's head, the boy resolved not to dig further into the women's secrets. He didn't have to add himself to their list of disturbances when these poor women secluded themselves away from the world. They were disgusting, sure, but weren't they the ones who had saved him? If he waited patiently, they would reveal their secrets.

The boy turned around to go back to his room. Just before he blew out the candle and climbed up the ladder for the last time, he spotted a frame he had kept his back toward the whole time. He slowly started to approach it. In his dim vision, he saw what looked like a photo of the mannequin, but interestingly, it was grimacing, as if it was horrified by something, and holding a candle in its hand. The boy took one step, and then another, toward the frame. The mannequin inside it scowled more and more, until the boy stood right in front of it—then it gaped in shock. The candle fell onto the floor and went out, leaving a thin, long trace of smoke. The darkness engulfed everything instantly, but the image the boy had just seen remained in sight.

What was inside the frame was a mirror.

Chapter 2

[Dazzling ✫★ Stars of the New Generation]
I Will Never Leave Your Side Again

Your first concert last weekend at the Jangchung Arena was a huge success. It's been a while since you met your fans in person. How did it feel?

—To be honest, I worried about it so much. Would people come? Could I sell out such a huge arena? I was terrified. As you know, I've been on hiatus for a while. So when I saw the silver-gray balloons filling up the venue, it brought me to tears. Going forward, I would like to do better for those fans who came. Show something new that they've never seen before.

Something new—that sounds full of infinite possibilities. You're famous for writing your own music and lyrics while completely changing your style for every song. Many fans say they love you for your chameleon-like talent.

—I'm just trying this and that to find my own way. Things change so quickly these days. Many younger idols debuted while I was on the hiatus, too. Despite the situation, I want to maintain my balance and create what makes me me.

It's interesting that you said you're "finding your own way." Even with everyone's help, you'll have to fly solo in the end. Don't you feel lonely sometimes?

—I'd be lying if I said I don't. (laughs) This is slightly off-topic, but it still feels strange coming back to a dark, empty house and having to turn on the lights. I'm turning twenty-one soon, but I'm still a child at heart.

I suppose I can't not ask you this question. Given you're in your prime, are you dating anyone?

—My fans are my lovers.

What a perfect answer.

—(laughs) Nowadays, I think of my fans as friends, moms, and lovers. I'm just so grateful that they waited for me.

We now have a wistful wait ahead of us until your next comeback. How do you plan to spend the next few months?

—First, I'm going to recharge before working on the new album. Read books, watch movies. I need to fill myself with good content to make good music. Personally, I'd like to go on a trip somewhere without telling anyone. My manager would scold me for that, though. (laughs)

Click. The interior of the car suddenly sank into darkness. Ahnna, in the back seat, had turned off the dome light without saying a word, and Mihee, in the passenger seat, lifted her gaze from the magazine she was reading and spun around toward her. As she flung the magazine over her lap, its pages—well-thumbed from being read hundreds of times since last year—fluttered weakly. A few flies lost their destination and vanished into the dark like an ownerless herd of sheep. *Tsk.* Mihee clicked her tongue before she could stop herself.

But Ahnna didn't get mad. Instead, she warned her in a low voice, "Be careful, Mihee. What if someone sees your face?"

"Oh, sorry, I didn't quite catch what you were saying."

Feigning politeness, Mihee deliberately raised her voice and looked Ahnna straight in the eye, but Ahnna, either ignoring Mihee's provocation or from nervousness, replied calmly, "A car's coming toward us."

Nami reached over to turn on the hazard lights. Frowning slightly, Mihee looked where Ahnna was pointing. A pinhole-sized light was flashing up on the hill in the direction of the city. As it approached, it appeared and disappeared, forming a giant S shape that grew faster and faster until it passed by the three women. Mihee identified the vehicle almost immediately. A white convertible. Two young men and two young women. Deafening hip-hop music blasting away, and heat that gushed into the night. They were probably some punks who had met up and decided to go for a drive. To come all the way out here, so far even from the suburbs, meant they were probably drunk or high. Mihee glanced at Ahnna in the rearview mirror, expecting her to have a word or two to say about them, but Ahnna was frozen stiff, unable even to blink. *I knew it*, Mihee thought to herself sarcastically. Ahnna must have been shocked that the two young women were exposing their white breasts, as if they were mermaids from the ocean depths.

As expected, Ahnna muttered hoarsely, "Disgusting bitches."

But what really seized Mihee's attention were the red smudges on the convertible's front bumper and green number plate. Even with her eyes closed, the violent splashes wobbled in her dark field of vision, inverted into green. She tapped Nami, who kept herself deeply buried in her car seat as she turned off the hazard lights with only a stretch of her arm.

"Did you see that?" she asked.

"See what?"

"The blood."

"What blood?"

"Just now . . ."

Mihee clammed up. The shadow of a four-footed animal that had jumped in front of their car, which bounced off into the bushes on the other side of the road, its dark eyes open and its long legs twisted outward—those incoherent images flashed before her eyes, making her skin already suffocating under the seat belt prickle once again. She placed her hands on her chest and took deep breaths. She rubbed her eyes hard. She must have been mistaken about the bloodstains. The shock of hitting that animal earlier had left her disoriented. Besides, she wasn't in her best condition; she had not slept well for the past few days, and whenever she squatted to pee only a feeble flow like that of an old woman oozed out. Her eyes were sticky from mucus, and she waved her hand to remove the honeycomb pattern persistently floating before them. When she changed her position, her thighs let out a ripping noise as they separated from the leather seat. She tried her best to ignore the wild animal road sign, radiating like luminous paint.

"Nothing," she managed to murmur.

Nami looked away, her interest lost.

It was the first day of a new lunar month. The road was submerged in darkness. A brief shower during the day had ceased, leaving behind worms split in half on the road. The wet fog from the nearby river had drifted to where the women were stationed. Except for a few moments when the clouds scattered, it was completely dark without a single star shining. A drop of sweat trickled down her nape, and Mihee slapped at it to rub it off. When the chirping of grasshoppers suddenly stopped, the reality that only the three of them were left set in, terrifying her.

The same thing had happened when she had surveyed the place a month ago. That day, Mihee had been with a dumb college student who claimed to love her gloom and tried with all his might to get between her legs. She left the guy and went for a walk by herself but got lost. After wandering for a while through the wet fog, she spotted a rock and an old man with his fishing rod. "Any luck?" she asked, relieved, to which he pointed at his bucket. Inside were three carp as big as her forearm. "Quite the catch," she exclaimed. The old man started to rave about how his catches of the day were actually small and he would typically hook fish as thick as an adult's thigh. She wondered why the place wasn't teeming with people then, and the man said there were reasons. The reservoir was known for taking human sacrifices, and since a young man had drowned when the dam was built, eight out of ten tourists who wet their feet in the water died within six months, especially if they were virgins.

"So you should look out, too," the old man said, scanning Mihee from head to toe. *How interesting*, she thought at the time. She had forgotten about it, but now, recalling the conversation, she let out a high-strung, rageful laugh. Virgins, did he say? Did he mean unmarried women? Or did anyone who'd never been penetrated count? What about oral intercourse? Or anal? What if only one's body was chaste, but one's soul was absolutely filthy? Or the opposite? What about a virgin who declined all courting and decided to live alone, or a virgin who wanted to become a slut but failed? Could those two be considered equal?

"Are you okay?" Nami suddenly asked.

"I'm fine."

"You look a bit tired. Did you get some sleep?"

Mihee said nothing.

"Want a cigarette?"

Nami pulled out a crumpled cigarette pack from her pocket. Mihee took it from her.

"Did you switch brands?" she asked. "You have the taste of a middle-aged man."

"This brand's supposed to be for young women. It's called Virginia."

"So?"

"As in 'virgin'?"

Unsure whether Nami's remark was a joke or not, Mihee shook the pack to pull out a cigarette and nipped at it between her teeth. Nami reached out to light it for her. A deep inhale instantly cleared Mihee's head. She lightly rubbed at the inner corners of her eyes to bring her eyesight into focus. The road far away from where people lived was quiet like at dawn, but the dashboard clock showed ten at night. That meant about an hour remained until Yosep would depart. Nothing was wrong, but Mihee's mind was filling with anxiety again.

What if he didn't come? No, that would never happen. Whenever he was free, Yosep stuck to his daily schedule to a pathological degree, and that was why this plan had legs. But it was also true that everything had its variables. Rain was expected tonight and tomorrow, and the wet road in the night wasn't suitable for an enjoyable drive. He could change his mind and drive downtown, his car could break down, he could suddenly fall ill, or he could just be a bit tired. Mihee could name hundreds of other reasons why Yosep might not come. These thoughts weirdly relieved her yet agitated her at the same time. After all, Yosep had to come today. If he didn't, then their operation had to be postponed to next week, and she couldn't tell if her nerves could hold up until then.

Unlike Mihee, who couldn't voice her anxiety and only pretended to be relaxed, Nami acted convincingly like someone out for night fishing. She tapped on the steering wheel like she was listening to music only she could hear, her profile bearing no emotion. Even if she were flagged down by the police with a corpse in her trunk, she could probably assume the same nonchalance. And because of her composure, the police would tap on the trunk and bid her safe travels. All of this was possible because she was convinced that everything would go as she desired. Mihee stole a glance at her before looking away. Nami was indeed a formidable person. She created her own prophecies and made them come true. How could she fail if she just kept trying until she succeeded?

Mihee believed in neither saju fortunetelling nor prophecies. As a citizen of a country that had hosted the Olympics, she found such unscientific nonsense comical. But within ten minutes of meeting Nami, she understood why the wealthy ladies who came seeking her advice trembled before her. In a way, Nami had a charm that overpowered others. Charisma of a sort. So when she had said that today was a lucky day that might come once in a century, Mihee had been relieved, thinking that they could at least avoid any bloodshed. But even so, the woman was still a nutcase. Mihee clicked her tongue out of habit and glanced back at Ahnna. How could she ask a shaman to decide on such an important day? According to Ahnna, seeking advice from the gods was not optional but required. She wasn't wrong. For this kind of venture, they had better scrape together all sorts of divine power, whether it be of the Christian God or of Allah. Regardless, Mihee thought the ajumma still was out of her mind, and soon laughed to herself. Out of her mind? Who here was in her right mind?

Mihee recalled her first encounter with Ahnna, outside a broadcasting station. She had grabbed a woman who was about to get into a cab. The woman looked bewildered, and the cab driver, annoyed and in a hurry, yelled, "Aren't you going to get in?"

"Not now!" Mihee yelled back, and after shutting the door, she whispered into the woman's ear. "That's not Yosep."

The woman looked surprised.

"That's an empty car, and Yosep went through the back door. He has a magazine interview later."

Mihee regretted it as soon as she'd said it. She wasn't sure why she had just done that. She then muttered to the woman with a dumb expression like a goldfish, "Then . . . I guess I'll go."

This time, the woman grabbed at Mihee's arm.

"Um, you didn't eat yet, did you?" she asked, slightly panting for some reason.

Mihee was unsure what to say.

"Let's go. It's on me."

The two went to Rose, a coffee shop in Gangnam. They descended the stairs to the basement and opened the door with a stained-glass window in the shape of roses. Because of the cigarette smoke billowing from each table, the cafe gave off the impression of a torture chamber or a brothel. It wasn't just Mihee who mistook the place—a middle-aged man who followed them inside had asked how much it was per hour.

"Mister, we are not that kind of business," the waitress spat.

A manager in a burgundy paisley vest rushed out. He kept his expression purposefully stiff until he locked eyes with the woman, at which point he relaxed his face and bowed. The woman waved her hand slightly and headed inside. Whether it was faulty construction or intentional interior design, Mihee wasn't sure, but one corner of the floor was a couple of steps higher than the rest, with two tables placed on the raised platform. The woman sat at the table on the right and surveyed the room.

"Choose whatever, as many as you want," she announced, in a somewhat dramatic tone.

Mihee flipped through the menu in the candlelight. The velour couch that looked like it'd been upholstered with curtains you might find in a gym, the reproductions of paintings on the wall, the gawking servers—every aspect of this coffee shop felt cheap, but the food was preposterously expensive. After giving it some thought, Mihee picked shrimp pilaf and orange juice; the woman chose coffee. She raised her hand, and the waitress rushed over to take her order. Not too long after, she returned with a tray. Despite its fancy name, the pilaf was just fried rice served in a large bowl, but freshly cooked food held astounding power over Mihee. The aromatic smell of butter trampled the stench of mildew and cigarettes that had seeped into the walls, and Mihee's mouth watered instantly. How long had it been since she had a proper meal like this? Her jaw ached from salivating so hard, but as usual, she donned a bored expression and slowly moved the spoon. The woman half-heartedly wetted her lips with her black coffee before she cautiously asked, "How did you know?"

"Sorry?"

The woman blurted out in a choked voice, "That I was . . . after Yosep . . ."

"Oh . . ."

Mihee carefully chose her words while chewing. So, this lady . . . she really had thought Mihee wouldn't notice? When she loitered near the broadcasting station on the day of the music show? When she had clasped her hands and stood on tiptoe every time shrieks came from the front of the crowd, when she had smacked her lips as she turned around at the sight of Yosep's car leaving the broadcast station? She really had thought no one would notice her, when she had been doing all that as a well-dressed grown-up?

Instead of answering, Mihee asked, "Uh, you know that baldy, right?"

She was referring a girl who shaved her head and wore a Buddhist monk's robe. A lot of rumors about her had made the rounds, including that she was so obsessed with idols that her parents shaved off her hair as a punishment, that she escaped a gang after being forced to beg for money on the street, and that she was an actual apostate monk. But when Mihee had asked the girl herself, she had replied that the bald head was simply to grab Yosep's attention.

"That's . . . how much you stand out," Mihee said to the woman, who was now blushing.

"I see."

"Yes, you know . . ."

Because you're old. Mihee gulped down those words along with the rice. A short silence followed. With an ambiguous look that gave no hint of whether she understood what Mihee was trying to say, the woman changed the subject.

"Are they friends?"

"Who?"

"Those girls who always hang out around you."

"Sure, something like that."

"What about you?"

Mihee laughed. If the woman had been a bit more observant, she would have noticed that Mihee had been left out of the group's inner circle. When Mihee didn't answer, the woman didn't pry further and sipped her lukewarm coffee. At any rate, the woman was behaving carefully around her, and that made Mihee feel uncomfortable and proud at the same time. It had been a very long time since anyone had treated her like that. Or should she say it was the first time?

Since the woman seemed finished discussing what she had wanted to discuss, Mihee resumed her meal. The rice grains had already gone cold and stiff, and the yellow grease pooled at the bottom of the bowl disgusted her. She hated when someone struck up a conversation while she ate.

"Thank you for talking to me today," the woman said. "I was always curious, like, about where Yosep . . . went and stuff."

Mihee said nothing.

"I suppose you can't tell me . . . how you found out?"

Without answering, Mihee swept the remaining rice into her mouth. That was enough.

"Thank you for the meal," she said.

The woman reached for the menu and said, "Order something else, you must still be hungry." Her words made Mihee gulp in reflex. Her body yearned for warm, aromatic food, but the hunger and chill from her life on the streets that had welled inside her was overpowered by her pride.

"No, thank you, I'm full."

"You really should have more."

"I'm okay. I have somewhere to be."

"I see. Do you have to leave right away?" The woman fidgeted nervously before she asked, "Could I have your phone number, by any chance?"

"I don't have a phone at home," Mihee replied.

"What about a beeper?"

"No beeper, either."

"I see."

The woman scanned Mihee for a while, but soon smacked her lips, deciding she wasn't lying. Mihee awkwardly smiled while smoothing down her pants pocket with a beeper inside. The woman forcefully pulled up the corners of her mouth to reciprocate her strangely pitiful smile.

Overcome by a strange sense of sympathy, Mihee said impulsively, "Let's say hello the next time we see each other."

The woman's face brightened.

"Yes, let's do that," she smiled. "My name is Ahnna. Seo Ahnna. You can call me Ahnna unnie."

Unnie, my ass. Mihee snorted to herself, but in return for the free food, she docilely repeated the woman's word and replied, "Yes, unnie."

Who would have guessed *that* kind of meeting would develop into *this* kind of relationship?

After that, Mihee began running into Ahnna on the regular. Initially Ahnna kept her distance, but soon began to follow Mihee closely. Mihee later learned that Ahnna was skillful at getting what she wanted while being seemingly well-mannered on the outside. Whenever there were outdoor events, they could sit right next to the production crew without pulling all-nighters. Being young and dumb, the staff mistook Ahnna for a big shot whom they didn't recognize, leaving her to roam around backstage. Ahnna brought back autographs from a variety of celebrities. Mihee found them fascinating and cherished them for a while, but it wasn't long before the scribbled pieces of paper would be crushed under the audience's feet even before the event began. Yosep was the only thing that mattered in their eyes, and the problem was that his very presence rendered Ahnna's arrogant charm worthless. Even at the sight of his shadow from a distance, Ahnna stiffened like a pillar of salt. A deep shadow cast across her face, and the staff who had been bowing their heads and avoiding her suddenly began questioning how she had gotten there and called for security. Those in love plunge to their lowest place. Mihee learned that fact from none other than watching Ahnna, whose veneer crumbled in the blink of an eye.

"Did you fight with the other girls recently?" Ahnna asked Mihee while they were sitting in the coffee shop, which had become their safe space.

Mihee had been sipping kiwi juice, but the lighting made it look like she was slurping tasty mud. Did they "fight"? Ahnna's demure expression forced Mihee to choose her words carefully while holding the sticky drink in her mouth. How should she put it? It was more like . . .

"They don't seem to like me," she finally said.

"Why not?"

Ahnna's question was foolishly naive. Couldn't she just tell? Mihee also found it awkward to talk truthfully about herself and simply cocked her head sideways to feign innocence.

"How would I know?"

Ahnna didn't ask her anything more. At the center of the table the candle shimmered. The glass statues decorating the corners of the cafe reflected the candlelight in Mihee's direction from time to time, and a few men stole glances at her, pretending to watch the reflected light. As she tucked her long hair behind her ears as if in response, Mihee burst out laughing. The gesture reminded her of the girls who badmouthed her for her slightest movements. She pretended to be pretty, did they say? She wasn't pretending; she was born pretty. What were they going to do about it? She often disregarded them, but she couldn't fend them off when they swarmed her. They slashed at her hair and clothes. They smashed her face until it bled and swelled. Until the girls changed their strategy and began ignoring her, not a single day had gone by without acquiring a new bruise on her body. Mihee actually preferred to be ignored. Someone had described being ignored as an erasure of the soul, but lack of interest allowed her hair to grow and her cut lip to heal. The only drawback was that she grew bored. Maybe that was why she had talked to Ahnna that day. She shook her head to dispel the stray thoughts.

"Yosep smiled at me one time," she said.

Ahnna seemed to be at a loss for words.

"I'd climbed up a tree," continued Mihee. "Yosep usually ignores the fans up there, but that day, he must have been in a good mood, or maybe he found it funny that I was hanging like a piece of fruit, because he laughed. I suppose the other girls couldn't stand that."

"Why not?"

Again, Ahnna sounded clueless. *So she really doesn't get it.* Mihee rubbed at her soft cheeks with both hands and shrugged nonchalantly.

"Not sure. They just followed me and hit me from the back."

"Hit you?" Ahnna's eyes widened. "Gosh, why?"

"It's okay. I'm totally fine now."

"What scary girls they are."

"They're quite tolerable, actually. If you don't make mistakes in the order of your thinking that is. When you get beaten, you have to focus on that moment, and after that, never think about the past. This order is what's important. If it switches, you could go crazy. From feeling like it's unfair."

The conversation that day ended there. The two never again talked about what Mihee had gone through, but the conversation prompted Ahnna to take better care of her. Ahnna offered Mihee, who had been living homeless on the streets, a part-time job at the cafe and let her sleep in the small resting area for staff. The coffee shop turned out to be Ahnna's property. Since there were enough employees and Mihee was an "additional hire," all she had to do was scrub the tables or serve dishes from time to time. She wouldn't do even that much on the days she went out to see Yosep, but Ahnna didn't say anything. Rather, she seemed to encourage Mihee to do so.

After Mihee accidentally discovered that Ahnna was being beaten by her husband, their relationship became more relaxed. Ahnna seemed to believe that Mihee pretended not to know about her married life out of consideration, which led her to rely more on Mihee. But the truth was, whether Ahnna was getting beaten by someone or even beating someone didn't interest Mihee at all. Maybe it was different for a wealthy ajumma, but violence was a dime a dozen in Mihee's world. In fact, violence was what this world was built on. Mihee kept her mouth shut only because what Ahnna was going through was nothing to her, but Ahnna mistook Mihee for a dependable person and trusted her more as time passed.

That peculiar employer–employee relationship was what had led Mihee to this night. Well, she had nothing to lose from joining in on this undertaking. She had thought the ajumma had finally gone mad when she had first heard about it, but what Ahnna had suggested was what Mihee had always dreamed of doing. Everyone harbors a weird fantasy or two. It just happens that some people actually have the means to carry them out. Ahnna was one of them, and tonight, Mihee was going to be reborn as one of Ahnna's kind.

"Oh my, look—what's that?" Ahnna murmured.

No one responded at first.

"Must be a deer. Poor thing, crossing the road in the middle of the night."

"A water deer, you mean?" Nami retorted.

Mihee's eyes could see only the darkness. In response to the other women's apathy, Ahnna started to wave her hands in midair.

"Look! Over there!"

Are you absolutely sure you saw it? Mihee nearly asked. Instead, she repeated what Nami had said:

"You must be tired. Why don't you get some rest? You can hand me the phone."

"No, but really . . ."

"Yes?"

"Oh . . . It's nothing."

"Are you sure you're okay?"

"Yes," Ahnna nodded.

Mihee went quiet. She dug up an old mint-flavored chewing-gum packet from the glove compartment and handed it to Ahnna and Nami. Ahnna raised her hand to refuse, and Nami took one and put it in her pocket. Mihee raised her eyebrow slightly before unwrapping and popping two in her mouth at once. The minty sweetness numbed her tongue and made her salivate behind her molars. She gulped as she reached over to the car stereo.

"Shall we listen to music? It'd help wake us up."

No one objected. When Mihee turned on the system and set the radio station, a familiar pop song started to play.

"I haven't heard this in a while," she said.

In a gleeful voice unbecoming of the tragic melody, Ahnna asked, "How do you know this song?"

"I heard it on TV."

"Weren't you only in grade school back when the incident happened? You remember all sorts of things, don't you?"

Ahnna started to hum excitedly. Images of filthy, unkempt heads began to barge into Mihee's mind. The criminals who broke into a family's home and took them hostage in a standoff against the police. That was all she could remember clearly about the incident, and she couldn't recall how it had ended. What had happened? Did they shoot themselves in the head? Mihee stroked her own head, feeling as though her brain was spilling out of her hollowed skull. Cold sweat trickled down her scalp, but her long, pinned-up hair remained as tidy as ever.

Mihee stared at Nami, who tapped on the wheel out of sync with the song, grooving to her own rhythm. Mihee didn't believe in fortune-telling, but to calm herself down, she recalled what Nami had said. Ahnna, Nami, Mihee, and Heeae. Saju of the four women was under the strong influence of metal, earth, fire, and wood, respectively. Since Yosep's had water, the five of them were destined to help each other. So far, Mihee had never gotten the impression that they got along well together; something felt empty, perhaps because Yosep was missing. The same held true for today. Everything was going smoothly, but that was the very problem. If today were the day of once-in-a-century luck, if they were all indeed complementing one another, there had to be a clear sign. Without thinking, Mihee brought her hands together. *Please, send me a sign*, she prayed. But Nami only tapped on the wheel, Ahnna kept humming to the song, and the smudge like a bloodsplatter started to waver before Mihee's eyes again. The smear grew bigger and bigger, approaching the car they were in. Mihee rubbed at her eyes as if trying to gouge them out. Faster, even faster. Exerting enough force to almost squish the pair of round jellies into her skull, she tried to focus on this precise moment. All the while, Ahnna's ostentatious English pronunciation of the song further frayed Mihee's nerves. Should she say something to her? Tell her to be quiet? To please shut up?

Right at that moment, a couple of knocks on the window. Mihee lifted her hands from her eyes. The sight of a silhouette standing on the driver's side and the fact that it wasn't her hallucination sent chills down her spine, but her eyes glistened from the hope that this might be some sort of sign.

—

At a wave of the man's hand, Mihee turned off the radio. The man sniffed and swallowed his mucus. He gulped more of it as he pinched and shook his nose sideways, after which he blurted out, "Scorpions."

"Sorry?" Mihee replied.

"Isn't this by Scorpions? 'Holiday'."

"Yes, but it's a Bee Gees song."

"Did you say the Bee Gees?"
"Yes."
"Isn't it 'Holiday', though?"
"It is, but it's the Bee Gees' 'Holiday'."
"Do the Bee Gees also have a song called 'Holiday'?"
"Yes. That's the more famous one."
"Yeah? More famous than Scorpions?"
"Yes, because it was on TV."
"On which channel?"
"All of them."
"Yeah? How come?"
"Um . . ."

When Mihee's voice trailed off, Nami, facing forward, answered instead.

"There was a hostage situation that was all over the news, and one of the offenders played this song on air during the police standoff. A bunch of them took their own lives."

"Did they?" the man muttered, and this time, he spat onto the ground. Then, he asked as if he had just remembered, "Have you seen my deer?"

"What?" Nami asked back.

"A deer. Have you seen it?"

"We haven't."

The man let out a deep sigh. He had a bucket hat pulled down low and work gloves hanging from his waist; beneath his worker's overalls, he was wearing a pair of high boots and a thick plaid shirt. He leaned against a cane in one of his hands, his leg seemingly uncomfortable. Maybe in his forties? It was hard to tell, but he seemed around that age.

"Goddamnit . . ." he murmured, before he abruptly stuck his nose into the cracked-open window and sniffed around, like a deer looking for food.

"Cigarette," he observed.

"Excuse me?" asked Nami.

"Young ladies like you are smoking cigarettes."

Nami fell silent.

"Young lady, it's better to quit as early as possible," the man lectured. "You'll have trouble conceiving a child, you see. You might think you don't care about having children, but when you come to regret it, it'll be too late. What could a human leave behind but their children? The same goes with deer. Those who can't bear fawns are cheaper. I could still sell them to newbies who have no idea, but that's not how you should do business. In the long run, it's better not to lie."

He drew close to the car as if to smell the cigarette again. His eyes, almost hidden beneath the hat, seemed to flash. Nami didn't flinch. With a single, nearly closed window in between, their faces grew closer and closer, and then . . . a loud *thud*. The man had bumped his head on the window. Rubbing at his forehead with a low groan, he shrieked in anger and embarrassment.

"This isn't the first time you young ladies have come here, is it? What are you doing here, anyway? What are you up to this late at night?"

"What do you think we're up to?"

The man seemed taken aback at first by Nami's response, but then asked in a hostile tone: "Aren't you from the cult? The Deer Farm?"

"The Deer Farm?" Nami's voice was low and calm. "I've never heard of it. What is it?"

The man, dejected, began to whine.

"There's a cult called the Deer Farm located near here. I get calls about them all the time. I have to grow pumpkins and corn and cut grass, too, but answering those calls takes up my entire day. I can't complain about that to people who've lost their children and parents to the cult, though. I miss calls from my regulars sometimes because of them. I worked so hard to build up my customer base."

"Do you . . . sell something?" Mihee asked cautiously.

The man heaved out a deep sigh.

"Yeah, I have a deer farm. A real one. Before going to bed, I came out to see if they were doing okay, and one of them was missing. A buck that's only ten days old, he's gone. He's still a baby . . . So you're saying you haven't seen him, right?"

"No," Nami shrugged. "This is our first time night-fishing here. Our friend is on the way with the equipment, but she's running late."

"Yeah? I feel like I've seen you somewhere."

"You know how young people look all the same."

"True," the man agreed curtly. Then he suddenly seemed to think of a good idea and asked with a grin, "Are you staying overnight?"

"No."

"If you are, then my place is great. We also do bed and breakfast. My mother grows every single ingredient for the meals. I used to only treat the guests coming from far away, but after they raved about how her cooking was better for their health than deer antlers, I couldn't help but start the business."

"Thank you for the offer, but we'll be leaving soon," Nami replied, bowing her head slightly.

The man proceeded to stand there silently, his hand placed on the car's roof. He stole glances at Nami, who didn't shy away from staring him straight in the eye, until he sighed and turned away.

Nami summed it up. "What a total nutjob."

Mihee nodded in agreement. "Motherfucker, we should just run him over," she commented.

The two began to hack the man into pieces with their snickers and snide words, diffusing the tension in the air and strengthening their bond. Ahnna didn't join in. Weirdly enough, she was dwelling on what the man had called them. He had referred to them as "young ladies." That young ladies had come here in the middle of the night. Certainly Mihee and Nami were young ladies. But what about herself? . . . She wasn't. It was painful but true. Had the man ignored her existence because she wasn't a "young lady?" Or had the darkness concealed her wrinkles? If Mihee and Nami hadn't been in the car, what would the man have called her? After much thought, Ahnna concluded that due to the darkness, he had assumed she was younger than her actual age. If not, she had the right to step out of the car right now and smash his skull.

To calm her rage, Ahnna closed her eyes. As she did every time her blood was about to boil over, she pulled out the drug-like delights from her memory. Recalling Yosep's eyes that gleamed like glass beads, the wrinkles on the bridge of his nose when his face crumpled into laughter, and the soft flesh that connected his ears and chin overjoyed her, which then triggered a nauseating carsickness. Fighting against the lurching emotions, Ahnna covered her mouth and bent forward. As she nearly ground her head against the back of the driver's seat, her tears dropped to the floor. The only way to put a stop to this confusion was to hold Yosep in her arms. To caress his cheeks rough with stubble, to burrow into his armpit giving off confusing body odor. Otherwise, she couldn't stop this hunger, this nausea from her empty stomach. She pressed both her eyes with her palms and held down the refluxing acid.

The first time Ahnna had begun to yearn for young bodies was in a city in Central Europe. It had been a year since she had belatedly followed her husband to his Ph.D. program. Their new home was a studio apartment in a multi-unit building. The elevator had been broken for decades, and the bathtub was in the kitchen. On the first day she moved in, grunting as she climbed up to the fifth floor and thawing her feet by an old oil stove, Ahnna thought there must have been a mistake in the housing contract. But her husband told her that he had been living there for the past four years, and they would be living there together from then on. He wore only the old jacket he had bought from a weekend flea market, never so much as pulling out the leather coat that Ahnna's father had custom-ordered for him. He ate bread and potatoes without any butter or oil, and he commuted more than two hours by bicycle, or even walked sometimes. In the years that Ahnna hadn't seen him, her husband had grown gaunt and his face haggard, but his eyes glistened like a saint who found enlightenment through self-mortification. She had very much expected that. When she had first met him as a rosy-cheeked man, he had often worn an old man's expression and said enjoying too many things made him gloomy. The end of an era, the collapse of politics, the flourishing of capitalism—the landmines that snatched joy away from him were scattered everywhere. Once, Ahnna had loved her husband for that. She had felt guilty at first and feared that he might despise her for her vanity, and later, she had considered him cute for saying her expensive lingerie was awful when, in fact, he was helplessly captivated by it. The problem was that living as a married couple was completely different from dating or mere cohabitation. Ahnna quickly realized that her husband resembled the city they were in: they both seemed romantic at a glance, but in reality, they were antiquated, horrendous, and bleak. More than anything, they were unbearable.

Ahnna soon became depressed. She used the damp, cold weather as an excuse to spend most of her time in bed. She would lift her heavy body only when the setting sun cast its long shadow through the western window. Sometimes, she would belatedly regret wasting her time and rush out of the apartment, but by the time she reached the nearest riverside, the sun had long sunken into its cold coffin. She would then stare at the flowing water before returning home like a defeated soldier.

Ahnna started receiving money her father secretly wired her. She used it to purchase clothing from Gucci and Chanel and wandered the city among the tourists, who thoroughly examined everything with bright smiles that seemed out of place. She carried a camera and took photos at the same places every day. Old buildings, remains of a giant wall, parks, and bridges not yet reconstructed . . . Her day ended around dusk when the tourists left her, alone. They never struck up a conversation with her, let alone asked her to join in their photos. Perhaps her face was too ridden with the exhaustion of a resident to talk to in good cheer.

One day, when she was standing alone under the bridge, facing the wind blowing from the river, someone struck her on her arm. A mugger? When she looked around to see who had hit her, she dropped the camera she was holding into the water. (Later, when she looked back on that moment, Ahnna thought she had hurled the camera into the river herself. In other words, she had unconsciously chosen to do it so that she could commit the boy's face forever only in her memory.) Before she could even feel bad about the loss, the camera sank into the water. But that wasn't what mattered.

The person who had struck her arm was a boy one might find in a Raphael painting. Unlike one of Raphael's subjects, though, he was scrawny in a nylon jacket, jeans worn shiny at the seat, and an old pair of military-style boots (maybe they were real military boots; Ahnna didn't know much about teens' clothes), all suitable for a twentieth-century boy. He looked malnourished even at a glance. The dirty blond hair covering his slender neck was tangled and matted, and a loose worn-out T-shirt revealed his bony chest full of freckles. His cheeks were coral-red, not from health but from being chapped by the cold. As Ahnna stood speechless before the boy's icy ocean-blue eyes, he started to speak.

"What did you just say?" Ahnna asked, bewildered. The boy looked straight into her eyes and said it again while caressing her palm with his fingernail. Ahnna's face flushed instantly. She stuttered, her tongue stiff and near-convulsing, before she could shake the boy's hand off and flee the scene.

Back at home, Ahnna immersed herself in hot bathwater and her thoughts. She had heard rumors that boys from the Eastern Bloc engaged in prostitution near the Central Station in exchange for a burger from McDonald's. She had thought it was an urban myth mocking the fall of communist ideology and never imagined it to be true. The boy had probably seen her camera and taken her for a wealthy Japanese tourist. But she lived there. She didn't want to get herself into an embarrassing mess. Ahnna kept clicking her tongue without realizing the bathwater was growing cold. *The world is seriously becoming a strange place . . .* But against her will, her hand was gradually heading down and down.

The next day, Ahnna went back under the bridge. After meeting the boy again, she sternly gave him a few instructions. To clean his teeth. To clip his nails. To wash his member. Ahnna became the boy's regular customer.

His name was Josef. Since Josef had no phone number, every time they parted could be the last. Meeting with him granted Ahnna sweet uncertainty. Ambiguity and agony. The tension that the police could kick the door in and raid them at any moment. A sharp pleasure, a sensation like snatching up a boutique's new seasonal product that everyone coveted, shot through her spine. Ahnna felt alive only when she met Josef. He was the sun, and she stole his light from him. Even if he was too hot and burned her, it'd be okay. Josef was worthy enough for her to fling herself into destruction. Tamed under Ahnna, he was no longer a filthy animal. He still laughed like a child and didn't mind soiling his small mouth in exchange for Levi's jeans and Nike sneakers, but his face started to exhibit a melancholy that drew women's attention. In a few years, he might become famous as a model or an actor. Ahnna dreamed of such a future. Her delusion was sweet yet cruel, and she vaguely envied the things that hadn't even happened. But as a brave adult, she had to watch Josef growing up. Their farewell would be beautiful, but maybe, just maybe, it would never happen—forever. From some point on, Ahnna began to ponder words like that. Those words that couldn't exist between them, like "forever."

The time to say goodbye always arrives. When Ahnna and her husband returned to Korea shortly after parting ways with the boy, she was awarded a peaceful middle-class life in exchange for love. A spacious high-rise apartment overlooking a river and a high-end imported automobile. Her husband no longer imitated poverty; the conversion was quicker than turning his hand over. Ahnna also decided to put everything behind her and faithfully play the role of housewife. She grew tropical plants on the balcony and flipped through interior design magazines in search of a living room similar to yet different from her neighbors'. The story about a bar with male hosts she had heard at a housewives' gathering was tempting, but she never went. Because those men weren't Josef. They were filthy. Her telephone and tables were dressed and undressed in knitted lace. Yellow goldfish were flushed down the toilet. Flowers in vases withered away, and ingredients in the refrigerator, beautifully organized like a Japanese garden, slowly decayed, untouched. Other than being childless, Ahnna and her husband were picture-perfect. Even though that picture was a subversive one in which the painter had hidden secrets, they were a happy couple. On the outside, at least.

Then, at a friends' summer gathering, Ahnna met the boy again. Of course, he was a different boy, with only his name similar to the blond Josef. But he also possessed blessed beauty and had several moles, and his face was saturated with peculiar melancholy. Only when she heard that he was adopted did she realize the source of his sadness. "Poor thing," Ahnna whispered to her friend who had brought the gossip. She thought the boy needed another adult on whom he could rely and wished to be that adult herself. She approached the boy through his adoptive parents. Neither the couple nor the boy suspected her, but Ahnna herself was aware of the twisted desire settled deep inside her heart.

"What if that bastard saw us?" Mihee abruptly asked. After the bouts of laughter had passed, she had been listening to the music. "Our faces. He must have seen us. What if he starts talking later?"

"It's okay, it's dark," Nami replied. "He was blind, too."

"Really?"

"Yes. I looked at him up close, right? His eyes were cloudy. He wasn't holding a flashlight or anything when he came out at this time of night, right? He only had a cane."

"Oh, so it's not like he had a limp."

"If it'll make you feel better, how about we go up the hill for a moment?" Nami suggested. "We have to go up at least once. What do you think, Ahnna?"

Ahnna didn't respond.

"Ms. Ahnna?"

Only when Nami called again did she react: "Huh?"

"What should we do? Should we move?"

"Do whatever you like."

"Then let's go up the hill."

Nami turned on the ignition. The car with three women moved slowly. Ahnna stared at the mountain as it approached them. Unsurprisingly, halfway up the hill was a deer emitting yellow light from its eyes. A snow-white stag with massive antlers and a glistening body was strolling in the dark mountains. By itself, ever so lonely . . .

Unsurprisingly, the boy was lonesome. Yosep had no affection for the family who had adopted him as an adolescent. Yet he felt rather comfortable around Ahnna, a complete outsider. Taking advantage of her status as the family's acquaintance, Ahnna gave the boy private tutoring for the rest of his summer vacation. The two often met at the fast-food joint near her house. Teaching and learning were set aside, and Ahnna devoted most of her time to listening to the boy's anguish, as they sat on those hard red plastic seats. Even then, her mind was teeming with other thoughts. She let his words slip out of one ear while mapping constellations of the moles on his nape, visible under his T-shirt. Completely unaware, the boy tore down the wall to his mind in front of Ahnna.

As with every kid his age, Yosep thought only about himself, to Ahnna's tedium. He behaved like the world's only orphan and instilled life into his own pain without realizing it. What he had gone through wasn't even worth turning into a trite soap opera. Neither was his dream of wanting to become a singer or finding his mother once he succeeded. But while his backstory was banal, that didn't mean Ahnna wasn't affected by it. Yosep was the only thing in her world, and Yosep's pain colored her world. The pain that others experienced was as meaningless as explosions in nameless cities. The world she'd known before Yosep was as good as non-existent. An angel who fell from the sky without history. That was who Yosep was. Ahnna felt like life itself had only begun when she first met Yosep.

One day, her pity and love mingled and swelled to the point of bursting. They had only one lesson left before Yosep was to return to the United States for the new semester. Though Ahnna had secretly been anticipating some kind of event that would trigger some tension, nothing had happened between them. Using their last lesson as an excuse, she invited Yosep to her home. The bell rang, and the boy entered hesitantly. Ahnna hid her excitement. She had no motivation whatsoever to teach him, but she led the lesson calmly and rather strictly. Sensing the strange tension in the room, Yosep also said nothing. The short lesson was over. Ahnna quickly got to her feet and served him a glass of orange juice.

"Have dinner before you leave. Food's all ready," she said.
"I think I should go."
"It's okay. I've already talked to your parents."

Ahnna slipped on an apron and went to the kitchen. Unable to refuse, Yosep sat on the living room couch, his hands folded together. Ahnna craned her neck and talked to him in between her prepping.

"Does your family often cook at home?"
"No. The housekeeper cooks for us, and if not, we eat out."
"Oh yeah? We usually cook at home."
"Do *you* cook, Miss?"
"Yes."
"I envy your husband. When I grow up, I'm going to marry someone who cooks well. That makes a house feel more like home, don't you think?"
"Yeah?"

Ahnna responded quite bluntly, but when she turned around, her face was smeared with peculiar joy. After lining up her signature California roll in a long dish with artistic dashes of mayonnaise, she brought it to the living-room table along with a bowl of salad. As Yosep expressed his admiration, she poured him a glass of non-alcoholic champagne.

"Do you like fusion dishes, too?" she asked.

Yosep quickly emptied the glass and nodded with a smack of his lips.

"I eat fusion a lot. There aren't many Korean restaurants where I live, so I end up having Japanese when I want to eat rice."

"It won't be as exactly the same as what you've had in Boston. I made it in my own way. I hope you like it."

"Looks yummy. It has a nice shape, too. Did you say you majored in art?"

"Sculpture," Ahnna smiled wryly. "It's been a long time since I worked on anything, though."

"That's so cool. Your skills shine even in cooking."

Yosep gathered his hands together to show thanks for the food and picked up his chopsticks. Perhaps he had become sloppy with his chopsticks after his time in the States, or perhaps Ahnna didn't roll up the maki tightly, but for whatever reason, the piece that Yosep picked up came undone before it reached his mouth. Avocado, cucumber, and crab meat mixed with mayonnaise fell on his white T-shirt.

"Oh!" Yosep cried.

Ahnna grabbed some tissue for the flustered boy. While he was scrubbing the mayonnaise off his clothes, she went into the bedroom and brought out one of her husband's T-shirts.

"Take it off. Here's something you can change into."

"It's okay."

"No need to be modest."

Yosep hesitantly took the new shirt and stood up. He seemed to contemplate whether he should go into a different room but, encouraged by Ahnna's nonchalant expression, he began to take off his T-shirt in the sepia sunset. As if conflicted between a child's innocence, a boy's shyness, and a young man's boldness, he kept his torso slightly twisted away from Ahnna. The posture emphasized his scrawny ribs and the diagonal stretch of his abdominal muscles. Ahnna was impatient and made a classic mistake: she hugged the boy's back, which was studded with moles like a starry summer night's sky.

"Wait," Ahnna panted, drooling on Yosep's back without realizing it. "Wait, wait, wait."

Her hand went downward. Then Yosep's body broke out of its stiffness and quivered, and a strong force immediately pushed her to the floor. Looking up at his unreadable face, obscured by the sunlight behind him, she prepared herself for name-calling. In fact, she secretly looked forward to it. But Yosep neither yelled at nor criticized Ahnna. With darkened eyes, he simply said: "I . . . thought of you like my own mother, ajumma."

And he ran away from her.

Not long after, Yosep returned overseas. What had happened was kept secret from his adoptive parents, and Ahnna didn't reflect on it, either. The incident bore something more embarrassing than romantic failure. Like some sort of detonator that shouldn't be touched—was that what she should call it?—she kept that memory buried. With no Yosep to light the fuse, what had happened that day could have remained an unexploded bomb.

Two years later, when she met Yosep again, he was on

television. He had become a singer like he had always dreamed and had received lots of love—the kind of love that crossed into fanaticism. Yosep received girls' overflowing yet aimless energy with his entire body. He acted like a saint. He said he loved each and every one of the girls, who from up on stage looked like countless dots scattered throughout the stadium. And he meant it. But there are multiple types of love, and inside, he was just your average boy.

Just last year, a dating scandal broke out involving Yosep and another idol member. Both sides denied the allegations, but the fans must have taken them for fact and attacked the female idol. Ahnna watched everything from a distance. She felt neither disappointment in Yosep nor hatred toward the girl, only inexplicable displeasure. To find its source, she rewatched the variety show episode where the two had supposedly met each other for the first time. Standing next to each other on the screen, Yosep and the girl were like a pair of deer with their fair skin and long necks. The two never faced each other. But for just a moment, Yosep stole a glance at the girl while laughing at someone's joke, and Ahnna didn't miss it. With the frame paused on the screen, she sat in front of the TV for a while. Finally, in the bluish light of dawn, she shed streams of tears with sore eyes and admitted it to herself. When he gazed at the girl, Yosep's eyes were so warm. They looked so unlike the cold gaze she had received after she had suddenly hugged him after their last lesson. For the first time, Ahnna recalled and reflected on what had happened that day. And while leaving deep scars on herself, she plucked out a thorn that had been bothering her ever since. *I thought of you like my own mother, ajumma.* Yes, that's what he had called her: ajumma, a woman who looked married and middle-aged. Ahnna remembered the disgust that had quickly flickered across Yosep's eyes when he had spat out the word.

No one had ever called Ahnna that before. Most people she met respected her. Not because she was rich or had graduated from a prestigious college, but because she was a woman. With Yosep, it was the opposite. She could be respected as an adult or a tutor, but she couldn't be a desirable woman in his eyes.

The exhaustion from having stayed up all night was weighing on her, and Ahnna went into the bathroom. The woman under the sharp, white light, with the ashy skin and gaunt face, wasn't the young and beautiful Ahnna. It was a being that time had noiselessly weathered away. An *ajumma*.

After wandering the streets for a while, Ahnna went to the river. On an excessively wide and long bridge, she had only one thought. That she wanted to die. That she wanted to throw herself into the gray, gloomy water. She felt like she could be reborn if she could immerse herself in the roiling stream. She might become milky-white again, like a lamb pulled out of a boiling cauldron. But she didn't let herself fall to the river bottom. Yosep held her back at the last moment. Even if she were to go, she had to embrace him, Yosep, one last time. When she arrived at that thought, Ahnna scoffed at herself. Embrace Yosep? There was no way she could achieve that unless she kidnapped him or something. Yes, unless she kidnapped him . . .

Nami slowed down and on the hilltop stopped the car at the roadside. The wet fog had not reached that point, and they could clearly see the light from the faraway village between the mountains. The women enjoyed the nightscape for a while.

"Romantic, right?" Nami muttered to herself.

Ahnna nodded, but she thought it wasn't as beautiful as the orange sunset slowly falling upon the city on that long-ago evening, or the countless moles her eyes had traced on the boy's back while relying on that faint light. That beauty was at a place as unreachable as the stars, but not anymore. Tonight, she was going to pull down a star. The star was either hot like ice or cold like fire, so the moment she embraced it, she would evaporate. She would be as frozen as a rock and shatter into pieces. But no matter. She was already a dead woman. She had been a living corpse ever since the day she threw something off the bridge.

Nami left the car and spread out her arms as if inhaling the evening air with her entire body. At the sight, Mihee turned around to the back seat.

"Unnie," she called. "Ahnna unnie."

"Hmm?"

"It's not your fault. Things happen while you drive."

Ahnna remained silent.

"It was just a water deer," Mihee continued. "People hunt them, too. Running over one by mistake is not a big deal."

"Yes, thank you." Ahnna said, smiling broadly.

No matter how much they had been through, kids were just kids. Babies she could wheedle down to their bones. She nearly choked up from the affection she felt toward her naive accomplices. Yes. Whatever happened later, tonight, they were a team. But why wasn't she hearing anything from Heeae? Ahnna bit her nail. She wanted to pluck out her heart, noisily beating as if it were the only organ left in her body, and soak it in the cold river. But as always, she strained her legs and assumed good manners. Recollecting the scattered moles on Yosep's body against the light beyond the open window, she felt she was alive, truly alive.

—

The old man was in a deep, calm sleep. The light on the ceiling was subtle, and the damp night air flowing in through the open window carried a strong smell of soil. Heeae remembered how she had put her baby to sleep one evening a long time ago. She and her child had lived in a rented room in an old colonial Japanese house located at the corner of a bustling market. The specialty of a poor neighborhood is noise: the noise of something breaking, drunkards shouting, and dogs barking had intermingled under the moonlight and showered down all night, but the child had never woken up. Heeae had drowsed with her finger placed underneath her son's nose. While going back and forth between her dreams and reality that night, she had learned that it was possible to grow anxious from loving too much.

But now, the one lying beside her with their mouth open

was not a child but an old man. Peering inside his mouth, which looked like an arid limestone cave, Heeae pictured herself at the man's age. Perhaps they wouldn't be too different. Everyone was bound to become lonely and immobile in the late stages of their lives. But the old man had a lot of money, while she didn't. The man had her next to him, but when Heeae started to have difficulty moving, she would be lucky to get help once a week from an unkind care worker who would pray for the pesky old granny to die already. The thought weighed heavily on her heart. Dying at the right time was also a blessing. Barely dragging your life out was no good for anyone. *Things were better in the past*, Heeae muttered to herself. Times when the aged would dress in their best clothes, finish their meal, and be carried on a jige pack frame up to the snowy mountain to wait for their last moment alone. And the one who shouldered the jige would be . . .

Heeae got up from the bed and headed to her room. After closing the window, she pressed her forehead against the cold glass and stared outside for a while. The mansion she was in was located on the very top of a hill in an affluent neighborhood and offered a view of the entire downtown area of Seoul. Once just a vast sandy field, the riverside had been transformed into a public park that beckoned happy families. Whenever she spotted people yachting under the midday blue sky, Heeae supposed that was what a carefree life looked like. Unlike her, who had lost everything, they had so much clutched in their hands and knew how to laugh. Heeae lifted only the corners of her mouth when brushing her teeth three times a day.

She liked that the old man was rich, at least. His mansion had a staircase that spiraled up like a cochlear duct, chandeliers that gleamed even without the lights on, and old pine trees boasting peculiar vigor scattered across the garden. Heeae felt like she was working on a film set. There wasn't much time left until filming would wrap, and she had to perform the most complicated scene in the movie before returning to her daily life. Until the director called "Cut!", she had to put up with sweeping and mopping this giant mansion, with the old man surveilling her from the second floor, inhaling the sour odor emitted from behind her ear as he fondled his crotch. If the actress woke up from the dream, everything would be over. Sometimes, like the veteran of life that he was, the old man would attempt to draw out Heeae's real emotions. He would deliberately soil the clothes he had just changed or knock over his meal to get on her nerves. When Heeae played along and improvised, by flinging a towel on the floor or slamming a rice bowl on the table, the man would smile in a way that only the two of them could recognize. He was a villain that any director would covet. He was wise, knew how to control the scene, and sometimes would conjure mild sympathy from the audience. But even a man such as him didn't know this: from some point on, Heeae began wanting to strangle him even after the camera went off.

Heeae thought back to the previous winter when she had first met the old man's daughter. The appointment was at 3 p.m., but the woman didn't show up at the cafe until after half-past three. As she took off her gloves and lit her cigarette, she glared at Heeae and did not even glance at the menu the staff offered. Her face bore an odd annoyance as if it was all Heeae's fault that the interview was delayed. Or was it just her eyebrows drawn too high up that gave that impression? Heeae sat up straight and donned a smile, but the woman only slightly pulled up her quivering lips. After puffing smoke for a while with an icy expression plastered to her face, she must have finally made up her mind.

"Ms. Kim Boksoon," she said abruptly.

"Yes," Heeae replied to her fake name.

"You're younger than I thought. I imagined you'd be over sixty."

"I'll be forty this year."

"I heard you've worked for over twenty years."

"Yes. I've been working since I was fourteen."

Hmm. Brimming with curiosity, the woman gave Heeae a second look before pouring out her words.

"He's an old man, so he doesn't eat much. He's a bit picky, though. He must have his Korean food for breakfast. The stew has to be made from scratch every morning. The rice, too, needless to say. He always eats meat for lunch. Steak. The doneness depends on his mood."

She didn't bother hiding her suspicion and scanned Heeae up and down.

"Do you know how to cook Western dishes?" she asked.

Heeae nodded. "I cooked them often for the family I used to work for. I don't have certificates, but I can cook pretty well if it's Italian or French. I also know how to bake cakes."

The woman didn't miss the chance to attack her.

"You know how my father is at risk for diabetes, right?" she snapped.

"Yes, yes, I know. I . . ." Heeae blushed. "I thought I'd just mention it."

The woman narrowed her eyes to stare at Heeae for a while, then stubbed out the cigarette and murmured, "You should be fine. Ahnna did recommend you, after all."

She was about to pull out another cigarette, but changing her mind, she began to tap her nails lightly on the table. Heeae held up the matchbox sitting on it.

"Do you want me to light your cigarette?" she asked.

The woman seemed startled by her initiative but soon shook her head. "No, I've got business to attend to . . . I'll call you."

A moment later, the chime rang, and a cold wind infused with the smell of gasoline wafted in. Heeae stayed seated for a while and drank the citrus tea that had turned cold then left the cafe. She couldn't say that the interview had gone well, but given how the woman had mentioned Ahnna, she figured she wouldn't have a problem getting hired.

But the woman never called. Heeae was living alone in a rented room without a telephone, so she had to pretend to go to the restroom several times a day to skulk outside the landlady's doorstep, but there was no sound of the phone ringing. Only after a few extremely distressing nights of waking up and rushing to the bathroom did Heeae realize she had failed the screening. Had she seemed like she wasn't good at Western cuisine? Or was she too young, was that the problem? Maybe the woman imagined the worst-case scenario in which her father fell for Heeae and bequeathed his entire fortune to a young woman like her. One wouldn't normally associate Heeae's fatigued look with a temptress who robbed old millionaires' pockets, but the woman would likely know that the relationships between men and women were never that simple. Unlike Heeae, whose worries ate her away inside, Ahnna was as cool as a cucumber.

"Don't worry, she'll call soon," her high-pitched voice sang down the phone.

"Would she really?" Heeae gulped and brought up the words she'd feared to say. "I'm afraid that she's figured out who I am."

"Hey, don't worry over nothing. *I* had shrewd enough eyes to recognize you for who you were back then, but that unnie? She never pays attention to other people. She doesn't even recognize the waiter working in the cafe she visits every day if he isn't in his uniform. She's probably pretending she's being thorough in making her decision, so all you have to do is wait. Okay?" Then, Ahnna added with a loud snort, "She always plays hard to get like that, as if."

As she pulled herself far away from the phone, Heeae was impressed by Ahnna's scornful tone and the way she looked down on such a fierce-looking woman. She was no ordinary lady, Ahnna. She had been that way ever since she was young. She had a sort of pride or arrogance rooted in herself that couldn't be fully attributed to her wealthy background. Heeae feared yet admired Ahnna for that. In other words, she wanted Ahnna's approval. The wish lingered even after all those years had passed, and Heeae agreed to whatever Ahnna said. When Ahnna said it was okay, it really felt like it was.

Just as Ahnna had said, the old man's daughter suddenly called after ten days or so.

"I was a bit busy, getting ready to leave the country." She opened with vague civilities that verged on an excuse and asked, "You can come starting tomorrow, right?"

The time was tight, but that wasn't a problem. Heeae didn't ask anything more and accepted the woman's request. When she rushed to the nearest payphone and delivered the news, Ahnna didn't sound surprised.

"What did I tell you?"

But inwardly pleased with how things had gone according to plan, she took Heeae to a dealer that night and bought her a cell phone that made Heeae's jaw drop: the latest flip phone.

"Use this from now on," Ahnna said. "You know how to, right?"

"Yes."

"Good. It'll be any day now."

Heeae nodded. Anxiety, pride, and longing boiled in her chest and brimmed over as clear tears.

"Don't cry," Ahnna told Heeae, who wiped her cheeks. "It's only the beginning. You can save your tears for when we succeed."

The next day, Heeae took the clothes, French and Italian cookery books, telescopes, and other items that Ahnna bought her and went to the old man's house. The mansion on the top of the hill was impeccable. No matter how hard she tried not to, Heeae couldn't help but think about her own place. In that shabby neighborhood lived old people who split a cucumber into three and ate a piece with red chili paste for each meal. Poverty and fatigue begot violence, and the houses as crowded as a cluster of crabs became shadows of their inhabitants, gnawing at their minds. On the contrary, the mansion was directly receiving the blessing of the sun. It stood aloof, far from and high above the rest of the world. Inside and out, it was just like heaven.

Heaven wasn't unfamiliar to Heeae. Since she was fourteen, she had spent most of her time in a tiny cell of heaven. She had served as the gatekeeper that guarded paradise from all kinds of filth, overlooking hell with heaven on her back. Sometimes, angels had given her tender meat and cheese as if out of mercy. During those moments, she could delude herself that she had also become an angel. Some of her colleagues couldn't stand the confusion and jumped off the clouds, but Heeae had held on, unwavering. She was strong. It was Yohan who had made her strong.

Yohan! The thought of the name filled Heeae's heart with proud sadness. Her lost child. But to have lost him meant that she had had him at one point. The loss she felt now was proof that she once possessed his little hands, his round head. She always carried a photo of her son close to her breast. The man had overlooked it when he forcefully took Yohan away. Now all that was left to Heeae was the photo and her memory of Yohan. The joy that welled up in her heart when the boy first started to walk and called his mother, and the scar that had been borne when he wailed about why he didn't have a father and why they were so poor—no one could take those away from her. She licked the wound over and over again with her weathered tongue. She did so without knowing if that healed it or worsened it. That was what let Heeae live. The scar. She wanted to cherish the scar that Yohan left only to her. It would rot away with her if she died, so she had to live.

When Ahnna had called her a few months earlier, Heeae had been working a building cleaning job. She had to wake up at 5:30 in the morning to arrive on time. The bluish light right before sunrise possessed an energy that made one look forward to a sprightly day, but Heeae was heavy-hearted. The victim in a controversial kidnapping case was found dead not too far from her home. Every time Heeae passed by the crime scene, blocked off with the yellow police line, she felt like the pain might kill her. Kidnapping was one of the things she most dreaded while raising Yohan. She feared the story of the boogeyman more than children did. She worried that someone would take away her son lying on the floor if she took her eyes off him even for a moment. As his beauty multiplied with his vernix coming off and limbs growing longer, her anxiety swelled.

The fact that the boy, her son whose beauty made Heeae stay up all night in fear, was indeed taken away right before her eyes ailed her. That was when the crime that reminded her of Yohan took place. Every time she passed the building where the victim had been abandoned, she felt as if someone were gouging her heart out with a frozen blade. Perhaps as a result, on her way to work one morning, Heeae collapsed unconscious. When she opened her eyes, she found herself in hospital, and after lying for a while with an IV drip, she returned home in a daze. She suffered in ambiguity, unclear whether it was a dream or reality. She lost her job and met young Yohan who came to visit, until a woodpecker pecked at her skull and she had to go to the toilet and vomit. Only after barely managing to rinse her mouth with cold water did Heeae realize that the knocking noise wasn't her hallucinating. Outside, the old landlady said she got a call. There was no one to call her. Strange, Heeae thought, but she still picked up the receiver. A lively voice that made it hard to guess the owner's age came from the other side.

"Hey, it's the weekend. What took you so long to answer?"

An unfamiliar, yet strangely familiar voice. Heeae rummaged through her dusty memories.

"Who . . . is this?" she began.

"It's me, Ahnna. Hey, who doesn't have a landline these days? I'm totally shocked, you know. That means your landlady has to holler for you every time you get a call. Doesn't she complain about how inconvenient that is?"

Heeae fell silent.

"Hello?"

She was unsure what to say.

"Hey, Heeae. Are you listening?"

"Yeah," Heeae finally managed to reply. The only Ahnna she knew was the youngest daughter of the family for whom she had her first job as a live-in maid. Suddenly, the cold early spring wind that had blown as she had left that house seeped back into her bones. How long had it been? Twenty years? She felt confused as if the time had been distorted, but Ahnna went on over the phone with her still-girlish voice, "You're doing well, right? I have something to say. Come over tomorrow. That way, we can see each other's faces, too."

She sounded like she was suggesting to a friend that they go sightseeing in the city over summer break. Her simplicity, cheerfulness, and, most importantly, her firm belief that there was no way she'd be rejected intimidated Heeae. So she wet her chapped lips and said okay, just like she had to for everything she had been told to do during her time at Ahnna's house.

Ahnna had summoned her to a coffee shop named Rose. To reach it Heeae had to change subway line several times. They said the economy was down, but ever since the Seongsu Bridge had been reconstructed, the neighborhood's businesses seemed to have been brought back to life, with its strange, otherworldly vitality gushing through the streets. Passing between men in racy outfits like tight shirts underneath their jackets with hair slicked back with mousse and women whose white teeth glistened between their wine-red lips, Heeae felt squeezed between two walls. When she finally found the sign to the coffee shop and stood outside the building, her forehead was sweating even though it wasn't hot.

The coffee shop was in the basement. Heeae felt her way down the steps. Once she'd pushed her way in through the thick wooden doors adorned with rose-patterned stained glass that made the place look like a church, a cross and an old religious painting welcomed her and the painting's scrawny man, bleeding with his arms wide open, zoomed into her view. A slight dizziness halted her. A quickly repeating harpsichord melody twirled around her head, and the light reflected from the waiter's gold earring stabbed her eyes. As she faltered from gravity pulling her down, someone shouted loudly, "Heeae!"

Heeae blinked hard, and faced the direction the sound had come from. In the innermost corner, against a flawlessly finished stone wall, a bob-haired woman wearing a sky-blue halterneck sweater sat at a table where the floor was elevated about a handspan. The woman's face looked unfamiliar, but Heeae approached her slowly.

"Miss . . . Ahnna?"

At that, the woman grabbed Heeae's hand, nearly pulling her towards her.

"Come on, 'Miss'? That makes it sound like we're strangers," the woman laughed.

Heeae could see her dimples sinking deep, visible even in the dark. Only then was Heeae convinced that the woman, her true face barely recognizable due to heavy makeup, was Ahnna.

"How have you been?" Ahnna asked in a silvery voice. "Did you eat yet?"

"Oh, not yet."

"I thought not. You must be hungry. Go ahead, order something." She opened the menu before the hesitating Heeae. "Go on. Never mind the price. I own this place, after all."

Heeae stared blankly at Ahnna.

"Heeae?" Ahnna called.

"Oh, thank you. I was just, just a bit dizzy. No wonder the cafe looks so amazing."

"Right? A famous designer from Germany worked on it. This table is made of the finest walnut, and the couch is velvet. Go ahead, touch it. Isn't it so soft? Our chef is from a hotel over in Tokyo, and his skill is simply outstanding. So much so that I feel sorry for making him cook these dishes . . ."

When Heeae simply blinked, Ahnna called again, "Heeae?"

"Huh?"

"What's wrong? Pick something already."

"Sorry, I'm just a bit out of it," Heeae said apologetically. "I'll have this kimchi thing . . . and an orange juice."

"Kimchi pilaf? That's just fried rice. You can order anything, you know."

"It's okay. I got a little carsick, so."

"Sure . . . Coffee for me," Ahnna said briefly, handing over the menu to the waiter who had been standing silently. The waiter, who kept his hair neat with hair gel, bowed slightly and walked over to the counter. Ahnna followed him with her gaze for a while, before she suddenly grasped Heeae's hand and rubbed it as if she were handling a small furry animal.

"It's been too long. Hasn't it been nearly twenty years? Your work must be taking a toll on you. How come you've lost so much weight?"

"Speak for yourself, you . . ." Heeae tried her best to pick words that wouldn't sound rude. "I wouldn't have recognized you if I ran into you on the street."

"Two decades' time is enough to change the rivers and mountains twice, as they say." Ahnna made a satisfied smile. "When was the last time we saw each other? The year we turned twenty-one?"

"Yeah."

"Yes, that spring. It was when I'd just entered college. Gosh, it's already been twenty years. Can you believe it?"

Heeae had nothing to say to that.

"Tell me you've been well," pressed Ahnna.

"Of course. You, too?"

"Oh, me, you know. Just getting by." Ahnna grinned widely.

Heeae also smiled, but their conversation disintegrated as easily as buckwheat noodles. The background music cut through their silence. A husky-voiced woman repeated some lyrics over and over again, with a tone that sounded both pleading and jubilant. Heeae tightened her stomach so that her voice wouldn't get drowned out by the music. She pointed at the painting that occupied the shop's front wall.

"That's . . ." she began.

"Oh, I brought it from home. Those, too," Ahnna said, pointing out the old Christian paintings. "They used to be in my brother's room. They're decorations. I'm not religious or anything. Did you believe in the Savior?"

"Yes."

"Yes, I remember. That's why my mom liked you so much.

She said she wanted to get a daughter-in-law like you, I think."

Another lengthy silence sank between them. Again, it was Heeae who spoke first.

"Is that . . . supposed to be a painting of Heaven?"

"Oh, that? Yes. The left is Heaven, and the center is the human world. The right is Hell."

"Ah, Okay. I remember now."

"That one's quite expensive even among the reproductions. An antique, too. I think my father bought it as a gift for my brother's eighteenth birthday. His taste was a bit bizarre, my brother."

"Yes, he treasured the gift quite a bit," reminisced Heeae. "He would always tell me to be careful with it in case I damaged it while polishing the frame."

"So you remember."

"Yeah."

Another long silence followed.

"I'm sorry," Ahnna said, lowering her head over the table.

Heeae scratched her eyebrow and did her best to sound indifferent.

"What for? It wasn't your fault."

"I'm so sorry." Ahnna lowered her voice even though no one was listening. "You know, I'm really sorry about what happened. We shouldn't have done that to you. If I hadn't been running around so much at the time, I could have done something about it. I was scatterbrained then, too. Not only did I enter college later than others, but the thing with my dad happened . . . This might sound like an excuse, but

I learned about the real reason you left only way later. If I knew then, I would've helped you no matter what it took. I wouldn't have let you go like that."

Heeae let Ahnna continue.

"I was really all over the place. Or should I say I was confused? As you already know, I really loved my father. So when people were talking about how Dad oppressed the workers and stuff, I just couldn't believe it. I was mad, I was in pain. I still remember how I would play in the front yard of the factory, and unnies with faces as pale as flour would come and tell me how pretty I was. So I never imagined my dad would treat them so badly . . . Seriously, I just hated everything that had to do with my family at the time. One day, I was trying to swallow a spoonful of rice, and the rice grains literally stood up inside my throat. That's why I didn't notice what had happened to you. Well, how could I have known? Everything was good until you left. You remember, right? Before the Seollal holidays, my mom, you, and I went to Myeongdong and ordered custom-made hanbok clothes. For the silk, you chose yellow for the jeogori top and red for the skirt, and I picked a green jeogori and a red skirt . . . I said we'd look like sisters if we wore them together . . . Remember? We went to Namsan and had pork cutlets, and you didn't even touch your plate . . . I thought that was strange since it was our first time in a while dining out, but I never imagined . . . Looking back, Mom probably knew everything already . . ."

Ahnna's murmurs died down. In an attempt to change the mood, she brightened her voice.

"Right, do you still talk to Miyeong?"

"No," Heeae replied.

"Oh, you don't? You two were so close. From the same hometown, if I remember correctly?"

"No, Miyeong is a Seoul girl."

"Oh, really? How strange, working as a live-in maid when she already lived in Seoul . . . But you two *were* close, weren't you? You hung out together a lot. At parties and stuff."

"It was just work."

"I see. I thought you were quite close . . ."

With that, Ahnna fell back into silence again. The two didn't dare to resume the conversation. Unable to bear the silence, Ahnna cleared her throat and pressed her empty water glass against her lips. The waiter with the slicked-back hair artfully filled the glass from a long-spouted pitcher and brought out their order. Ahnna didn't even glance at him as he slightly adjusted the coffee cup so she could easily hold the handle. When he set down the orange juice and kimchi pilaf and turned around, she abruptly cursed.

"Sons of bitches."

Heeae remained silent.

"Yeongki oppa is a son of a bitch, but Seo Sucheol is a worse son of a bitch for offering you to him. That dirty bastard. Coward. Motherfucker. How could he . . ." Ahnna continued, unable to stop. "If Miyeong hadn't said anything, we would have never known. Should I be thanking her for that? I don't know . . ."

Heeae still remained silent.

"But you, you were being so you. How could you not say a word about it? My mom would've helped you if you told her."

Ahnna pretended to sulk and gave Heeae a cutesy frown. Heeae could do nothing but laugh at her naivety. Ahnna stared at Heeae's face as if she intended to read her mind, but soon sighed.

"Well, it's all in the past now, so what's the use talking about it? But I have good news, too. Seo Sucheol doesn't belong to this world any longer."

"Did he . . . pass away?" Heeae asked.

"You mean, 'go to hell'? It's okay. It wasn't just you that he messed with. He did the same to me, too. And to Seohee. You know Seohee, right? My friend." Ahnna chuckled, unbecoming for her, before she continued. "Hey, you know what shocked me? All the women I talked to had older brothers who molested them at least once, big or small. What in the world is wrong with older brothers? Anyway, I'm glad that mine died off early. If not, he would've squandered all of Father's fortune a long time ago. Then I could never have married a professor. My husband's smart, but he is penniless, you see."

Ahnna twitched her dark-brown lips. As if she had just noticed the plate of kimchi pilaf, she offered, "What are you waiting for? Dig in."

"What? Oh, okay."

Heeae lowered her head toward the shining rice grains soaked in oil. Once she had a spoonful, hot and spicy air slammed her nostrils hard and made her cough. Finely chopped kimchi and rice grains scattered across the table with saliva droplets.

"I'm sorry."

Flustered, Heeae fumbled the table for a napkin.

"No, it's okay, that happens," Ahnna waved. Then, she added, "But let's not order rice when you meet Eunyeong unnie, okay? She's a clean-freak, you know. If you spatter so much as a single grain of rice, you're out right away."

At the sound of an unfamiliar name, Heeae asked, "Who's Eunyeong . . . unnie?"

"You don't remember? I suppose she didn't come over to my house that often, maybe once or twice a year . . . I'll have to fill you in, but long story short, I'd like to ask you a favor."

"What favor?"

"Nothing much. It's to get in as a live-in housekeeper in her father's home and keep a lookout for another house nearby. I heard that the ajumma working there is quitting after this year. The work itself shouldn't be hard. The rest of the family lives in the U.S., so you won't have other people nitpick at you. The man has a limp, but he doesn't have trouble walking with his cane. He's prediabetic, so you'd have to pay some attention to his meals, but that's . . . nothing difficult. You took care of my entire family when you were just fourteen, am I right?"

Keep a lookout? Why would she? For what? Heeae tried to put things together in her head. Wait, how did Ahnna know that she'd quit her job? How did she find her number?

Even before Heeae could start asking, Ahnna threw a question that encompassed all the answers she could give.

"You know Yosep, right?"

A silence colder than ever lingered over the table. Ahnna quietly rummaged through her handbag and pulled out a cigarette pack. Her relaxed movements—tapping the pack twice on the table and picking up and lighting the cigarette that slipped out—were as organic as a flowing river. Elegant. She released thin, soft smoke a couple of times before she smiled.

"I learned that he's your son. Oh, right, Yohan is the name you gave him."

Heeae was at a loss for words.

"I was surprised. I heard that you'd aborted the baby," Ahnna continued. "And that baby became a celebrity. What a shock. Reporters would totally flip out if they found out about it." She fluttered her long eyelashes, smiling. "Hey, heredity is the most mysterious thing, don't you think? No matter how absolute it seems, it often goes against our expectations. Like, the ugliest couple can give birth to a pretty baby, or it can be the other way around. There are Black couples giving birth to white babies, too. I always thought those stories were nonsense, but reality is more shocking than any TV drama, isn't it?"

Heeae barely managed to produce sounds; her throat had dried up from astonishment.

"How did you . . . know?" she asked.

"I didn't, until a few days ago. I knew Yosep was adopted, though. I lived abroad for a few years, following my husband. Just when I was taking some rest after coming back to Korea, Yeongki oppa called and said that his kid was also in Korea for the break. So we all met, and Yosep's face looked completely different from when he had been younger. It wasn't like I'd seen him often, so I thought I was just imagining things. But it turns out, the kid had died, and oppa took in his other son born out of wedlock. I heard that unnie was having issues getting pregnant. I knew they always obsessed over having a son, but I never imagined that they'd adopt a fully grown child like that."

Heeae's heart thumped like a drum.

"How's, how's Yohan?" she asked, stroking her hot ear and cheeks.

"How what?"

"Is he . . . doing well?"

Ahnna slurped her coffee and spat nonchalantly, "What do you think? Of course not."

Heeae had nothing to say.

"What did Yeongki oppa even tell him? What could make the boy tremble like that and tell me, 'I can't meet my mom, not when I'm alive'?"

At Heeae's silence, Ahnna went on.

"But he should be doing better than you, at least. Hey, do you know how shocked I was at first? I thought you could just talk normally after it passes, your aphasia, you know? I never knew it could damage your voice so much . . . Anyway, after I heard that, I promised Yosep that I'd find his mother no matter what his father says, no matter what it takes. The boy's still young, so he might shake like a leaf at every word his father says, but to me, finding a person isn't that hard. We're living in convenient times, aren't we? I can find out anything with money. That's how I heard about your aphasia after losing Yosep. Which is to say, I didn't plan to meet you in the first place."

Then, like a middle-schooler who'd prepared a secret treat for her classmate's birthday, she added brightly, "Surprised to hear from me after all these years, aren't you?"

Heeae kept quiet.

"I was surprised, too. My shaman said I'd meet an old acquaintance again this year, but I never imagined it would be you."

Ahnna stubbed out the nearly burnt-out cigarette on the ashtray and sat up straight.

"Well, I suppose it's a bit late, but I'm going to keep my promise," she declared. "That little kid, he's all grown up and making his own living now, but he must miss his mom, right? Yeongki oppa can't do that. He can't just tear you two apart when you gave birth to the boy and raised him yourself."

"But what do I do?" Heeae screamed. "He won't let me see him, he won't! So what can I possibly do?"

It was as if a burning-hot stone had been tossed inside her. Her painstakingly suppressed mind began to rattle, and her eyesight blurred. She rubbed her wet cheeks just like a child would. In her distorted vision, Ahnna was staring at her without saying a word, wearing an expression hard to read as sadness or pain.

"Here."

When Heeae calmed after a long while, Ahnna offered her some tissues. She raised her hand to order a cup of warm black tea, pulled out a flat stainless flask, and poured something into the tea. Before Heeae could ask what it was, Ahnna resolutely said, "Whiskey. You'll come back to your senses once you finish it."

Heeae usually didn't drink, but she trusted Ahnna and emptied the slightly lukewarm cup. Either because of having a good cry or because of the drink, she felt her body and mind relaxing. When she covered her mouth to stop the hiccups, Ahnna flashed a light smile.

"I didn't call you without any plans," she said cheerfully. "I thought of some of my own. I'm going to discuss them now. You've got time, right?"

Heeae nodded. She had nothing important going on in her life, anyway. Except Yohan. Ahnna put on a satisfied expression and raised her hand straight up in the air.

"Here, two more coffees!"

Heeae opened her bag and pulled out a pair of binoculars that she had wrapped in her clothes. Pressing them against her eyes gave her temporary dizziness, but soon, between the curtains, she could see Yohan pacing the living room. Seemingly conflicted, he sat on the couch one moment and fiddled with the remote control the next, before he finally stood up as if he had made up his mind and turned the lights off. In the darkness, Heeae noticed Yohan standing against the window to check if any girls were roaming around near his house. There were three or four despite the rain forecast, but it didn't matter even if there were more. The girls wouldn't know that Yohan had changed his car. Heeae didn't either, until two months ago, when she had spotted a hand carelessly stuck out of an open window of a tinted Grandeur.

That day, having been jolted from her sleep, Heeae stared out of the window. The season was spring, and curtains were drawn in Yohan's unlit room. Would he be sleeping okay these days? Aching from the sudden thought, Heeae placed her right hand on her chest.

Yohan had been a weak child ever since he was a baby. Before bedtime, she had fed him toasted ginkgo nuts, mantis eggs, and even ashes of earthworms burned inside hollowed eggshells, but he would still wet his bed once every ten days or so. That had become his habit, and he would wake up several times in the night. When he finally seemed to be getting better at sleeping through the night, that man had taken Yohan away, and she had no way of knowing if her child had broken entirely out of the habit.

Heeae leaned outside the window into the dark. With cherry blossoms pouring down like rain, the spring evening was breathtaking. The time was late, and no girls were lurking, either. She usually disliked them for pestering Yohan, but that day, their absence made her feel lonely. She wiped the tears pooling in her eyes.

A car was driving up the hill. Was it fresh out of the factory? Or just well taken care of? A neat New Grandeur halted in front of the mansion on the other side, waiting for the parking lot's shutters to go up. Heeae was about to look away casually at the cherry blossom tree. But just then, the Grandeur's window rolled down, and a hand came out.

Oh? She didn't need the binoculars. It was undoubtedly Yohan's face that peeked through the window crack. Yohan grabbed a flower petal and drew in his arm before closing the window, and the car drifted into the parking lot. Yohan's car was a Tiburon. Heeae hadn't heard anything about him buying a new car. *But just maybe,* she thought, and jotted down the date and time she witnessed the car. Three weeks later, she noticed that the Grandeur left and returned at the same time on the dot, once a week, and reported it to Ahnna.

"It must be his personal schedule," Ahnna whispered, her eyes sparkling. "I was waiting for that."

The plan that gushed out of her mouth was absurd and sounded like something out of a movie. Heeae would have stopped her, but this time, she simply nodded and replied, "Yes, let's do that." Heeae was exhausted. Exhausted from caring for a fussy old man, only stealing glances at her own son's shadow, and at times, resisting the impulse to shriek like the girls who stalked him.

When eleven o'clock came around, the tinted Grandeur emerged from the parking lot. As expected, the girls didn't react. One of them, worn out, turned away. Heeae opened her cell phone, made a call, and hung up after it rang twice. Then she stood by the window and made sure she saw the little lights descend along the hill before she returned to the old man's bedroom.

The man slept like a log. Even though all he had left now was his mean temper, he must have loved his children at one point. He would have promised to pull down the moon and the stars for them. Heeae thought about how the man's daughter never called. Would she also have jumped into her father's arms in her childhood and claimed she was going to marry him? As time passed, the love given to one's child was bound to be betrayed. Such was nature's way, and Heeae didn't deny it. She was just jealous of the old man. She envied him for having been able to give enough to be betrayed. She wanted to be betrayed. But by whom? If she didn't have someone to grow tired of the love she showered, someone to abandon and trample over her at the end, there was no reason for her to keep living.

Once again, she thought back to the olden days. How would those old parents in nice clothes have felt when they had been carried up the mountains on jiges? They must have been happy, at peace. Leaning against their children's steaming backs one last time, they would have thoroughly enjoyed the the younger generation's brimming vitality. Touched by the fact that their own blood was coursing through those bodies. But at this rate, Heeae would have to wade through the snow with her own two feet. No way. Even if that were to be her future, she had to meet Yohan at least once more in her lifetime. She had to confirm that he was once her cells, a piece that had fallen out of her body.

Kneeling beside the old man, still fast asleep, Heeae clasped her hands. The prayer that she had been whispering in her mind soon turned into tongues, and in the end, she lay on the floor, her face stained with tears. It was going to be midnight soon. The moment was near to meet her child, the boy who had split her body open and come into this world twenty years ago.

She could meet him. She could see Yohan soon.

Through her fuzzy vision, Heeae saw herself embracing Yohan in her arms.

"N-Nami."

A voice squealed. It was Ahnna, stepping out of the car while panting as if she had sprinted a hundred meters.

"It's here."

"He left?" asked Nami.

Instead of answering, Ahnna raised her cell phone to show the screen. Nami quickly leaned in through the open window. As expected, it was exactly eleven o'clock. She listened closely to the road conditions announced by the radio broadcast. Late night on a weekday. No accidents. The road was completely empty, but it sounded like not many people had the nerve to glide down it. Or maybe all the luck had aligned and prevented anything from happening.

"Don't you need to head down now?" Ahnna asked impatiently. "You should be there getting ready."

"Isn't it too early?" asked Nami. "Will you be okay by yourself here?"

"I'll be okay. You go ahead."

"What about the battery?"

"It's enough." Ahnna suddenly squeezed Nami's hand tightly and said, "You have to do it right, okay?"

"Don't worry."

Ahnna stole a glance at Mihee in the passenger seat and whispered, "I'm not sure this is gonna go well."

"It's okay, I'll be with her," Nami assured her. "Remember,

you have to call me right when he passes by, okay? I might be mistaken otherwise."

Ahnna nodded.

"I'll be counting on you," Nami said in farewell.

She got in the car and made a U-turn to head down the hill. The noise of water falling rang louder and louder inside the car, probably from the dam's open floodgate. Was it getting cloudy? The air felt damp. Listening to the thundering waterfall, Nami immersed herself in the memory of one rainy afternoon.

In a word, Nami's mom was a nutcase. She mostly lay at home without moving a muscle, but she would sometimes rush out of the house and dance until she passed out or talk nonsense to old folks at the village pavilion, only to be shooed back home. Nami could now see that it was sort of a sinbyeong, in which the gods told her mother to become a shaman. But her dad opted not for hospital treatment or a mudang initiation ritual, but for a Christian exorcising prayer. A reverend and some ladies from a prayer group came to Nami's home. Nami grumbled about how pointless it was since she didn't want to harbor false hope, but to her surprise, their prayer healed her mom. The next thing she knew, she came home from school and was welcomed by doughnuts generously sprinkled with sugar or a tower of mini pork cutlets. She grabbed the food with her bare hands and stuffed it down her throat. When her mother asked her to eat slowly, she nodded, praying that the suffocating joy would last for a long time.

One summer day, an unexpected shower came down. Seeing a long queue in front of her school's payphone, Nami sprang out from under the eaves. The night before, she had watched a movie with both her parents for the first time. It was titled *Singin' in the Rain*. Nami absolutely loved how the man in love danced in the rain while splashing away. She hadn't forgotten those steps. She hippity-hopped while soaking her whole body with love and raindrops.

Nami waited for the signal to change at an eight-lane road. She soon spotted a person in a white gown-like house dress holding an umbrella—it was her mother. Nami's chest swelled like a baby pigeon's. She waved excitedly.

"Mom!"

But her mom didn't react. Nami stomped her feet from anxiety. She wondered why she was so glad to see her mother when they saw each other every day. The time dragged on. The light turned green. Her mom took her first step. Nami also took her first step. And—

Crash!

That was the last of her mom. Even after hitting her mother, the car skidded along the rainy road and didn't stop until it had slid fifteen meters and slammed into the building on the other side of the intersection. Both Nami's mom and the driver died on the spot. The driver was Nami's dad. *How sad*, people would say. Dad, who had rushed back home lest his daughter should get drenched in the rain. Mom, who had brought herself out of the house despite her illness. They said it was a tragedy concocted by coincidence. Nami was only curious about one thing: was it her mom getting run over by her dad, or was it her dad running over her mom?

Asking and answering the same question over and over again made her doubt not more vivid but more obscure. Dismantled and squashed. The person who pulled Nami out of the dense fog was a woman who claimed to be her mom's older sister. Nami had never seen her before, but she couldn't deny that the woman shared the same blood as her mom. From the woman's sonorous voice to the strange glow in her eyes, it was as if Nami's mom had returned from the burial after snapping her neck back into place and changing her clothes. Nami was entrusted to her aunt. When she awkwardly entered her aunt's house for the first time with her scant belongings, her eyes popped at how fancy it was. Her aunt turned out to be a successful shaman. Her fortunetelling pinpointed which areas in Seoul would see a rise in land and apartment prices, shooting her to a sort of stardom among Gangnam housewives.

Nami graduated middle school under her aunt's care. She entered high school but soon dropped out to help with her aunt's business, mainly answering calls and confirming appointments. When her aunt was in a good mood or customers were told good fortunes, Nami would receive a small amount of pocket money, but not a fixed salary. Yet she didn't care. What she wanted more than money was to learn how to captivate others. Her aunt led high and mighty madams by their noses. Women who glowered at other people in the outside world bowed down flat on the floor as soon as the door to her aunt's room opened. Nami was very interested in why people kept visiting in spite of her aunt's rudeness—why the crowds only grew bigger, in fact. Like an actor wearing a mask, she mimicked her aunt. She washed with cold water, didn't eat meat, and smoked and drank in secret.

At one point, Nami realized that customers had started to call her the baby bodhisattva. She was neither a baby nor a bodhisattva, but her aunt merely laughed and didn't stop her customers. Instead, she carved out about an hour or so of her time after work to teach Nami how to read the saju fortune. Nami was a diligent student. She had always thought that shamans rambled about revelations shot down from the beyond, but once she began to think of it as something like statistics, saju didn't seem difficult at all. On top of that, she mimicked the way her aunt spoke, glared, and sat, making her look quite plausible.

Soon, Nami placed her own desk in the former waiting room and read simple fortunes for visitors. Since she couldn't be tasked with important readings, she specialized in love fortunes and compatibilities. Those seemed to hit the mark pretty well and gained her regulars who sought only her. As if having predicted everything, her aunt encouraged Nami and said the talent to become a fraud, just like the ghostly possession to become a shaman, was heaven-sent.

The regulars that Nami accumulated one by one made her a big deal. Just as she did with her customers, Nami began brainwashing herself. Her aunt seemed to think that Nami's confidence was a marketing skill of a sort, but that wasn't true. Nami truly believed in herself. She was like a person who had only ever read one book, and the title of that book was herself. That was like the Bible to Nami.

One rainy day, Nami met a woman. She was her aunt's patron, who visited out of the blue without a reservation. Her face was familiar, but Nami felt awkward as they had never had a conversation before. She could barely look straight at the woman's scrawny face and sharp eyes. The woman said it was okay, but her aunt's consultation with the previous customer was taking longer than usual. It was Nami who grew impatient as time went by. Was it really going to be okay? Her frightened mind conjured up a vision in which the woman knocked over all the candles in the shrine to set it on fire.

"Excuse me." The woman started to speak.

Her voice was like a child's. Her soft and high tone that betrayed her looks startled Nami.

"Sorry?" she asked back reflexively.

"Uhm, can I watch some television?"

"Yes, suit yourself."

The woman blushed and bowed down. After fiddling with the remote control, she landed on a channel airing a music show. Nami asked her if she liked pop music, and the woman slurred that she sometimes listened to it as a hobby. But her gaze suggested it wasn't as simple as that. Her eyes looked fierce, like a beast preparing to hunt in the shadows. What was she after? Nami glanced at the screen in curiosity, but the woman didn't react to any of the singers' performances. The emcee then announced the next performance would be the last for the day. That was when the woman flinched. *Was that it?* Nami mused. What in the world could it be?

The performance began.

There was a boy.

He sang, danced, sparkled. And that was it.

When Nami looked back at the woman, her face was gleaming with ecstasy. The woman had clearly fallen in love. And she wasn't the only one. *It's him*, Nami thought. The moment she saw the boy, she felt it was fate. It was as though a new chapter in her life had opened. The experience was powerful, untouchably hot. And the woman's eyes, locked on Nami, were just as scorching. Even though she didn't say a word, the woman sensed that Nami had also fallen in love with the boy. There was no need to hide any longer.

"What's his name?" Nami asked.

The woman replied, "Yosep."

That was how Nami and Ahnna met for the first time.

The radio chimed at midnight. *Happy birthday, Yosep,* Nami muttered to herself. Mihee, who had been outside while checking over the plan, leaned in and knocked on the window.

"Hey, Nami. Did you hear what I said?"

Nami didn't say anything.

"Would you please focus?" Mihee asked impatiently. "We've only got one shot . . ."

"It's okay. Everything's going to be fine." Nami opened her eyes wide with a smile. "Trust me. Today's our lucky day."

Mihee wore a complicated expression and, determined to say what she had to say, went on to review the plan by herself.

"So, when Yosep comes, we will turn on the traffic wand. I'll get out of the car and wave it around. Yosep would ask if we need help, right? Then I'll tell him that it looks like the engine has broken down, and ask him if he could get out of his car and take a look. When he says okay and sticks his head under the open hood, then . . ." Mihee flourished the stun gun in her hand. "It's over."

Nami flashed a toothy smile. "Perfect."

"I hope it goes well," Mihee muttered, hugging her arms closely though it wasn't even cold. "I'm a bit nervous."

"Don't worry, we've got this." Nami nodded while looking Mihee straight in the eye.

Mihee seemed relieved and revealed a more relaxed smile, but Nami had her own agenda. Instead of knocking Yosep out, she wanted to run him over. After all, crisis was the most suitable seasoning for a fateful love.

They would surely fall in love the moment they saw each other. Nami had no doubt about it, but to simply fall in love would be boring. What if someone asked, *How did you two fall for each other? It was love at first sight.* The end! Love at first sight was cool and all, but it lacked drama. It was like a painting of a dragon that looked like it might soar into the sky, but with its eyes drawn without pupils. Or a parfait beautifully topped with whipped cream, but missing a cherry on top. Which is why Nami decided to devise the perfect meet-cute: a fun, bloody story that people would like. So far, she had plotted out the following scenario.

When Yosep's car approaches, Nami drives over the centerline. The two collide, almost meeting their demise. Given his personality, Yosep might ram into the guardrail so as not to hit Nami. But it would be better for the two to run into each other, wouldn't it? Because love is all about collision. The two cars' bumpers crumple like paper. The shattered glass scatters like sugar all over the black road. Nami might pass out for about ten minutes or so. But she eventually opens her eyes. Even though her entire body feels like jelly, she wills the car door open and limps toward Yosep. She falls at least once and dusts the glass particles off her palms as she approaches him. Under the new moon, Yosep's eyes are closed like Pygmalion's sculpture of Galatea yet to be kissed. It would be great if his pale forehead, tilted sideways, let a streak of dark-red blood trickle down. It would be much more romantic that way. Then one day, after having been brought to the mansion in her car, Yosep opens his eyes and finds Nami, a holy angel, passed out next to him, left exhausted from nursing him back to health. Surprised, Yosep brushes back her hair to check her face, and at that moment, Nami wakes up and meets his gaze. Just as ducklings imprint on their mother duck, the two become the one and only love for each other.

Nami trembled as she pictured how their meeting would unfold; she could see everything so clearly, as if it were happening before her eyes. Just the thought of it made her giggle. She forced her lips into a frown to conceal her active imagination. Then suddenly there was a knock on the window—Mihee was outside, grumbling, her head covered with her hands.

"Gosh, it's raining. Do you think it will pour?"

"Looks like it'll pass soon," answered Nami.

Mihee got in the car. As soon as she closed the door there was a furious downpour, but just like Nami had predicted, the heavy rain stopped almost as soon as it began. Everything was going as Nami had hoped. She had cited all kinds of reasons as to why today was their lucky day, but in truth, she had chosen today for their operation for only one reason: it was Yosep's twenty-first birthday. What other day could be luckier than that? She lightly tapped on the steering wheel.

Amused, Mihee asked, "Aren't you nervous?"

"Why would I be? There's nothing to worry about."

"You know, just because. Life is full of unfortunate coincidences."

"Coincidence is an invention of a weak mind. All you need is a strong conviction that you'll succeed. Then nothing can get in your way. Mihee, you want to succeed, don't you?"

After a short silence, Mihee replied, "Yes."

"Tell me. Do you want to succeed?"

"Yes, I do."

"Then you will."

When a yellow dot seemed to loom beyond the hills, the cell phone rang. It was Ahnna, as expected.

Nami answered. "We spotted the car."

"Is it him?" asked Mihee.

As soon as Nami nodded, Mihee sprang out of the car. Nami turned on the headlights and shone them on Mihee, who waved the traffic wand. Nami felt her neck and shoulders growing stiff, just as they had when she first learned how to drive. She took her hands off the wheel and massaged her neck. Mihee also lowered her arms and stood still.

Even after a long wait, the car still hadn't arrived. What was going on? As Nami and Mihee waited in confusion, Ahnna called again.

"Did you do it?" she asked in a trembling voice.

"No. He's not here yet," Nami replied.

"What? He passed by a few minutes ago!"

"Are you sure it's Yosep's car?"

"Yes. I checked the plate."

"Well, he's not here. Wait a second."

Nami pulled the phone away from her cheek and waved at Mihee. Once Mihee stuck her head inside the driver's window, Nami said: "Ahnna says it *was* Yosep."

"Are we supposed to believe his car disappeared, then?" Mihee asked incredulously.

"I guess. You also saw the light on the hill just now, right?"

"Yes."

"It wasn't some animal's eyes shining or anything, right?"

"I'm sure it was a car."

"Strange. Where could he have gone?"

"Oh," Mihee widened her eyes and whispered. "Maybe he went to the reservoir."

"The reservoir?"

"There is another path before coming down this way. I spotted it during my previous visit." Mihee bit her lip in anger. "What should we do? Should we go up and see?"

"Wait!" Nami held her hand up and relayed Mihee's words to Ahnna over the phone. "Yes. Yes, turns out there's another road. What should we do?" Then she nodded before hanging up. "Ahnna says she'll join us. Let's go pick her up."

The two went back up the hill, picked Ahnna up, and turned the car to head down to the reservoir. They decided to check first to see if Yosep was really there and parked their car by the roadside. Muted footsteps waded through the grass. Their thighs were drenched. The reservoir was much bigger than they had thought. The moonless night slowed down their movement more than usual. They gave up being stealthy and turned on their flashlights. After wandering for a while, the three women found a car parked among the tree shadows.

"That's it, right?" Mihee nervously took a deep breath. "What do we do? Better to pretend that we're here to fish, right?"

"Yes, that sounds good," Ahnna nodded. "But wait, we don't have fishing poles. Should I bring them now?"

"Isn't that weird? Who carries around fishing poles? We can say that we've set them up far away . . ."

Mihee and Ahnna's murmurs of devising a rubbish plan were mixed with the bugs' chirping. Nami didn't care. That wasn't what mattered.

Something was off.

It was less of a hunch and more of a conviction. Nami left the other two behind and approached Yosep's car. The two women merely flailed, unable to stop her.

"Wait, Nami!"

Ahnna's hushed voice came a moment later. Nami lost her grip on the flashlight, letting it fall to the ground. But now wasn't the time to worry about that.

She stood in front of the driver's window. She knocked on the tinted glass but received no response. Still, she was certain that Yosep was inside. He was sitting asleep, yet not exactly sleeping. She stopped moving and simply stood there. She wasn't sure what to do. Ahnna approached from behind, panting.

"Why are you standing like that?" she whispered. "Is Yosep not there?"

Nami didn't answer. She simply stood there, silently sensing the cogwheels of fate that had begun twisting out of joint. Thick droplets of rain started falling again. They wouldn't stop this time. They would fall ruthlessly, savagely, as if to tear down the heavens. Nami shuddered at the gripping premonition. She closed her eyes as Ahnna began to shriek, banging at the window. The feeling that something had gone awry swept along her spine like a cold thumb.

Chapter 3

"You have to pretend you're dead."

What did Yosep's face look like when he said that? Did he stare like he was looking at a madman? Was he expressionless? Or . . . was he smiling?

"We got another one," Song spat as he walked in. "The bitch is totally out of her mind."

Unsure whether Song was angry or excited, Park opened the box Song handed him. He flinched and nearly lost his grip for a moment, but fortunately, the box didn't drop on the floor. Putting on a straight face, Park returned the box. No matter how often he had seen it, the sight of a dead rat with nails driven into its eyes gave him the creeps. The Chinese character "死", meaning death, written in red on the enclosed paper, had been imprinted on his mind and floated before his eyes as a green letter against the white wall.

Park recalled the packages that had been steadily arriving since the summer of last year. Some contained smashed cassette tapes and Yosep's photo torn into pieces. There was a box with voodoo straw dolls, as well as one with a partially burned photo and a decapitated baby deer plushie inside – Baby Deer was Yosep's nickname. All those threats had ended up being one-offs, but the dead rats were different. They arrived in different packages every week. Some days, they'd receive two or three dead rats in the mail. It was cruel and consistent.

"But just this one came today," Song said slowly. "The rest of the mail is all normal. Oh, and there was a cake, too. Ms. Kim Mijeong took it just now."

Park shook his head. "Tell her to throw it away."

"Excuse me?"

"Throw them all out. Who knows what's in them?"

"Oh, you're right." Song nodded. Then he gave an exaggerated shudder and added, "Crazy bitches."

Song's voice had somewhat lost its vigor while saying those words. When Park glanced back, Song frowned immediately. But Park had caught his face just before it changed. Jealousy. Yes, Song was jealous of Yosep. Park knew that Song, despite his beady-eyed glares and heavyset body, was an extremely delicate man, so delicate that he had to enclose himself within violence. Song would curse loudly and throw his fists at the girls who got close to Yosep, all the while yearning for them. He badmouthed them as horny bitches, but whenever they hollered at Park, "You're so handsome!" Song's blank face hardened even more, unable to hide his envy. Even when he knew the girls were only joking and heard the giggling and snickering that followed, Song still wanted to be the target of those words, to blush just once.

Park stared at Song, who suddenly seemed like a stranger.

If Song, who scratched the eczema scabs on his face out of habit, were handsome, Park thought he would have worked at a host club. Sweet-talking women. Satisfying them, using them before deserting them, and sometimes getting deserted, living like a lone wolf. That was the life Song wanted, and perhaps closer to his heaven-sent nature. But his looks and his acorn-sized genitals—a consequence of childhood obesity—ruined everything. Park thought about advising him to get his penis beaded but didn't. His acquaintances who had gotten it done raved about how they could drive their women crazy now, but that would all be useless for Song, who froze in front of a naked woman.

Park heaved a deep sigh. What Song needed was the experience of satisfying a woman, of being loved by one. Whether it was merely a need for acceptance or based on real hunger for love, Park didn't care. Without it, Song would break down, harder and faster. But what woman would love a man who considered the very feeling of love shameful, a man who didn't know how to swallow his meager pride?

"Do you think she sent it, too?"

Song's question pulled Park out of his thoughts.

"What?"

"The sanitary pad. Do you think the person who sent that sent something again?"

"Oh," Park answered vaguely, "she might have."

The nasty boxes had begun to pour in right after the scandal. They didn't quite compare to the death threats hurled at Yosep's supposed love interest, but Yosep had also received pretty serious attacks. Employees from his agency could now tell if something dangerous was inside just by the look of the boxes. But the bizarre package that Song was referring to had arrived before all this had happened, among countless gifts that celebrated Yosep's transfer to the agency in late spring the year before. A hundred artificial roses were enclosed in the parcel. It would have been somewhat romantic if it hadn't been for the letter written in blood with a curled-up sanitary pad placed at the center and the maggots swarming out of the stinking box.

In fact, the letter-writer's handwriting was rather shapely, and the note's content elegant. What had it said? Right, written next to a small droplet of blood was the line, *I love you as much as this whole world minus this circle.* Song's member had bulged at the sight, but Park, finding himself immersed in an odd sadness, recalled an old fairy tale: a story about a princess raising geese. A queen gives a handkerchief dotted with red blood to her daughter, the princess, who leaves home to marry. Whenever the princess is in trouble, the bloodstain whispers: *Your Highness, your mother's heart would break if she knew about this . . .*

"Well, if you'll excuse me."

Having given up trying to read Park's thoughts, Song bowed from the waist.

Suddenly coming to his senses, Park called out, "Hey."

"Yes, sir?"

"Leave that here. I'll deal with it."

Song put down the box at his feet and stepped backwards.

"Hey," Park called again.

"Yes, sir?"

"Come here."

With Song standing there, teetering in fear, Park pulled out two ten-thousand-won bills.

"Here, use this to buy Mijeong a little something. Don't tell her I gave you the money for it, just tell her you bought it. And tell her not to eat that cake."

"You don't have to," Song stuttered.

Tsk, Park clicked his tongue in reflex. "It's not even your money. No need to be cheap."

Song's face flushed red. *See, that's precisely your problem*, Park wanted to say, but he waved him away instead. "You can leave now."

Song left the room in a hurry with his head dropped low.

When Park opened the door immediately after he knocked, the CEO hurriedly pressed the button on the remote control. The television screen flashed the shape of a cross before the light disappeared into a single dot. Park was almost certain that his boss was watching porn involving young boys: a fanatic of confession and martyrdom, the man was a devoted Christian whose sense of guilt pointed in a perverted direction. Turning his gaze away from the painting of a saint forever turning a spinning wheel with his ankle chained, Park casually put the box down on the desk.

"Hey, Seungtae. What's up?" his boss greeted him, as if nothing had happened.

"It's here again," Park said.

"Again?"

The CEO kept his body pressed against the desk and craned his neck to peer into the box. The fishy smell from his boss's body made Park's mood plummet, but he managed to maintain his calm.

"There's no address, nothing," Park reported. "Probably not even fingerprints. It looks like she climbed over the wall to place it in front of the building."

"Did you check the surveillance cameras?"

"We did, but nothing. She must have entered through the dead zones."

"What did security say?"

"She likely came in when they were on patrol."

"How long has it been?"

"Sorry?"

"Since we've been getting these packages."

Park quickly did the math in his head and replied, "It was since the scandal from last July . . . so about eight months."

"Eight months, huh . . ." His boss audibly sucked in air between his teeth and continued. "Seungtae, do you know why this country is called one of the Four Asian Dragons when there's not even a single drop of crude oil underneath our land?"

The question seemed to have come out of nowhere. In response, Park shook his head. "No, sir."

"It's all because our people did well. How did we make it all this way from the devastated battlefield using only our bare hands? That's all our people's doing. That's how relentless we are. Smart, diligent, persevering. Where do you think all that blood went to?" The CEO heaved a deep sigh, his admiration and disgust blending together. "In my opinion, those girls are talented. It takes a special kind of patience to live on the street, stay up all night stalking, and use your brain to send things like these. If they'd been born under the Japanese occupation, they would have fought for independence. If they'd been born just a decade earlier, they would have made their name in pro-democracy protests. The problem is, why are these girls wasting their talent doing *this*? It's just amazing. Amazing, but gross."

Park remained silent.

"Seungtae," his boss said.

"Yes, sir."

"What do you think we should do? Should we report them to the police?"

Park shook his head. "That'll just ruin Yosep's image for no good reason. It's better to let them be until things quiet down."

"So, we should stay put?"

"Yes, sir."

"I suppose you're right. Anyone can threaten to kill with words. Yes, let them be. It'll only cost us money . . . They'll all forget with time, anyway."

Isn't that exactly what we should be most worried about? Park wondered. *About the boy being forgotten? That no one cared about his love life?* That would prove that Yosep's career as a singer was going downhill. In fact, the number of gifts that Yosep received was noticeably smaller after the scandal. Not many girls lurked near his house anymore.

Maybe it was just one person who was sending all these weird packages. Was this person the same person who sent the sanitary pad? Deep in Park's mind was a groundless belief that that couldn't be the case. He was just making a guess from the handwriting, but this letter written in blood had a sort of elegance to it. A quaint and classic elegance that not only conveyed the message, but also possessed linguistic beauty . . .

The phone in the CEO's office rang. Although Park hadn't said a word, his boss lifted his hand and gestured as if to cover Park's mouth.

"Yes, Mr. Kim. Turn on the TV? Why, what's on?"

After a brief silence, he placed the receiver on his desk and grabbed the remote. The image that appeared stupefied Park. Only after blinking several times did he comprehend what he was seeing. People were being escorted from an office building into ambulances. Behind the reporter, who was bellowing with the veins in his neck bulging, a woman had passed out with blood streaming down her forehead. It was all airing on TV uncensored.

"A bomb," his boss said, dismayed. "They threw a bomb at the agency."

It was the agency Yosep's ex-girlfriend belonged to. Both Park and his boss kept their mouths shut. Only the sharp voice of the newscaster cut through the silence.

"Her agency had it rough, too," the CEO finally muttered. "They got so many death threats. Countless letters saying how dare she date Yosep, that she's gonna shed blood for this. But a bomb . . ."

He sounded uncharacteristically astonished. Then he called out, "Seungtae."

"Yes, sir?"

"We're fucked," he declared. "We're just fucked. What do we do now?"

Park didn't answer. He just stared blankly at the people broken down into small pixels. His eyeballs ached so badly that they felt like they might fall out. Streaks of tears fell from his unblinking eyes. While wiping them away, Park came up with an idea.

As his boss stood gaping at the TV, he asked, "Boss, could you let me handle this?"

"Handle what?"

"This mess. Let me clean it up."

"That's fine and all, but what are you gonna do?"

"Just . . . let me handle it. It'll be as quick as producing a song."

"You won't tell even me?"

Park kept silent.

"Sure, producing a song," his boss nodded. "It's about time. We gotta start fresh."

As he said this, he pressed his palms together and clacked his nails. After thinking it over, the CEO asked, "How many years has it been since you came to Seoul?"

"This year makes it thirteen."

"Really? It's been more than a decade since we first met? Gosh, how time flies. When did that scruffy little bastard just out of high school grow into the fine man I know today, hmm? Now you're as dandy as they come."

Park listened quietly.

His boss continued, "I'm sorry I ended up making you suffer like this. You know how much I care about you."

"Don't worry about it."

"Not that I need to tell you this, but our industry is full of wolves trying to bite you. You pretend to be a wolf, Seungtae, but you're a dog. Loyal . . . and in need of a master. I'm not saying you're weak. It's just your nature."

Park didn't respond.

"Where's Yosep?" the CEO asked.

"Probably in the basement."

"I see. You go ahead. Talk to him."

Park bowed to his boss and turned around.

"Seungtae," the CEO called again from behind him.

"Yes, sir?"

"Don't forget who your master is."

Park bowed once more before he left the room.

News of the terror attack had left Yosep confused. Just as Park expected, the boy didn't know what it meant. It didn't feel real to him.

Before Yosep could come to his senses, Park quickly said, "People are saying everyone made it out alive. The news called it a bomb, but the weapon was actually some kind of homemade toy, so not much damage was done. The only problem is that we can't tell how serious this could get if they target us next. What that agency received was a warning—we might get the real thing."

Yosep listened calmly to Park's outpouring of words. When

he blinked, his pooled sweat fell like tears. His long, tangled eyelashes were wet as if he had been crying, and underneath his left eye a small yellow twinkling piece of crystal had formed from all the saltiness. A grain of sand. A crumb of gold. Many would pay to lick at it, but the boy carelessly wiped it off with the back of his hand. Park caught himself making a regrettable expression in the mirror and pulled his gaze down to the floor.

They were in the basement practice room, pungent with the stench of sweat. The space reminded Park of his immature era, of boys throwing their fists before exchanging words and spitting onto filthy cement. But Yosep, standing in the middle of it all, emitted only a faint aroma of soap and heat. Suddenly overcome with fear of him, Park cowered. He might get burnt from the heat if he approached the boy any closer. From between Yosep's lips and teeth leaked light breathing sounding like steam. After a long while Yosep began to speak.

"It's because of me, isn't it?"

"Huh?"

"The attack on the agency, it happened because of me."

Park didn't answer.

"Hyung." Yosep was pleading. "I'm so scared."

Despite Park's silence, the boy continued.

"I can't do this, not anymore."

Yosep's eyes looked blank, as though they were made of glass. His cheeks flushed pink. Park stared at Yosep's face again. Even though Park saw it often, that face of his would sometimes stab his heart. It wasn't a figure of speech—it really did hurt. *If I start feeling sympathy, all bets are off,* Park reminded himself. He looked away from Yosep's innocent, childlike face and rummaged through his brain. He could bring up the contract, or even try something more tangible, like threatening or coercing him. There were several options, but he chose to coax Yosep with soft words.

"I know you're a nice, responsible guy," he began. "But you need to think about all the people who depend on you. You know that our boss, me, and the rest of the company are relying on you. Your pride is important, of course, but you have to survive, even if life gets a little messy. To survive is to win. You know that, don't you?"

"I feel so sorry for her."

"But not for us?"

Yosep didn't say anything.

"Sep," Park called him affectionately.

"What can I do, then?"

Park was waiting for Yosep to say that. He reeled off the rough plan he had come up with. When he said Yosep would have to pretend to kill himself, the idol's eyes grew wide. Two of his lower teeth peeked out between his loosened lips.

"Kill myself?" he whispered.

As if trying to put spilled water back in a cup, Park hastily replied, "Not for real. You just have to pretend you tried. It takes about five hours to die by burning charcoal, they say. You can take some sleeping pills and sleep it off. Then I'll wake you up before it gets too dangerous. All we need is for news to break about your suicide attempt."

"What good would that do?"

"You win sympathy. No one can blame you, and no one can attack you."

Yosep fell into silence.

"It sounds messed up, doesn't it?" Park asked apologetically.

Yosep shook his head. "No, it's okay. But . . . where do I do it? I can't do it at home. I don't want to cause a commotion."

"You can do it in a car."

"Can I? People would follow me."

"You can use my car. It's new, and the windows are tinted, so that should work. I'll leave it in your parking lot. Take it out on a fixed day and time every week for the next couple of months. Think of it as going for a drive, make a lap around the neighborhood. But remember, you have to go to the same spot every time. Make a habit out of it. That way, no one would suspect where I find you."

Yosep asked back slowly, "Would that really . . . work?"

"You think it wouldn't?"

"I mean, the people. Would they really understand me? It's like I'm putting on a show . . ."

"Sep."

"Yes?"

"Isn't that what we all do, put on a show?"

After a long while, Yosep murmured, "You're right, hyung."

"Let's start with the driving, starting this week."

"Okay."

"I'm sorry to put you through this."

"No, it's okay," Yosep said, shaking his head. "It's all my fault. I trust you, hyung. Who else would I trust?"

Yosep's gaze stabbed at Park again. Park closed his eyes as if he could avoid it that way.

—

"Did you get all of it down?" Mihee asked.

"More or less," Nami replied. "What is the magazine called?"

"Any one will do. An entertainment magazine, though."

"Okay."

Nami checked the shopping list written in her notepad again. After making sure she hadn't missed anything, she put the notepad and the pen in the front pocket of her shirt, shouldered a hiking backpack, and threw on her raincoat over it.

"I'll be back," Nami shouted into the house.

Ahnna rushed out, yelling, "Wait, wait, I nearly forgot. Get a bag of flour, too."

Watching Nami put on her boots near the doorway, Mihee asked, "What for?"

"What do you mean, what for?" shrugged Ahnna. "We can make sujebi or noodles with some broth, griddle some pancakes, fritters—you name it. With this rainy weather we're having, it's only right to cook something with flour at least once."

When Mihee didn't react enthusiastically, Ahnna asked, "Why? Do you not like flour?"

"No, it's just that, I just had too much food made of flour growing up and got tired of it."

"Yeah? Did your parents sell it or something?"

"Sorry?"

Ahnna sounded more curious than Mihee was. "You just said you had food made of flour all the time. Your parents didn't own a noodle restaurant, then?"

"Oh," Mihee smiled and fudged, "Well, something like that."

"I'm off." Nami stood up straight. "I don't like flour that much, either, so I'll get a small bag."

"No, it's fine. Don't bother, then," said Ahnna.

"Are you sure?"

"Yes. It's not much fun if I eat it by myself, now, is it? Oh, get dried jujubes if they have some. I'll put them in when I boil water to drink."

"Got it."

Ahnna turned around swiftly at Nami's reply, but Mihee walked out to the door barefoot and opened the door for Nami.

"I don't know what that unnie eats to sustain herself," Mihee muttered. "I think she might collapse at some point."

"Should I get a bag of flour, then?" asked Nami.

"No, she'd barely eat it, anyway. We don't need another thing to worry about." Then Mihee added, "Be careful out there."

Without a word, Nami waved and put on her hat over her headphones. As soon as she stepped out of the door, the fierce wind and light rain flapped her raincoat. It wasn't the best weather, but at least the heavens weren't opening. Among the noises raging around her, she could hear Yosep's voice. *I am going to feed the owner of this voice.* The thought gave her a surge of strength. Not one to shy away from puddles,

Nami marched on, playfully splashing away. The boots she'd borrowed from Mihee were too small for her, and her toenails ached as though they would break at the slightest bump. If this weather were to continue, she'd better get a new pair. She mused over the idea while nearly sliding down the hill.

Nami drove to a big supermarket situated near a tourist spot. The three women had staked out the place, judging that the location would draw less attention to an odd outsider. With the bad economy and prolonged rain, the supermarket hadn't received much traffic despite the vacation season. Even when the speaker high up on the wall blasted the latest pop music, the store was engulfed in the gloom of a business threatening to close. Instead of taking a leisurely stroll inside as she had originally planned, Nami diligently crossed items off her shopping list. She bought dried jujubes and looked for a pair of boots in the fishing section. All the sizes they had in stock were too small, so she didn't bother buying any. The only thing left on the list was the magazine Mihee had asked for. Nami stood next to the metal rack at the checkout and scanned through the magazines littered with yellow and red in their titles. Most of them were luring readers with scandalous headlines. Without realizing it, Nami ended up browsing the magazines for quite a while. At one point, she felt alone and lifted her head to find that the cashiers had all left their stations to gather at the storefront.

A young man wearing only swimming shorts that reached his knees was babbling something. His skimpy outfit stood out, but the clerks seemed to be more interested in what he had to say than in his nearly naked body. Intrigued, Nami hovered nearby, pretending to pick out items as she eavesdropped. The man was saying that an unidentified body had been found on the beach close by. It wasn't unusual for a corpse to float ashore at this time of year, but those incidents had become more frequent.

"It's not the same as the last time, though, is it?" a young clerk asked. He looked fresh out of high school.

"It is," the man replied. "Another young man."

He made scissors with his index and middle fingers and imitated a snip. The women around him groaned.

"Gosh, how horrible. Must be a suicide."

"What kind of crazy bastard would castrate himself before taking his own life?"

"Maybe he's a gang member."

"No, he's gotta be from the North. Remember all that hullabaloo about the submarine coming down? I'm sure they're going to block this area off soon."

The man shrugged awkwardly. "Maybe. Anyway, the police came and kicked me out right away."

Nami was captivated by the story, to which everyone was adding their two cents, until someone tapped on her arm. She flinched but stepped aside calmly.

"You can go ahead," she said as she turned around, only for her jaw to drop at the outfit of the woman standing behind her.

The middle-aged woman was wearing a white dress with a slightly creamy tone. It looked a little ridiculous to wear to a supermarket; it was the kind of dress that would stand out anywhere except at a wedding. The woman seemed unbothered by Nami's shock, and looked her straight in the eyes.

"It's not my oppa," she said.

"Excuse me?"

"That's not my oppa. The real one's coming soon. My oppa . . ."

That was the last thing she said before fleeing the store.

"Geez, that lady. I told her not to come." One of the cashiers nearby tutted. He turned to Nami and asked offhandedly, "Miss, are you okay?"

Hiding her face with her hair, Nami nodded and placed the items on the counter. The cashier pushed in the swing door that came up to his knees and muttered, "Such troubled times we live in . . ."

He had said that to no one in particular, but everyone seemed to agree as they sighed and dispersed. Like peeing on frozen feet, the news of a dead body had only temporarily heated the atmosphere. It seemed like the persistent rain had transformed even the primitive toy called death into something slippery and sticky—something that couldn't be held or fiddled with.

Nami bowed to the sallow-faced cashier, who handed her a receipt under the bluish light, and left the store. She sat in the driver's seat, started the engine, and turned the car around toward the mansion, suppressing the impulse to drive along the coast.

After parking the car partway up the hill, Nami walked the remaining distance back to the mansion. She half-heartedly announced her arrival while unloading the purchased items on the table and rushed to the bathroom before she got cold. Stripping down and rubbing herself with a towel soaked in soapy water, she noticed that her arm ached from carrying the shopping bags up the hill. It would be so convenient if she could take the car right in front of the mansion. Yosep might have lost his memory, but he hadn't gone deaf. He might grow suspicious if he learned that the women were out driving around when he believed they were marooned in the mansion. What if his memory came back? They wouldn't be able to keep scaring him and bandaging him up the way they were now. They might have to resort to breaking his leg, like in *Misery*.

"That can't happen. He needs to dance," Nami said to herself loudly.

And even if they did decide to do that, who would take on the job? Breaking a leg? None of them wanted that. Probably. If no one volunteered, she would do it, but still. Nami remembered hearing that breaking a bone off cleanly made it stronger when it healed. Even if she made a mistake and inflicted a serious injury, Yosep's singing was decent enough to continue his career. Wouldn't it be nice, in its own way, to rely solely on singing skills as a singer? A handsome young singer who became incapacitated from an accident. Kind of romantic, wasn't it? Nami sank deep into her thoughts while staring at the water in the basin. On the surface floated Yosep, sorrowfully singing in a chair. *You win one when you lose one*, Nami thought, crouched. Maybe Yosep would really become a master singer. A singer who tugged at people's heartstrings not with skills but with sincerity. Take the movie *Seopyeonje*, for example. Real vocals came only after going blind.

These thoughts helped Nami accept the unexpected turn of events as fate, more or less. Yosep's suicide attempt and memory loss, and the persistent rain. All those were producing better results than the four women's original plan. Maybe, just maybe, this was what was meant to happen from the beginning. In this world, mistakes often turn out better than plans, and this might be one of those cases . . .

By the way, Nami wondered, *is it true that Misery isn't the name of the scary lady but rather of the pretty girl who appeared in the novel written by the man who got kidnapped?*

Nami ruffled her hair as she left the bathroom. The dining table had already been tidied up. Mihee was presumably upstairs, and Ahnna was preparing a meal in the kitchen. The blunt kitchen knife made her chopping look laborious. She asked to sharpen the blade with a whetstone later, and Nami nodded. Then she stuffed a dried piece of bread into her mouth and scooped up some rice and soup before heading to the guest room.

Awoken by the sound of the door opening, puffy-faced Yosep blinked a few times. Nami looked into his eyes and smiled slightly. Yosep returned the smile but soon looked away, probably feeling too shy. Nami reached to close the door behind her.

"Were you sleeping?" she whispered.

"Yes, though not for very long . . ." Yosep nodded, and stared down at his hands.

Nami pulled a chair to his bedside and gazed at his face.

The boy kept his eyes fixed on his hands, except when he stole glances at Nami as if to gauge her thoughts. Every time their eyes met, Nami smiled or twitched her eyebrows in support, but she was busy observing Yosep's face and didn't realize that her expression was stiff most of the time.

Even in the delicate darkness of a cloudy afternoon, she could see Yosep was blushing. She grew deeply emotional over the sentiment blossoming in their relationship, which was as intangible and vague as mist. Yosep was finally breaking out of his shell. He didn't realize it himself, but in her eyes, he was as transparent as the intestines of a mutant ectotherm. *Any moment now.* Nami's chest heaved with pride. Yosep would soon realize that she was the only one who recognized his true self. He would also come to understand that the two of them would be perfect only after they formed a couple, like sea creatures that lived in symbiosis, with one fish hiding, feeding, and one fish protecting the other.

The woman Nami had met during the day suddenly occurred to her. The woman wandering in a wedding dress without her groom. A madwoman may be happier than anyone else; it is just the observers who are driven to pain. Humans need to depend on each other. Nami was lucky to have found her mate in time, but some weren't. She had to be compassionate toward them.

Overcome with happiness, Nami spoon-fed soup to Yosep. His parting lips induced a spontaneous awe. *Ah, so pretty. How pretty.* Nami pretended she was clumsy with the spoon and grazed her finger against his upper lip. Watching food going into Yosep's baby-chick-like mouth fulfilled her more than watching a goose's liver fattening pleases a farmer.

As if to test him, Nami placed a pill on her palm. *Lick it. Lick it, Yosep. Let's put an end to today's game.* Suppressing the urge to pull back her hand mischievously, she stared at Yosep's face. The moment he slowly lowered his head and was about to reveal the crown of his head, voices floating in through the open door snatched Nami's attention away. The sounds were muffled, and the words couldn't be made out, but someone was certainly losing her temper. Nami wanted to ignore it, but the commotion nagged at her. Should she go and have a look? She was unconsciously frowning in irritation, when she felt a tickle on her palm like a baby bird's peck. Startled, she withdrew her hand and gawked at Yosep, but he simply drank his water, smiled and opened his mouth like a child to show that he had taken the pill. *Ah, how lovely! How adorable!* As she stood up, Nami wiped away her grin. *My better half, where in the world did you come from?* Excited at the thought of recalling the ticklish brushing against her palm later that night, all the while trying hard to hide her rage and annoyance at the ruckus outside the door that had interrupted their time together, Nami waved at Yosep as she stepped backwards and closed the door. Thinking how stupid the noise outside was for ceasing as soon as she turned the doorknob, she nearly danced her way to the living room.

In the kitchen, a pot of broth was boiling. Foam threatened to spill all over the stove as steam from the pot furiously shot up above it, but no one was paying attention. Nami scuttled across the living room to turn off the stove. After the pot quieted down, she turned around to face the two women confronting each other.

Heeae was standing at the doorway. Her face was flushed red, and her short hair, wet from the rain, was slicked back behind her ears. Across from her was Ahnna, also red in the face, but unlike Heeae, who looked as shabby as a country mouse, Ahnna was as frightening as a goblin.

"It's been a while."

Heeae was the first one to speak. She revealed a meek smile to Nami and handed her a plastic bag.

"I brought some medicine," she said. "For Yohan. And for Ahnna, and a little bit of chocolate for everyone else . . ."

"I told you to send it to the post office. Then I'll go retrieve it," Ahnna spat, her voice soft yet annoyed.

"But—"

"No buts. I told you we have to be careful for a while, you can't just come over here. Can't you stay put for a few more days? Soon enough, you'll be able to see him all you want."

"But there hasn't been much talk about him on TV. It looked like no one has contacted or followed him so far, so . . ."

"That's what *you* think. You think everyone else gets followed because they're dumb?" Ahnna snapped coldly. "You're just being selfish. You can't just barge in here because you want to see him. You think that'll work? You haven't forgotten that he's a celebrity, have you? What if a hit piece on him comes out? Then what?"

Heeae stayed silent.

"Go home. Right now. Why do you think we're hiding all the way out here?" Then, Ahnna muttered through clenched teeth, "Idiot."

She began to shove Heeae's back. Little by little, Heeae was pushed out of the door by the mysteriously strong power emanating from Ahnna's scrawny body. Puzzled, Mihee came down the stairs and tried to interject, but Nami grabbed her hand to stop her. Mihee quickly figured out what was happening and observed the two women's quarrel with her lips sealed. Things had gotten a bit ugly, but no one could stop them now. Ahnna was so enraged that the others could nearly feel the heat surging from her. Amidst the swelter, Heeae quietly blurted out:

"I can't leave."

"What?"

"The last bus of the day has already gone."

"What are you talking about? It's not even six yet."

"I'm serious. Here, look at the timetable."

With her face now even redder, Heeae pulled a folded piece of paper from her pocket. Ahnna glared at the paper for a long while, and then sighed. "This is why I can't stand the boonies."

"Also . . ." Heeae said in a barely audible voice, trembling like a skinned mouse. "He's my son. You have no right to stop me from seeing my son . . ."

Mouth agape, Ahnna clenched her fist. Fearing that Ahnna might strike Heeae in her fury, Mihee butted in.

"That sounds like a good idea. Why don't we let her stay

the night? So she can enjoy some nice mother-and-son time."

Unable to find a reason to oppose it, Nami also nodded. Three to one. Ahnna was outnumbered. In the end, she nodded with an irritated look.

"Fine. But only enter when he's asleep."

Heeae seemed to want to say something but didn't.

"You're not telling me you want to see him when he's awake, are you?" Ahnna frowned. "Imagine how shocked he would be to see you all of a sudden when he's already sick."

Heeae nodded, her face drained. "Okay. I'll go see him when he falls asleep."

"Good." Ahnna then turned to Nami. "Nami."

"Yes?"

"Did you give him his pill?"

"Of course. Don't worry."

"Good. And don't forget to medicate him, okay? He's a sick child," Ahnna sighed. "We should eat, too. You, pull out the dishes up there."

Nervous, Heeae stood still before hesitantly entering the mansion and, with trembling hands, arranged the dishes as she was told. Ahnna turned the stove back on and swept chopped green onions into the pot, while Mihee set spoons and chopsticks on the table. Watching all of them in action, Nami thought: why did they all try so hard when, in the end, she was the one who was going to win Yosep's heart?

—

The wind grew stronger as the night wore on, the sound of it whipping the window becoming more frequent. Ahnna sat at the table, staring at the branches bending in the gusts as she drank a cup of freshly brewed tea. It had tasted quite bland when she had only boiled mushroom, but the brew now had a subtle sweetness with the dried jujube blended in. The tree out the window twisted and turned along with the wind, but its clumsy dance wasn't interesting enough to kill time. Especially when Heeae was in Yosep's room.

I should do *something*, Ahnna thought, and opened the weekly magazine Nami had bought earlier. It was a sleazy rag, mainly focused on sensationalized political scandals, celebrity gossip, eschatology, and sex counselling, with ads running on the bottom of the pages highlighting pills for erectile dysfunction and hair-loss, penis enlargement surgeries, and phone sex services. Ahnna read a few paragraphs of trashy erotica—about a bald man and a woman who fetishized bald heads—before flinging the magazine away. She then turned to Mihee, whose head was dense with hair. The young woman was plopped on the table across from Ahnna, fumbling with a radio.

"What's that?" Ahnna asked.

"A radio."

Well, I know that much . . . Ahnna hesitated a bit before acknowledging Mihee's flat response, but she soon asked again, "Did you bring it here?"

"No, I found it." Only then did Mihee meet eyes with Ahnna. "It was in my room. Someone must have left it a long time ago."

"Does it work?"

"Not sure."

Mihee fiddled with the fully extended antenna and pressed the power button. Only static mixed in with the sound of rain. With the tip of her fingernails, she carefully turned the dial, one click at a time. After straining their ears for a while, the two suddenly received a response in Japanese.

"I suppose Japanese radio signals reach here, too," Mihee muttered as she pulled away from the radio. Her face serious, she listened attentively to the broadcast before turning the radio off.

"Was it boring?" Ahnna asked.

"I don't know. I can't speak Japanese."

A testy response. That girl could get touchy sometimes for no reason. *I can never understand young people these days,* Ahnna thought, as she rose from the table and headed over to the kitchen sink. Nami was crouched over the kitchen knife, her fingers gathered together to sharpen it. The shuddering sound of the blade rubbing against the whetstone harmonized with the wind raging outside. Ahnna felt a chill run down the back of her neck, but upon seeing the blunt knife—once unable to cut a single stalk of green onion—now emit a cold sheen after a few dashes of water and friction, she felt a pleasant sense of satisfaction.

"Are you done?" she asked Nami. "If so, there's a pair of scissors in the bathroom. Could you sharpen those, too?"

"Scissors?"

"Yes, they're in the water cup. I'm thinking about cutting Yosep's hair next week or so."

"Okay," Nami answered without lifting her head. After a deep exhale, she turned around and examined the whetted knife under the kitchen light.

"I'll work on them after I'm done with this," she said. "I need to whet it more."

"Okay. You can take your time to make sure they're sharp. All the metal tools in this place are in bad shape."

"Leave it to me. Sharpening knives is my specialty."

"Did your aunt also perform gut rituals?" Ahnna asked.

"She still does," Nami answered. "Though she's quite pricey."

"Yeah? How much does she charge?"

"Depends on the matter at hand . . . Why, are you interested?"

"You know. Just in case."

"It's okay. I should be able to handle things. No need to go to my aunt," Nami said resolutely before lowering her head back over the knife.

Ahnna sat at the table again and sipped the cold tea for a while. As Mihee and Nami hung their heads over their projects, she murmured that she was going to the bathroom, and slipped out of the kitchen.

Just washing her face made Ahnna feel refreshed. She stood in front of the mirror and scrutinized herself. Under the low lighting, her dark eyes looked profound and melancholic. She spent some time examining every inch of her face. Whether it was because of the clean mountain air and water, or because of Yosep's presence, she appeared much livelier than she had in Seoul. Something similar had happened to her before. When she was seeing the blond Josef, she had looked so beautiful that passersby would check her out. Whenever she walked down the street, a man or two always let out a whistle. People's gazes used to be the cushion that made high heels on hard pavement tolerable. The memories brought a subtle blush to her cheeks. It is said that medieval witches bathed in the blood of virgins to retain their youth. But as far as Ahnna knew, nothing was more potent than a beautiful boy.

She giggled to herself for a while, then headed over to the guest room and knocked on its door. Not to complain about the mother–son reunion taking too long, but to check and see if Yosep was sleeping soundly. But the moment she saw Heeae holding a rag with a dumbfounded expression, her mood immediately plummeted. She came all this way just to keep playing maid? The sight enraged her. She couldn't take it any longer.

"Come out for a second. We need to talk," she told Heeae, who only cranked her head out the door.

"Can't it wait?"

"It won't take long," Ahnna pressed. "I just have something to ask you. Besides, now you'll get to see him every day."

Heeae forced herself to nod. Before she left the room, she examined the dresser and brought out an armful of Yosep's clothes.

"What is it?" she asked.

Seeing the bunch of laundry, Ahnna forgot even the excuses she had made up and snatched Heeae's wrist.

"Hey, what do you think you're doing?" she snarled.
"What?"
"Aren't you here to see Yosep? So why—what . . ."
"Oh, this?"
Heeae broke out of her blank expression and smiled bashfully.
"If you don't handwash his laundry, it'll get a bit . . ." Her voice trailed off, embarrassed. "You know how washing machines can't wash grime off properly. They just make lint fly everywhere. When I lived with your family, I handwashed almost everything at the creek behind your building. Even if they say they purify tap water with chemicals and whatnot, it's still gross Han River water. But that creek had the cleanest water you can imagine. It had crawfish in the summer, too . . ."

Ahnna pursed her lips and didn't say a word. She was thinking about how another woman she knew had claimed the same thing: her mother-in-law. While visiting Seoul for a relative's wedding ceremony, the old woman had stayed at Ahnna's house and scrubbed the floor with a rag each day and night. She had prepared a tableful of breakfast and pulled down all the underwear that Ahnna had hung out to dry just to handwash all of it again, deliberately making up things to do without a moment's rest. From a distance, it had looked like Ahnna was lazing about while working her mother-in-law to the bone, but in reality, that wasn't true. She was constantly subjected to her mother-in-law's passive-aggressive nudging, as the woman demonstrated to Ahnna how to look after her son. Ahnna snorted. Did she really think that would make her move even a finger? In her mother-in-law's eyes, Ahnna's husband was a precious little boy who needed to be treated like a king, but to Ahnna, he was just a pathetic bum. Did that woman think her son would have become a professor without Ahnna? If it weren't for her, the man would still be living in a flophouse and drinking soju with kimchi juice as a side dish—her mother-in-law should be thanking her. Why in the world did Ahnna have to get on all fours like a dog to wipe the floor? Did she really have to wash his underpants and wield kitchen knives so early in the morning?

Ahnna's glare burned with fury. Puzzled, Heeae avoided her gaze with a smile. That scared face. As if she was saying, *I don't know anything, I just like to keep things clean.* It enraged Ahnna even more. *Trash,* she thought. *You got that? You're trash . . .*

At that moment, Mihee's cool voice fell upon the two women's heated faces.

"Better forget about it." Still sprawled over the dining table, she told Heeae, "It's raining."

As if she had only just realized, Heeae flailed. "Oh, right, it is. Gosh, I'm sorry. I'll fold them again. I'm a bit all over the place . . . It's because I haven't seen Yohan . . . that boy . . . in so long. Too long."

Heeae circled round and round on the same spot before disappearing up to the second floor. Ahnna was glaring at the staircase for a while when Mihee's voice called out from behind her.

"Unnie."

Ahnna didn't reply.

"Ahnna unnie."

"What?" she snapped.

"Let her be," Mihee urged. "Telling her what to do will only wear you out. Some people are like that. Like lions at the circus. They feel most relaxed when they're in a cage. And they both need the occasional beating to come to their senses."

"I just—"

Before Ahnna could say anything more, Mihee stood up and stretched.

"What time even is it? How come I'm so tired? I'm gonna go to bed now," she yawned. "Nami, are you done with the headphones?"

"Oh, I put them on the couch," Nami replied. "Thank you."

"Did you get a new pair?"

"No."

"What? Why not? Did the store not sell them?"

"No, I just forgot. But I figured I'd be fine since you have a pair."

It took a moment before Mihee replied, "Then let me know when you need the headphones. You can borrow them when I'm not using them." She then added, "Excuse me," cocking her head in a bow and climbing up the stairs to the second floor.

Nami hunched over the whetstone again, scrubbed the blade a few more times, and raised it up against the light. Even when it was sharp enough, she still examined the knife, dissatisfied. Ahnna sat on the living-room couch, pretending to be deep in thought while pricking her ears for noise coming from the guest room. She was hoping to hear Yosep groan in his sleep, but no sound caught her ears. The rainfall drowned out all the other noises. *So loud . . .* Ahnna thought to herself, slowly closing her eyes. She removed the sound of the bombarding raindrops one by one—their rapping on the window, falling into puddles, shooting down on leaves. Then the room became completely tranquil . . .

Until she heard knocking. She followed the noise to the front door. When she pressed her ear against the door, someone called her name. *Ahnna. Ahnna.* She opened the door. But no one was there. At first, she thought it was a prank, until someone tugged at her clothes. She looked down to find a small child. A stranger.

Let me in, the child said. Confused, Ahnna nodded instinctively. The child shook his head.

No, tell me to come in.

Okay, come in.

As soon as she said so, the child rushed through the door. Out of nowhere, other children followed him in. Mischievous children. They began to frolic in the mansion. Some jumped on the couch, some covered themselves in soot while prodding the fireplace, and some dragged Ahnna to the kitchen and constantly poked their heads in. *How do you do this? What about that?* She took away the kitchen knife from one child's hand, lifted another who was frantically opening and closing the fridge door and seated them at the table, washed another child's dirty hands with water, and spanked yet another child, scolding them not to kick up dust. Oddly enough, Ahnna was delighted by the chaos. Even though the arm she used as a pillow began to feel numb in her sleep, she made an effort to stay in the dream and wondered, *Do I want to have a child?* No, she always considered the very idea awful . . .

When she woke up, her chin ached as if she had dislocated it in her sleep. With her eyes closed, she wiped the drool that dribbled down her chin. She could feel a blanket sliding down her shoulder. Someone must have covered her with it while she was asleep. She reached over and pulled it up. As she was rubbing her body, trembling from the chill, she heard knocking at the front door.

"Yes, come in," she replied, still dazed.

No one replied.

"Please. Come in."

And no one came in. Ahnna sprang up as if someone had splashed her with cold water. Outside was inexplicably bright. She dashed toward the living-room window and peeked between the curtains. The rain was as loud as ever, and the wind was still wild enough to break branches from the trees. But she didn't remember that car parked in the yard, headlights blinking. Before she could make head or tail of it, the lights vanished. She could hear a car door close. A shadow, its identity unknown, began to climb up the front porch stairs. Her mouth let out a strange groan as if her tongue had plugged up her throat.

Were they done for? She squeezed at the front of her shirt.

Maybe the shadow had already sensed that something was wrong. As though to prove her speculation, its strides were a bit off. It seemed to have noticed that people were present in the mansion. Given the place was supposed to have been empty for several years, its steps were instinctively vigilant. There had to be a reason why the shadow had come all this way in the middle of the night. It was led to the front door by a will stronger than instinct. The shadow pulled a key out of its pocket. It inserted the key into the hole.

After flipping the switch it had fumbled around for, the shadow seemed surprised to find that the mansion had working electricity. At the sight of Ahnna's puffy face, it merely raised its eyebrows, too shocked to say a word.

"Uh . . ." the man stuttered. He lowered his head almost reflexively. "Sorry, but, uh, who are you?"

Apologizing was his first mistake. Ahnna scanned him, seizing the upper hand in the encounter. The man, with a plain hairstyle and a dumbstruck expression, blinked incessantly as Ahnna stared. Only then did she realize who he was. In a coy tone a girl would use with a boy she had a crush on, Ahnna said: "You . . . You're Seongwuk."

The man stood stunned.

"Don't you remember me? It's Auntie Ahnna."

"Ah."

Seongwuk began to rack his brain. Finally, he seemed to recall the person he unknowingly had passed by at barbecues and church gatherings all those years ago.

"Oh, Auntie. How have you been?" he stammered.

How lucky. Ahnna suppressed the laughter that was

climbing up her throat. The Choi family who owned this mansion were insolent little bitches, but Seongwuk was so tender it made her wonder if he had been adopted. Thanks to nature's tricks, the young man had blossomed with an inferior gene that had become obsolete ages ago. He was a boy who resembled no one. It distressed his mother, Eunyeong, but that was who Seongwuk was.

"Yes. You didn't recognize me, did you?" Ahnna began to ask sharply again.

"No, it's just, it's been a while . . ."

"Sure. I mean, you were always so busy studying that I barely saw you at your family gatherings, anyway. So, is life at your dream college treating you well?"

"You know, it's good."

"My gosh. Hey, pull your shoulders back straight. Why are you crouched over like a wuss? Just how old are you now?"

"Uh, twenty-one."

"And the military? Did you serve?"

"Not yet."

"I see, that explains a lot. Why haven't you yet?"

"I studied another year for the college entrance exam, so . . ."

"Oh, right, right. I remember. That's why Eunyeong unnie had a hard time shuttling you back and forth last year . . ." Ahnna reminisced with a dreamy expression, gazing into the distance. "You'll be serving soon enough, then. Defending the country is important. Korea isn't a unified country yet . . ."

"Yeah," Seongwuk slurred. "There's also a troop stationed near here."

"Is that so?"

"Yes. We're not too far from North Korea, so . . ." He blinked for a while before he asked the question he had been putting off for a while. "By the way, what . . . what brings you here, Auntie?"

"Here? What, is it weird to you that I'm here?"

"No, it's not that . . ."

"I've been coming here since I was much younger than you are right now, kid."

"I'm sorry."

"Gosh, how come you're always apologizing? Look, your shoulders are hunched again. Straighten them." Ahnna slapped Seongwuk's shoulder and muttered as she picked dust off his clothes, "Your mom told me to come check the place out."

Rubbing his shoulder, Seongwuk asked, "M-My mom did?"

"Yes. A house deteriorates if no one lives in it. You must be on vacation. Why aren't you visiting your family in the U.S.?"

"Oh, well, I'm seeing some friends."

"Yeah? Your college friends?"

"Yes, something like that . . ." Seongwuk trailed off.

Suddenly, Ahnna gripped Seongwuk's arm like a meat hook would.

"Ow," the boy moaned, but Ahnna pretended she didn't hear and pulled him into the kitchen.

"Where are my manners? I should've at least offered you a cup of tea," she beamed. "Sit here. I'll get the water going."

Overwhelmed by her vigor, Seongwuk tottered down into a chair. Like a guest in an unfamiliar place, he stole furtive glances at his grandfather's mansion, which could become his own someday. Ahnna scurried around him to divert his attention.

"What would you like? Coffee? We have yulmu tea, and also hot water brewed with mushrooms and dried jujube. I picked the mushrooms myself, nearby. It's good for your health."

"Oh, I'll have yulmu tea. Thank you."

Ahnna filled the kettle, set it on the stove, and stood on tiptoe to pull out yulmu powder from the cabinet. Then she sat across from Seongwuk and mindlessly wiped down the spotlessly clean table. Seongwuk pulled down his hands which hung awkwardly over the table and gathered them over his lap.

"What do college students do these days?" Ahnna asked, eyeing his hands.

"I'm sure they do whatever you did back in your day."

"Back in my day? How would you know how things were back in my day?"

She was only joking, yet Seongwuk dropped his gaze, frightened. How in the world did this family produce such a nitwit? Ahnna nearly clucked her tongue but stopped herself with incredible restraint.

"So, when does Jinwuk finish college?" She managed to change the subject.

"He should graduate early next year."

"Yeah? I'm jealous of Eunyeong unnie. Her oldest son attends a prestigious college in the U.S., and her younger son goes to the best college in Korea just like his father and grandfather did. Am I right?"

To her flattery, Seongwuk sat up straight, blushing.

"Auntie, the water's boiling," he said.

"Oh, you're right."

Ahnna got up, turned the stove off, and reached for a mug. Then she opened the yulmu powder bag and scooped two spoonfuls into the mug.

"Sugar?" she asked.

"Um, just a teaspoon," answered Seongwuk.

Ahnna opened the cabinet again with the mug in one hand. No sugar in there. She crouched down and opened all the drawers that she could reach, chatting up Seongwuk all the while.

"I didn't realize it when you were young, but you take after your mother. I bet you get that a lot, don't you? Hmm?"

"Uh, not really."

"No? In my opinion, you do. It's a good thing. What if you resembled your father? He looks like a greedy cattle thief. Your mom is older now, but she was a star at her high school. They said she looked like Bette Davis."

Ahnna then feigned surprise and muttered, "Oh, there it is." She reached for the bag of sugar placed next to the rat poison in the corner of one of the lower cabinets. "What's it doing there?" She stealthily blocked Seongwuk's view with her body and with his spoonful of sugar, slipped a sleeping pill into his tea. This way, she could let the others out while Seongwuk was asleep. She hurriedly poured hot water from the kettle. Stirring the mug so the pill would dissolve quickly, she asked the question that had been at the tip of her tongue the entire time.

"By the way, what brings you here at this hour of night?"

Seongwuk remained silent.

"Hmm?"

Still no response. Instead, Ahnna could hear the noise of a chair dragging across the floor and some sort of air leaking. She turned around to see Seongwuk. The boy had stood up from his seat, his face heavily shadowed by the light glowing from behind him. But his puffed chest and straightened back, the blue veins bulging from his temples, neck, arms, and wrists, were all as vivid as close-up shots. He was a bomb about to explode. The blade that had just penetrated his chest was like a small fuse.

The mug fell from Ahnna's hand. When she saw the red blotch slowly growing before her eyes, she passed out on the spot. Two bodies fell onto the ground. The heart of one was pumping blood quickly, while that of the other flapped like a dying fish on the shore and soon ceased all movement. But the rain was undisturbed by such goings-on. It continued to pour down, regardless of what happened in the human world.

—

The headphones that Nami had returned to her sounded strange—some water had probably gotten inside them. Mihee used her blanket to wipe off the jack and slammed the earpads onto the pillow to dislodge the water, but she eventually gave up and lay down. With her eyes closed, she listened repeatedly to music that sounded wrapped in plastic. It made her feel as if she were submerged under the ocean. Immersed in the sensation, Mihee ruminated about her past.

When she was young, before she had learned how to love her mom she had learned how to pity her. Having come to Seoul at fourteen and begun to work in a factory, Mihee's mother was a sweet little beauty even in young Mihee's eyes. Everyone had told her she'd meet a good husband, but she always had exceptionally bad luck with men. The dads that wandered in and out of Mihee's life either had no jobs or had trouble holding them. Their gallant bluff about how they would buy her mom a huge diamond ring and a fur coat transformed into gallant violence. Whenever she passed the living room, making her best effort to ignore the household items shattered into pieces, Mihee became engulfed in shame and rage. She'd think, *What the hell is the problem? Why does this world have so many sons of bitches to offer?*

Less than a month after she ran away from home, Mihee learned that everything had been her mother's choice. In short, her mother was the type of person who grew bored with "just living." She craved constant stimulation. To her, a decent life meant she could find abundant happiness from "picking and choosing her fun every day," just like the ice-cream commercial said. But happiness in real life was like water dripping from a faucet that had run dry. After sticking out her tongue to barely a taste and glaring at the faucet until her eyes hurt, her mom could no longer stand the tedious wait. She refused to slowly wither away as nature directed, so she chose instead to set her tongue ablaze.

Some of the girls who wandered the streets with Mihee were the same type. Some really had nowhere to go, but many had decent families. Perfectly fine girls squatted along the road to see Yosep pass by for only a few seconds. They slept on the ground, peed in the bushes, and beat each other up while waiting for their idol. They yearned to know a human's mind one fathom deep, which was harder to know than the water ten fathoms deep. It didn't matter whether it was love or not. What did matter was that Yosep would appear before their eyes the moment boredom nearly drove them mad. No stimulation felt better than wholly devoting themselves to another person.

Mihee was turning twenty-two next year. At some point, she had become conscious of this thing called "the future." Soon enough, she would be too old not to feel ashamed of living on the streets and bouncing around other people's homes. It happened to be the end of a century, too. A new millennium would be here soon. The timing was perfect for her to change her way of life. Mihee thought that she wanted to give birth to a child. That was how she wanted to restart. But she was her mother's daughter. She couldn't be sure when that gene, whose sole talent was to step into the mire, would win over her willpower. Mihee was stuck with a dilemma: how could she break out of this curse?

If she were a princess in a fairy tale, her fairy godmother would help her. At first, Mihee thought Ahnna could be her godmother. But Ahnna turned out to be quite the calculating woman. She never did a favor without expecting something in return. She had once urged Mihee to call her unnie and acted as if she would give her anything, but ever since they had arrived at the mansion, Ahnna couldn't seem to stand Mihee even having so much as a meal, despite the fact that Ahnna herself had offered to cook. And since Mihee wasn't clever enough to lift her own curse, the only option that remained was a kiss from a prince. She was going to win, Mihee thought, gritting her teeth. She was going to win Yosep. Yosep was the highest-hanging fruit her hand could reach. And she had been cultivating that fruit with her love, support, and time. Picking it off its tree wouldn't be so easy. She didn't have a ladder, and her shoulder might dislocate, and maybe she'd sprain her ankle, but no matter. Once in her hands, the fruit would peel itself and drip juice. The moment she took a bite of the succulent fruit, she would be unbound from the old spell and ascend to the castle of eternal happiness.

Mihee was deeply immersed in her fantasies when she sensed someone's movement outside. She opened her eyes to see a window that had grown hazily bright. As she wondered whether dawn had already come, the light suddenly disappeared. She moved only her finger to turn the cassette player off. She lay motionless while pricking up her ears, but there was no noise except the rain. Her spine began to stiffen as though she had been skewered with a bamboo stick. She couldn't hold out any longer and got off her bed, half reluctant and half curious.

As soon as she opened the door, white light flared from

the living room. In the distance, Ahnna's voice faintly floated up through the splattering rain. *She's not in bed yet?* Mihee slowly descended the staircase, sliding her feet down the stairs. Just when she was about to call Ahnna's name, she heard another voice: a somewhat threatening, unfamiliar voice, seemingly belonging to a man. Frightened, Mihee stepped backwards on tiptoes. She returned to her room, locked the door, and perched at the edge of her bed. She caught her breath while listening to her own deafening heartbeat, soon realizing that Ahnna had softly called the man's name. That was strange, to say the least. She wouldn't address a robber like that.

Intrigued, Mihee went back down to the first floor. She took extra care not to make any noise, but before she could reach the last step, her eyes met Ahnna's, glaring back at her. Ahnna looked nervous and outraged at the same time. She had always been hot-tempered, but it was different this time. Her rage was real. The sheer intensity of her scowl stiffened Mihee like a statue, and while Mihee stood frozen to the spot, Ahnna snatched the man's arm like an eagle snatching a chicken and headed to the kitchen. She seated the man so that his back was turned to the living room. Then she placed her index finger to her lips for Mihee to see.

Someone you know? asked Mihee, moving only her lips, to which Ahnna blinked.

You want me to shut up? Mihee asked again.

This time, Ahnna nodded while pretending to swipe her hair behind her ears. Having received the sign, Mihee moved as if she had been released from a trap. She hid in the staircase's shadow and observed the two. Ahnna restlessly flung open the cabinet doors. Mihee couldn't hear the conversation clearly because of the rain, but from what she could tell from a distance, things seemed civil. Mihee eased her mind and decided to let Ahnna handle the situation. At that moment, a breeze swirled right next to her, and someone's shadow swiftly passed by.

Huh?

Before Mihee could stop it, a knife had entered the man's back.

Ahnna sat leaning against the sink, exhausted. The feces leaking out of the corpse had created a horrid stench in the living room, as had Ahnna wetting herself, but no one mentioned a word. Not that anyone was in their right mind to. Of all the people present, Nami was the only one who appeared unruffled by the events. She calmly boiled some water and made coffee, then rummaged through the cabinets. She pulled out a bottle of brandy that Mihee had no idea about and poured it into mugs. Nami crouched in front of the trembling Ahnna and thrust a mug at her.

"Have some," she said.

Ahnna slowly lifted her head and whispered hoarsely, "Are you crazy?"

"Have some first."

"You're crazy. Definitely crazy. Crazy, it's all crazy."

"Just a sip."

Nami forcefully opened Ahnna's hand and handed her the mug. But Ahnna didn't grip the mug, and it dropped onto the floor. It didn't shatter, but it was now stained with blood. Hot coffee spread across the floor, blending with the smells of ammonia and blood, as well as a whiff of alcohol that seemed to have drifted in from afar. Ahnna's low voice emerged above everything.

"You're crazy. You're clearly out of your mind."

Nami didn't respond.

"How, how could you—"

Suddenly, Ahnna drew in a breath and covered her mouth with her hands. Mihee thought she was going to burst into tears. But the next moment, what spurted out between Ahnna's fingers like a fountain was yellow gastric juice. Mihee, Heeae, and even Ahnna herself winced in surprise, but Nami, who got covered with it, didn't so much as blink. She stood up as if nothing had happened and poured the remaining coffee into a new mug. Then, to wash up the vomit, she stuck her head below the faucet like a middle-school boy who had just sprinted the school grounds. After she finished, Nami handed Ahnna a new cup of hot coffee mixed with brandy.

"Drink," she urged. "It'll bring you back to your senses."

Nami's face stayed blank as she spoke. The water droplets falling from her wet hair made concentric circles on the pool of blood. As if enchanted by Nami's spell, Ahnna drew the coffee mug close to her lips. One sip. Then another sip. The more the mug emptied, the more tears rolled down Ahnna's cheeks.

Nami squatted to Ahnna's eye level and said, "That helped, didn't it?"

Ahnna remained silent.

"What's done is done," Nami continued.

"Ha."

Ahnna clucked her tongue loudly. Her blazing eyes seemed to want to ask if it wasn't Nami herself who had made this happen, but she was silent. Judging that Ahnna was calmer, Nami rose up from her knees. There was a loud thud, and Nami suddenly disappeared from Mihee's sight. Startled, Mihee looked down at the floor to find that Nami had slipped on some blood, her arms and legs sprawled.

"I got a cramp," she muttered.

In spite of the other women's shock, Nami licked her finger, drenched in blood, and smudged it three times on the tip of her nose as per the superstition.

"Let me bring some rags for mopping," she said, struggling to stand.

Ahnna, silently emptying the mug, raised her hand to stop her. "Leave it. Don't you touch anything."

Nami hesitated.

"I said, don't," pressed Ahnna.

Nami stepped back with both her hands spread in surrender. Ahnna called Mihee instead.

"Mihee, I'm sorry. But could you?"

Mihee didn't reply.

"Please. I can't let her do it. She's the one who killed him," Ahnna pleaded, on the verge of tears. Sensing Mihee's hesitation, she quickly added, "I'm not asking for a favor. Over there, bring that to me."

Ahnna pointed at her wallet on the dining table. When Mihee handed it to her, Ahnna quickly pulled out a piece of paper without a proper look. Mihee was given the paper before she could say a word. She held it up against the light, flipped it, and counted the number of zeroes with her finger.

"Is this . . . real?" she asked, frowning.

Ahnna waved irritably as if the million-won check were some sort of fly. "Yes, so please . . . Please do something."

"I'll help, too." Heeae, who had been sitting at the table without saying a word, stood up. "This young lady can't do it alone. The body's bound to be quite heavy."

"No, Heeae." Ahnna's eyes brimmed with tears. "How could you say that? A person died in front of my eyes. You have to stay with me."

Heeae stared at Ahnna.

"Lee Heeae!"

Ahnna called pleadingly and began to sob. Heeae put her arm around Ahnna's shoulders and hoisted her up.

"Okay," she said. "Then let's take a bath first, shall we? You can't sleep like this."

Ahnna limped to the bathroom even though she wasn't injured. Bloody footprints trailed behind her. Heeae let out a deep sigh and cranked her head to mouth to Mihee: *Wait just a moment.*

Mihee nodded.

The rain seemed like it wouldn't be stopping any time soon. Mihee watched somewhat hopefully, but the corpse also seemed like it wouldn't move any time soon. *So he's really dead*, Mihee thought, staring down at the blood pooled on the floor. A person was dead. It had all happened so quickly. He was stabbed with a mere knife, and he died without so much as a yelp. Was it better that he died with a single strike? Even if he had survived, he would have been left unattended, unable to receive proper treatment. They would have been in bigger trouble if he ran into Yosep.

Mihee heard footsteps. She turned around and saw Heeae approaching her with an exhausted look.

"Is unnie asleep?" asked Mihee.

"Yes, she took some meds," Heeae replied. "What about Nami?"

"She went to bed. She seemed a little startled, but mostly okay. She hurt her hand, so I bandaged her."

Heeae rubbed at her face. "Why did she do it?"

"Sounds like she mistook him for a reporter or something. Still . . . she could have asked first."

"Oh, well. What's done is done."

"True."

Heeae inhaled deeply and rolled up her sleeves. "We should . . . probably bury him, right?"

"It's raining quite hard," Mihee pointed out. "Do you think it'll be okay?"

"But we can't leave him here. He's going to smell, too . . ."

After some hesitation, Heeae touched the knife stuck in the man's back. She tried pulling at it for a while, but soon gave up and put on a pair of rubber gloves. When she tried again, exerting force until her face turned red, the knife flung far away with a splatter of blood. Shocked, Mihee turned to Heeae, but Heeae calmly stood up and wiped the blood on her face with her arm.

"Do you have raincoats?" she asked.

"Yes."

"Then we should both wear one. And . . . Do you happen to have plastic bags for kimchi-making? Or old blankets. We'll also need shovels, and some twine would be handy."

"I'll look for them."

"Thank you. I'll clean up this mess in the meantime."

Mihee nodded. As she thought about how Heeae also wasn't in her right mind, judging from how nonchalantly she had rubbed off the blood splattered on her face, Mihee herself strode into the empty room on the second floor, the place she had thought was spooky and had been avoiding entering even in the daylight. In a daring, or rather, apathetic mood, she stripped the bedsheets from the two spare rooms and held them in her arms. Coughing at the dust, she headed down to the kitchen and found Heeae washing a mop.

"Did you find something?" Heeae asked, swiping her hair behind her ear.

Her cheek and apron were bloodied red. The scarlet liquid filling the bucket reminded Mihee of an art class, but the thickened metallic smell of blood pulled her back to reality.

"I took off the bedsheets," she replied, trying hard not to wrinkle her nose.

"Anything else useful?"

"No."

"There should be a shovel somewhere. That kind of tool is a must in mountains like these." Heeae rubbed her hand clean on the apron. "I'll clean up here first and look for it. Mihee, could you help me move the table?"

"Toward you?"

"No. Over there, on the other side. We need to spread the sheets here." In a brisk voice unbecoming of the situation, Heeae told Mihee, "Let's lift it together on my count. Okay, here goes. One, two . . ."

They picked up the table and moved it with a screech. The sound was louder than expected. The two turned to Yosep's bedroom door. All was quiet, but the chance of him waking made chills run down their spines. They hastily opened the blanket, placed the corpse on it, and rolled it up like a gimbap. The body was heavy and stiff. They had just begun cleaning up, yet their arms trembled from exhaustion. Giving all the strength they had, they sealed the corpse quickly. It looked pretty neat, with red twine tied at head and foot. All would have been fine if that was the end of it, but it just marked the beginning of their problems. Where in the world would they bury it? Since they were on private property, they could do it anywhere in the backyard. But what if the body got swept away with the silt in this rain? What if they couldn't find a shovel? Would they have to dig with spoons like jailbreakers? They could, but the corpse would rot and reek in the process. They were doing their best to ignore it, but the number of flies surrounding the corpse was only increasing, wasn't it? The moment her mind was about to collapse under self-doubt, Mihee caught the sound of a clap. She raised her head and saw Heeae, flushed red from perspiration, withdrawing her hands from her cheeks.

"I'm sorry," Heeae apologized. "I felt a bit dazed, so . . ."

Mihee shook her head.

"Why don't we go outside first?" Heeae suggested briskly to comfort Mihee. "Let's check out the spot to dig. We might find something useful in the meantime."

The two women brandished flashlights and went outside the mansion to search for tools. To save time, Mihee took the left and Heeae the right to circle the building. In the backyard, Mihee found an axe stuck in an old tree trunk. She also spotted a hoe, but neither would be helpful for digging up soil. She had already expected the worst, but the hopelessness of the situation drained her completely.

Mihee leaned against the outer wall of the mansion and stared at the dark forest. She so wished that a tiger would come down from the mountains: its thorned tongue would lick up and devour the corpse in the kitchen like candy. In her delusion, Mihee dozed off for a moment—a dreadful, shallow sleep with half a dozen dreams flashing immediately one after another. She felt like she was experiencing vertigo more than dreaming. Then she sensed something uneven against her back. Oddly bothered, she pushed herself up out of her temper and felt the wall. Her hand caught a door handle curved inward, and when she pulled at it, the door easily flung open. Now wide awake, Mihee shone her flashlight inside. A long staircase stretched down to the endless darkness of the basement. What was this place? Could she go in? As she stayed rooted to the spot in hesitation, Heeae approached her from around the other side of the mansion.

"Oh, it's a cellar," Heeae whispered. "A cellar should have it."

"A cellar?"

"Yes," Heeae continued, full of conviction and excitement, "I remember hearing the old man. He said he used the basement to clean and prep the animals he hunted. There should be something handy down there."

"Isn't it a bit strange? The door opened so easily."

"Why would they lock a door they'd expect no one to open?"

Before Mihee could stop her, Heeae strode down into the dark, musty underground. Mihee was left with no choice but to follow her. The well-built cement stairs were regular in height, so the two women made their way down in rhythmic steps. The further they advanced, the more they could feel the chill, which was categorically different from the cold air above ground that had been seeping into their bones.

The seemingly endless stairs finally came to an end. Mihee, floundering in the thick darkness, could hear a rustling against the wall. Lightly panicked, she fumbled for the switch. When the light came on, she grimaced at the sudden brightness and collapsed onto the floor. Heeae grabbed her arm to hoist her back up.

"Are you okay?" she asked.

But Mihee didn't open her eyes. She only gasped for a while before finally managing to mumble, "That, over there."

"Oh, it scared you. It's okay, it's nothing."

Heeae's grip around her arm tightened. That calmed Mihee enough to slowly open her eyes. While steadying her heart that had leapt to her throat, at the second look, what sat below a lightbulb was a mannequin the size of a boy. Only then did she relax and register the scenery inside. The cellar, seemingly located below the guest room on the first floor, gave off a vibe of someplace between a butcher shop and a leather workshop. A few empty bird cages hung from the ceiling, and various specimens and stuffed animals, ranging from insects to small birds, were on display. Unlike the taxidermies upstairs, which were as crisp and lively as if they had sliced a frame in time, the ones here were of poor quality, as though they would melt the moment the sunlight touched them.

Heeae picked up a glass eye from inside a glass bottle and held it up against the light. "I think he made these himself. That's probably why he hid them down here."

She carefully placed the eyeball back into the bottle and took a step back to look around the cellar. Judging from the foldable camping bed, some cooking ware, and simple toiletries, the owner must have stayed here for quite some time. There was even running water in the corner area, which was about three square meters in size and had been finished with tiles. When Mihee squatted by the tiles and twisted the tap, water came flowing out.

"Seems like the space is ready for someone to move in," Heeae said, staring at the yellow tiles soaking in water.

"It must have been an air-raid shelter," Mihee said.

As the two women became lost in thought over the peculiar design of the mansion, Heeae soon snapped back to her senses.

"We don't have time for this. We should be looking for things."

She began to go through the drawers nearby. Mihee was wandering close to Heeae, when something in the corner hijacked her attention: a commercial freezer with a sliding door. Mihee approached the machine. With a slight push, the door easily slid open. Though it smelled like aged kimchi, the inside of the freezer was clean and spacious. Mihee leaned inside and picked up a stiff, straight brown hair.

Before Mihee knew it, Heeae was standing beside her. "Must have been used for storing the game," she muttered.

Without replying, Mihee extended her arms to estimate the size of the freezer. The width seemed big enough if one were to keep one's arms close to one's torso when lying down, but she wasn't sure about the length. Mihee shook her head, frowning. Wasn't sure about the length compared to *what*? At that moment, Heeae stepped confidently into the freezer and lay down, waving at the startled Mihee.

"Mihee, come lie here for a second."

"I—"

"Just a second will do. You're taller than I am."

Heeae swiftly exited to switch places. Mihee dithered about stepping into the freezer. Even though she knew the power was off, her bare legs beneath her shorts touched the freezer's floor and the chill made her skin crawl. She placed her feet against the inner wall and stretched her hands above her head. Since there was about a head's worth of space above her head, she figured a decently sized adult man should also be able to fit inside. As soon as she finished her size estimates, Mihee bolted upright.

With a peaceful look on her face, Heeae murmured, "There's enough space for two, don't you think?"

Mihee didn't reply. And Heeae, who had squatted down and was fumbling around near the floor, looked as if she wasn't expecting her to. Moments later, the freezer lit up with a low but loud hum of a machine. Despite the noise, Mihee at first thought it didn't work, but the cold air soon started to gather from the bottom. Heeae reached into the freezer and swirled her hand inside a few times.

"It's in good condition," she said. "Pretty big, too."

The two women met each other's eyes. Before Mihee could speak, Heeae said:

"We have no other options. It's raining outside, and we don't know what will happen if it gets washed up in the rain. If you think about it, cremation is also setting a dead person on fire. Rich people even pay money to freeze themselves, you know—"

"No," Mihee cut off Heeae. "What I mean is, it's okay."

The two didn't say a word. A moment later, they raced up the stairs as if their backs were on fire.

He looks like Snow White, Mihee thought, examining the man's face under the bedsheet. With his eyes closed, he looked at peace.

Heeae muttered, "Doesn't it look like he's sleeping in a cradle?"

"You're right. He looks comfortable."

"I feel sorry for him, he's still young. Why did he have to come out here, of all places?"

"Do you know who he is?"

Heeae nodded tentatively. "I think he's the grandson of my employer. I saw a photo from when he was young, but I hadn't realized he'd grown up so much. The old man isn't the type to gush about his family, so."

"He does look young."

"Right? Maybe a year or two older than my Yohan . . . Look, he barely has any facial hair."

After caressing the man's cheek, Heeae pulled down her sleeve and wetted its edge with her saliva to wipe the bloodstain off his face.

With her hands gathered in prayer, she whispered, "Rest in peace, baby. I'm sorry." Then she lifted her head. "Let's keep it a secret that we put him here, at least for a while."

"Yes, it's better that way, isn't it?"

"Yes. If someone asks, we'll say that we buried him."

Mihee nodded in agreement. The two women closed the freezer door and turned the light off. As soon as Mihee placed her foot on the first step, the thought of having completed the task thoroughly exhausted her. She dragged herself into the kitchen, feeling heavier with every step. She plopped down at the table, before gathering the energy to climb up to her bedroom on the second floor. Meanwhile, Heeae mopped up the blood trails to the doorway, washed the knife and put it back, and left the mansion, not returning for a long while.

"Here." After she had returned, Heeae whipped out a mug of tea. "Drink while it's still warm."

"Where . . . have you been?" Mihee asked.

"I parked the boy's car somewhere else. I'd taken his car key just in case. Go ahead, drink it. We can't have you suffering from a cold."

Mihee couldn't even lift a finger. The steam rising from the mug and sneaking into her nostrils felt overwhelming, and the smell of blood lingering at the tip of her nose made it impossible to gulp anything down. But unable to refuse the favor, she managed to muster superhuman strength and drew the mug close to her lips. In the meantime, Heeae washed the rugs and scoured the floor several times, muttering how she should look for Clorox tomorrow. *How amazing*, Mihee exclaimed to herself, standing up to surrender to the sleep that was weighing her down heavier than gravity.

"Thank you for the tea," she said. "I'm going to bed now."

Heeae called out to stop her. "Hey . . ."

"Yes?"

"What should we do about the money?"

In response to Heeae's out-of-the-blue question, Mihee could only rub her eyes without producing a proper reply.

"Just now, Ahnna said that if you clean up, then . . ." Heeae trailed off, embarrassed. She drew a rectangle in the air with both of her index fingers.

Only then did the forgotten check re-emerge inside Mihee's hazy brain. Blinking her eyes, which felt as dry as if someone had poured sand into them, Mihee did her best to make a natural smile.

"Oh, of course we should split it. Fifty–fifty. Better to cash it out later, right?"

"Yes. Who should hold onto it until then?"

"I will. I'll write you an IOU instead. Hold on."

Mihee sprawled over the table and drafted a note. Her hand trembled from laboring away, and she had to rewrite repeatedly to complete the sentence. She handed the note to Heeae with a stiff smile.

> *I, Choi Mihee, will pay Lee Heeae Five Hundred Thousand Won out of the One Million Won that I received from Seo Ahnna.*

"This will work, right?" Mihee carefully asked Heeae, who glared at the paper. Heeae returned the note with an awkward twist in her lips.

"Sign it, too."

Her brazenness left Mihee speechless.

"Sign it for me," Heeae pressed.

Mihee bent over and was about to sign it, when she impulsively said, "You know what? You can just have it."

"Sorry?"

Mihee took the check out from her pocket and put it in Heeae's hand.

"You can have it," she repeated.

"What? Really?" Heeae exclaimed, her face flushed, though it was hard to tell whether from confusion or delight. "Can I really?"

"Yes, I'm fine without. You did all the work yourself anyway."

"Oh, that's not true. We both did . . . I feel bad . . ."

Without hesitation, Heeae pushed the check into her own pocket. Mihee's eyes met hers and smiled in encouragement. *It's really over*, Mihee thought. Despite the fact she had just hidden a dead man, she somehow couldn't feel a thing. She tried to swallow but couldn't. It was as though she had become a mummy. Her thoughts and her youth had shriveled like dried intestines. If she were to sit inside a burning pit, she would surely crackle.

As Mihee closed her eyes, Heeae asked, "Are you going to bed now?"

"Yes."

"I see."

A thought crossed Mihee's mind. She told Heeae, "I forgot you were staying overnight, so I removed all the sheets from the spare rooms. I don't think there's anything left for you to sleep under."

"Oh well."

"But there is a big towel you can use."

"Where?"

"It's hanging on the chair," Mihee said, jutting her chin toward the guest room.

Heeae silenced even her own breath and walked over to slightly part the door open. As the light from the living room poured in, the eyes of the birds, stuffed with iron wires, soft cotton, and a struggle toward eternity, began to glisten. Underneath the dignified guardians of natural history lay Yosep, sound asleep. His body, partly exposed under the summer blanket, was as pale as candle wax. Mihee found it hard to believe that he, too, was melting under the fire that was time, but if she were to slit his stomach, only fat would smear the blade. Even an angel would smell like grilled meat when burnt in the fire.

Mihee felt a surge of nausea and swallowed. As she continued to gulp down her acidic saliva, Heeae stopped in the midst of bringing out the towel and turned around. She picked up the pillow that had fallen onto the floor, returned it to the bed, and tucked Yosep's foot under the blanket. Even after locking the door, Heeae stood there silently for a long while before she turned around and whispered with an insipid smile, "How come he wriggles so much in his sleep?"

She said it in a disapproving tone, but her face was brimming with motherly pride. Mihee smiled, thinking about how Yosep would forever remain a boy. At least to Heeae. Heeae's eyes suppressed a fire, so that its blaze wouldn't melt and burn Yosep.

"Is he asleep?" Mihee asked, gazing into those eyes.

"Of course. You know how children sleep," Heeae replied, full of confidence. "He won't wake up until the sun comes up. Never."

Saturday

Mihee began to see Heeae in a different light. She had once jeered at the old saying, "You only become a real adult after you give birth to a child," but now there seemed to be some truth to it. Women who gave birth knew the secrets of this world. They had to; they were raising children, wiping up their pee and poo until they grew up to become proper human beings. In other words, those women were like butchers. They were the type of people who would slit open an animal, slice it up with sharp knives, and scrub the kidney, liver, heart, and intestines under cold water before serving them on a silver plate. They knew the dark side of living organisms. That flesh rotted, fruits softened, and flowers fell. That the world was encased in thin and delicate skin, and the dirty things inside spilled out like visceral fat at the slightest cut. And Mihee wished to remain forever ignorant of those facts. Some people wanted to wield shivs in their hands, but not her. What she wanted was cleanliness. Packaged meat. Like the cold, scarlet lumps of protein in the butcher's shop that made her forget that they were once flesh and bone.

Mihee entered the room and saw Yosep's emaciated face. He didn't gain any weight even though he was in bed all day under false care. No, he was getting skinnier every day. How much had he lost since he arrived here? Five kilos? Deprived of sunlight for so long, his skin was tinged a bluish-gray. Sympathetic, Mihee frowned. They had decided to limit his food intake to make it easier to handle him, but this was really based on the fact that Ahnna preferred slender bodies. Mihee couldn't say anything. She couldn't. Everything she ate and lived off came out of Ahnna's pocket.

Mihee sat quietly on the chair beside the bed. She believed she had treated Yosep wisely. At an adequate distance. With a nonchalant attitude. Promoting his self-reliance so that he could recover his masculinity. She didn't have to talk about herself that much, because planted secrets were bound to sprout into love. But for today at least, her indifference wasn't a performance. Mihee really was sick and tired of everything. She didn't bother waking Yosep up, and after placing his tray on the bedside table, became lost in thought. The only image that emerged clearly in the murk of her mind was the man lying in the freezer. That tranquility. That smoothness, which can belong only to the shell that one leaves behind, wavered before her eyes. Compared to that, how filthy was Yosep? His soft, fair skin had been his pride, but it made his freckles as prominent as birthmarks. Even in the pouring rain, his skin looked parched, and the sebum dotting his face like strawberry seeds gave her mild goosebumps. Not only that, but he also had not taken a proper bath since his arrival, which made him reek of rot. Before she even realized it, Mihee had scooted her chair back a little.

She could hear a bit of a ruckus coming from outside. Thinking that Yosep would help himself when he woke up,

Mihee left the tray as it was and fled from the guest room. Ahnna was downstairs, finally awake. Her face was bloated and a bit ashen. Are you not feeling well? Mihee was about to ask, when Ahnna spun around and threw up in the sink. The vomit resounded loudly as it plopped into the stainless-steel basin. Trying to forget the sensation of her own stomach rumbling, Mihee calmly approached Ahnna.

"Are you okay?" she asked.

Ahnna didn't reply, her head still hanging over the sink. The rising heat and smell made Mihee stop by the table as she stared blankly. Before she could say anything, Heeae snatched her hand and pointed to the table. The bowls of freshly cooked rice and bean paste soup made with large chunks of summer napa cabbage and dried anchovies were releasing warm white steam. What was happening? As Mihee wondered, Heeae whispered into her ear.

"She can't eat anything, she says. Because of what happened yesterday."

"Oh."

"She refuses to have anything sliced or chopped with *this*." Heeae shook the knife, tightly wrapped in a plastic bag. "I'm going to throw it away. Then we should buy a new one . . ."

"Are you leaving now?" Mihee asked.

"No, not me."

"Why not?"

"I have to stay by Ahnna's side. You saw her yesterday. She might look strong on the outside, but she's quite softhearted . . ."

As Heeae sighed, Mihee volunteered. "I'll buy it, then."

"Thank you. Are you going alone, though?"

"Yes?"

"I think it's better that Nami go with you," Heeae whispered in a low voice. "I worry that having them both in the same place would be a bit . . ."

"Okay. Then we'll have coffee or something to kill some time. Oh, but are you good for time?"

"Sorry?"

"Don't you have to go today? To see the owner . . . the old man."

"Oh." Heeae seemed flustered by the question and stammered, "It's okay. I'm actually taking some time off."

It felt like she was fudging an excuse, but Mihee didn't question her further. "I see. Then, please take care of Ahnna unnie. Where's Nami?"

"She's still on the second floor."

"Got it."

She left the kitchen and went up to the second floor. Nami was in the living room, sitting on an upholstered couch with her headphones on. She swiveled around even before Mihee could call her, her eyes asking what had brought Mihee here. Mihee was startled by her movement but managed to ask calmly, "Nami, I'm going to the supermarket. Do you want to come with me?"

Nami's voice was dubious. "I went last time. We said we would take turns running errands, didn't we?"

"It's just that, I'm not a very good driver, you know. I thought it would be nice if you could watch me. Since you know the directions well . . . And you also forgot to buy your own headphones, so . . ."

Nami awkwardly took off Mihee's headphones and handed them to her. "That's true," she said. "Then wait for me. I need to change before we go."

After she watched Nami head into her room, Mihee descended to the first floor. Ahnna, looking a bit refreshed, was sitting on the couch, covered in a blanket and sipping tea. She glanced up at Mihee. Heeae, who had been sitting across from Ahnna, placed her teacup on the table and approached Mihee. Mihee was about to put her boots on when she noticed that Nami's pointed feet had punctured holes in the toes. Strangely, she didn't feel like it was a loss. Changing into a pair of pink mule flats instead, Mihee had a short exchange with Heeae.

"What shall we do with . . . *that thing* in the basement?" Mihee asked.

"We'll leave it as it is."

"What if his parents or friends come looking for him?"

"They could . . . But how would they know he's here?" Heeae said, deep in thought.

It was hard to tell from that one encounter, but the old man's daughter didn't seem to have much interest in her own father. Considering the scrupulous interview, Heeae had assumed the woman would meddle with the caretaking to no end, but she hadn't contacted her once to ask how things were going. Heeae could only guess the woman would treat her own children the same way.

"Still, we should think about how to deal with it in time," Mihee suggested.

"Yes, we should."

"Once the rain stops, we should bury him as soon as possible. We can't leave him there like that."

Just when the conversation was over, Nami's footsteps came down the stairs. Mihee gave a slight nod to Heeae and left the mansion with Nami.

The two women headed to the supermarket on the beach. Having visited it only recently, Nami knew well where things were. They had a set list of items to purchase, too. While their shopping could easily have been finished within five minutes, Mihee left everything to Nami and deliberately roamed around the store. *How funny,* she thought. Even in times like these, the forest of neatly organized products had her eyes widening in amazement. Mihee strolled between the displays and caressed the colorful, alluring items with loving touches. As she walked on the smooth tiles, she forgot she was in some eastern seaside village during one of the last few summer days left in the twentieth century. Under the white light, everything was fair. Snacks in fancy eye-catching packaging, orange carrots, green vegetables, and red meat were all sold within a single category called "product." If she were to have Yosep, she could also have all of these. But, but—

What was the good in all of that?

Mihee stood in front of the magazine section and waited for Nami to finish at the checkout. She quickly scanned the titles of gossip magazines that only tourists took an interest in, but none of them talked about Yosep's disappearance. An idol had evaporated, but there had been no scandalous updates for over a month. Instead, the media buzzed about some actress's love affair. A relief, Mihee supposed, but her stomach still burned.

"Anything fun in there?" Nami struck up a conversation after finishing the payment.

"I was just browsing." Out of habit, Mihee nearly slipped the magazine unpaid for under her jacket, but she returned it to the stand. "Did you get everything?"

"Yes. Here's the receipt."

Mihee slowly counted the bills. Then she folded the money and receipt in half and put them in her pants pocket. When they were outside, she asked Nami about grabbing a cup of coffee nearby.

Nami frowned, "Do you think they'll have a place like that around here?"

"Why not? Coffee shops are a dime a dozen these days. Let's go. We could both use a cup."

"Are we going to pay for it with the change we just got?"

"Would that bother you? Then I'll pay. I've got money, too," said Mihee pompously. She had offered because of what she had discussed with Heeae, but more than that, she wanted to shake off the gloom that stuck to her like seaweed. Mihee wanted to meet people. She wanted to drink aromatic coffee, eat fried chicken paired with cold draft beer, and listen to music flowing along the walls. Her mind would be more relaxed if she could fling her head back laughing, enjoying the furtive thrill of other people's stares. Mihee thought Nami would feel the same. Sure, she was a fortuneteller and whatnot, but Nami was also an ordinary young woman.

Unexpectedly, Nami shook her head. She couldn't be treated like that without paying a price. A price? Strictly speaking, the reason why they were out here today and had money to spend was that Nami had recklessly stabbed a man.

"Why don't we do this?" Mihee suggested. "You can read my fortune, bodhisattva, and I'll pay the fee with coffee. That should work, right?"

"Well, I guess that wouldn't be a problem . . ."

Mihee linked her arms with Nami almost affectionately. "Then let's go. After all this, I just want to have a cup of coffee and relax."

Perhaps secretly wishing to have a bit of fun, Nami finally gave in to Mihee's urging.

The two women left the car parked at the supermarket and walked along the sandy beach strewn with white shells. After they climbed a series of steep stairs toward the pine grove, a coffee shop appeared before them. Because of the bad weather, it was empty except for an old man who seemed to be the owner and a nerdy-looking barista with bleached hair. Mihee and Nami sat by the window away from the counter. The barista seemed to have been newly hired for the summer, judging from how he stood so stiffly next to their table. He stole looks at their faces more than necessary. When Mihee exclaimed over how the place still served ssanghwa tea with raw eggs, his acne-pitted cheeks blushed so red they looked as if they would explode. Mihee found it funny. With her mood lifted, she changed her order a few times to tease him before finally ordering an iced coffee. Nami ordered a glass of kiwi juice. Mihee took off her raincoat and hung it on the back of her chair, using the opportunity to look around the messy interior.

"Well, I suppose this isn't bad," she whispered. "It's by the ocean, so the view wins half the battle, really."

Nami followed Mihee's gaze and looked out of the window. Immediately outside was a precipitous cliff, and on the top of it were a few trees that swayed ferociously in the wind yet didn't relent, as if waiting for someone. A black pine forest. Waves licking the cliff. The foam shattered to reveal sharp white teeth, but they couldn't scathe the rocks even one bit. The gray sky was cast above the deep-blue ocean that gloomily twisted itself as if in dejection. Mihee still liked it. The pine forest looked so different when seen not through the mansion window.

"It's nice," Mihee muttered, staring at the incessant flow of water. "There should be a path leading from the mansion to the ocean, too."

"Really?"

"You didn't know? Listen closely at night. When the rain lets up a bit, you can hear the waves. It's quite loud, so I don't think the ocean is too far from there. I thought everyone knew."

"I fall asleep as soon as my head touches the pillow."

"Yeah? I suppose I'm the same these days. I must be tired. I get bruised easily, too."

"Me too."

"It's all because we're not eating properly. Just between us, Ahnna unnie's cooking isn't the best, you know . . ."

While the two women chatted, the kitchen began to fill

with loud noises and the aroma of coffee. The mixer whirred as it ground together ice and fruit, and the owner's voice yelled, "No, this way, this way," to his slow-witted barista. Moments later, the barista approached the table, carrying the trembling tray. Though Mihee was skeptical at first, the coffee was decent for a cafe that served tourists. She relaxed and leaned against the couch. As Mihee blinked her exhausted eyes, Nami frowned slightly, then suddenly lowered her head over the cup, sucking the juice in. Her embarrassing slurping startled Mihee awake, and while she merely blinked, dazed, Nami stuck out her tongue. Upon taking a closer look, Mihee spotted a fruit fly on it. Nami rubbed the fly off her tongue with her index finger and peered at it.

Mihee picked up a napkin and said, "I'll tell the kitchen."

"It's okay, I took care of it."

"Did you see? That it was in there?"

"Yes. But I figured I couldn't scoop it out with the straw, so I used my tongue instead."

Nami then inserted the straw and drew in the juice. Mihee could hear the tiny black kiwi seeds bursting between her teeth. They reminded her of the freckles on Yosep's cheekbones and the sebaceous filaments on his nose, sickening her to her stomach. She gulped down the coffee, but its greasy taste made her feel worse. She scratched her chest through her thin T-shirt. The itch spread to her belly, arms, and back like wildfire. Seemingly oblivious to Mihee's condition, Nami sucked in the juice until her cheeks went hollow and smacked her lips.

"The juice here's pretty good," she said. "It's yummy with a lot of fruit in it. Do you want to have a sip, too?"

Madly scratching the nape of her neck, Mihee lied, "No. I . . . don't like sour things that much."

"No? It's not that sour," said Nami, pouting and smacking her lips to take out a seed stuck in between her teeth. *Smack, smack, smooch, smooch.* The sound overlapped with the soothing folk song playing in the cafe, annoying Mihee like a skipping record. As she clenched her teeth and slapped her burning arm with the opposite hand, her tongue ran ahead of her mind.

"I think you're quite fearless, Nami."

At the sudden remark, Nami asked, "Why do you say that?"

"Oh, you know. I never see you sweat."

As soon as Mihee spat those words, her itch instantly diminished, as though someone had splashed cold water on her skin. As she smoothed her arms filled with red nail marks, she hesitated a moment before continuing to speak.

"I thought you were a bit of a neat-freak at first. But I guess not really? Like, just now . . ." She lowered her voice. "And looking after Yosep, that's all you. Ahnna unnie wiping his arms and legs, that's more like playing house . . . *You* clean up all the mess."

"So what?"

"You know. Just . . . a human can get dirty very easily, don't you think?"

Nami barely reacted. Instead, she clutched at the straw and swirled her drink in an oddly weary manner until she spoke.

"Can I tell you a story? Since you're paying for the juice."

"Yes, go ahead."
"It's an old tale. Might be boring."
"It's okay."
When Mihee nodded, Nami began.

"Ānanda, one of the Buddha's disciples, was a beautiful boy whose good looks attracted a lot of attention. Women passing by would turn around just to get a glimpse of him. Normally, a disciple's robe should be worn with one shoulder exposed, but Ānanda had to cover both shoulders to avoid tempting women. While he had as many earthly passions as the people harassing him did, Ānanda earnestly practiced the teachings of the Buddha, until one day a woman appeared before him. She was different from other women and followed Ānanda around quite persistently—to the point that he thought he might have to resign from his position as a disciple. Troubled, Ānanda told the Buddha about the woman, and the Buddha summoned her.

"He asked, 'How much do you love Ānanda?' The woman said, 'More than anyone in this world.' So the Buddha asked again, 'Which parts of him do you love?' 'I love his eyes, his nose, his mouth, his everything,' she answered. The Buddha then said, 'Eyes have crust, nose has mucus, and mouth has saliva. Wax forms in the ears and bloody pus flows in the body. Do you still love him?'

"Enlightened by his words, the woman became a bhikkhuni, a nun. What do you think the moral of this story is?"

Mihee didn't answer. And Nami, slurping the remaining juice and chomping on the kiwi seeds, didn't seem to be expecting a reply.

"Well, I'm sure everyone has their own take," she continued, expressionless. "But in my eyes, the story seems to be saying, don't even think about loving someone if you don't have the guts to love their bloody pus. What if the woman told the Buddha, 'Yes, I do. I love his crust, his snot, his saliva, his earwax, his pus, everything.' Would the Buddha have allowed the woman to have Ānanda? And . . ."

A faint smile spread across Nami's face as she spoke.

"Don't you think even Yosep's excretions make him beautiful?"

Mihee detected an odd sense of superiority from Nami's expression. Nearly losing control of her temper, she let a barrage of disorganized words slip out as low groans, until the dopey-looking barista appeared. He was holding a tray of evenly sliced watermelon pieces. Even at a glance, the big, fan-shaped slices looked firm, juicy, and without any bruises.

Once he placed the tray on the table, Nami said sternly, "We didn't order this."

The barista stammered, "Oh, no, we bought this to eat ourselves, but it's quite delicious. So, uh, the owner says we should offer you some . . ."

While Nami continued to glare suspiciously, Mihee gushed over the ripe watermelon.

"Oh, what a treat! It must be rather expensive with all the rain this year . . ." She mused, then craned her neck toward the kitchen and called out to the owner, "Sir! Thank you so much!"

The owner, who had been watching them from inside the kitchen, raised his right hand to reciprocate. Mihee beamed and waved back, but her smile quickly waned as soon as the barista turned around.

"Aren't you going to eat it?" Nami asked.

"No, a fly sat on it," Mihee replied briskly and lit a cigarette. Taking a deep breath that filled her entire chest, she felt as if something was descending within her. Dickheads. Upon noticing their dumb gazes on her cheeks, Mihee deliberately prolonged puffing out the smoke. Ever since she had quit smoking when she was around Yosep, cigarettes made her head spin. Sweeping her hair back, Mihee dispelled her complicated thoughts along with the smoke.

"You know there's a saying," Nami said, watching Mihee across the table. "That people are bound to love someone who resembles them. Do you believe that?"

"Well, I'm not sure."

"I do. Yosep and I look alike, too."

"You do?"

"Yes."

Silence fell between the two. Nodding with full confidence, Nami stared at Mihee, her eyes wide open. Mihee squinted to examine the face in front of her, which still bore traces of baby fat.

"Nami, how did you do in school?" she asked.

"Why do you ask?"

"Just because. I'm curious. You did go to school, didn't you?"

"Only until high school. I didn't make it a full month there."

"Can I ask why?"

"Because I was bullied."

An unsurprising response, but Nami's eerie calmness caught Mihee off-guard.

"That's why I felt it was fate," Nami added. "Yosep and I have the same scars."

"Because Yosep was also bullied when he lived in the U.S.?"

"No, not on that kind of level, but more fundamentally speaking. I can't make Yosep happy. And Yosep can't make me happy, either. The very equation of happiness is impossible for us to solve. Instead, we can suffer together. Like the lovers sculpted in relief on the Gates of Hell, intertwined like snakes. Lovers naked in front of each other. Conjoined twins coalesced with pain and joy. That's what Yosep and I are."

At a loss for words, Mihee finally managed to croak, "Yosep isn't that kind of a boy."

"You might not realize it yet, but Yosep *is* that kind of a boy."

Nami's words hurt Mihee's pride. Lowering her voice as much as she could, Mihee rattled off.

"Nami, you are aware that I followed Yosep around, right? Literally all day? I know all his habits, his closest friends, and what he orders for Chinese delivery. I think I know Yosep better than you do, considering all you did was sit in the corner of your room and squeal when he showed up on TV."

"Can you graft a halved apple with grapes?" Nami asked.

"What did you just say?"

Confused, Mihee stared at Nami's face. Nami held her gaze and continued.

"Oh, maybe it is possible. Science progresses so quickly, I suppose. But that's science, not nature. Nature is this—when you plant half an apple, a tree grows from it. And you get a whole fruit from the grown tree. That's how nature works, that's destiny. Yosep is half an apple, and I'm the soil. We will grow a tree together. The tree will bear fruit, and that fruit will grow more new trees. And you, Mihee, are a bunch of grapes."

Mihee took offense and retorted, "You think you love him because you pity him."

"You're right," Nami replied nonchalantly. "I'm also a pitiful person. I never considered that to be a bad thing."

Doesn't miss a beat, does she? Mihee clicked her tongue. Deciding that there was nothing to be gained from their argument, she just puffed away at her cigarette.

"Aren't you going to have the watermelon?" she asked.

Nami shrugged as if the answer was obvious. "I don't accept favors without paying the price."

"Suit yourself." Mihee stubbed out her cigarette in the ashtray and stretched. "Let's go. I wonder if they even wipe the tables properly here."

The two went back down to the beach. Upset, Mihee hastened her steps across the hardened sand. She sometimes pretended to pluck the heels of her mule flats out of the sand and stole a glance behind her, but Nami was preoccupied with seagulls flying past and barely kept up with her.

After repeating her strategy several times, Mihee, frustrated, charged toward a black rock in the distance. A corner of her head boiled with fury, but she didn't know why. Actually, she did know. She knew Nami was right, and knowing that she couldn't refute what Nami had said enraged her.

Mihee stopped and let out a deep breath. Her quick strides had made her heart race and her breathing ragged. She squatted down and pressed her hands against her face, catching her breath. A siren far away woke her up from the short vertigo. She thought it was her ears ringing at first, but the noise grew clearer and louder. She raised her head. She noticed that people were gathered around what she had thought was a black rock. A dozen crows were forming a large circle above it, and a few people were rushing down the steps that stretched from the road to the beach. Just when Mihee sensed someone standing behind her, Nami offered her hand.

"Something must have happened," Mihee whispered as she pulled herself up with Nami's help, forgetting all the unpleasantries from the coffee shop. "People are gathered up there. Why?"

"Looks like someone died."

"That's such a horrible thing to say!"

"I mean, last time I went to the supermarket, I overheard people talking about it. Apparently, it's not rare for a corpse to wash up on the shore. What was it that they said? Something about how a pretty strange corpse turned up the other day."

"Really?" Mihee asked, her voice higher than usual. "Strange how?"

"I'm not sure. I didn't get to hear the whole thing."

"Why are you telling me this now? You should have mentioned it earlier."

"What good would that have done? It's not exactly uplifting," Nami reacted curtly.

"You know," mumbled Mihee. "It's just . . . nice to know how things are going outside."

Before they even realized it, the two had gotten close enough to the dark silhouette that they were able to distinguish the faces of the people surrounding it. Even though she knew she still wouldn't be able to see, Mihee craned her neck in both directions. Then a middle-aged man strode across the scene and blocked their view. He was shirtless, although he didn't look like he had been in the water. Mihee was instantly disgusted by the sight of his nipples, which resembled faded raisins. When she quickly looked away and tried to dodge him, the man struck up a conversation to stop her.

"Ladies, you can't pass through here," he began.

"Why not?" Mihee asked.

"Why, as in the twenty-fifth letter in the alphabet?"

"I don't have time for your dad jokes. What happened?"

The man smacked his lips in embarrassment and replied, "A corpse washed up on the shore."

Just as Nami had expected. Suppressing her curiosity, Mihee feigned indifference.

"Oh, really? How did that happen?"

"I wouldn't know."

"Does this happen often?"

"Now and then, I'd say . . ."

When the man smacked his lips again, a bubble of saliva burst at the corner of his mouth. He squinted at the two women and declared, "You ladies are tourists."

"How did you know?" Mihee asked.

The man's eyes, slowly drifting as if to see through their translucent raincoats, halted at Mihee's breasts.

"I know one when I see one," he smiled. "I'm sorry you didn't get to enjoy the ocean."

Bastard. Mihee quickly erased the frown from her face and flashed a light smile.

"We wouldn't be able to anyway in this weather. Besides, where else would we get to look at a corpse?"

The man snorted. "Ladies are so brave these days, aren't they? I was trying to save you from having nightmares, and this is how you thank me."

"Mister, how would we survive in this tough world if we were scared by *this*? We're not that fragile, don't you worry," Mihee snapped, exaggeratedly tugging at Nami's arm. "Nami, come this way. Let's go up over there and look."

Mihee's raincoat flapped as they climbed the cement steps. Once she reached the roadside, her mules clacking away, she was met by people who couldn't make it down to the beach or had been banished from the scene, now standing on their tiptoes between the randomly parked cars to steal a look at the corpse. Mihee squeezed in between them. Unlike what she had expected, the body on the beach wasn't swollen. *I heard those who drown bloat like a wrestler*, she thought. *Maybe the person didn't drown? Those people hanging around the body, they must be detectives, right? It looks like a film set.* As she kept her eyes glued to the scene, a woman came up the steps and began talking to a woman behind Mihee and Nami.

"Another young guy with his parts cut off."

"Again? What is going on in this town?"

"I don't know. But I don't think he's from the area."

"Could he be a spy?"

"Come on, do spies even exist anymore?"

"Of course. Don't you watch the news, unnie? A submarine or something came down here the other day, too. And you might not know because you're from the south, but spies really do come down a lot to this neighborhood. When I was young, my father would tell me not to play in the mountains. If we got lost, we could end up in North Korea, he'd say. You can ask oppa, too—"

The two women's conversation cut off. A few people were quickly swarming near the stairs, and in between the crowd, Mihee could see the corpse coming up on a stretcher. As people began to shift, she managed to push her way to the very front. The bag containing the corpse briefly passed in front of her. Mihee regretted not seeing see his pale ankles, if only for a moment.

Once the ambulance left, the crowd began to disperse. Mihee gazed at the beach closed off with yellow tape, its hardened wet sand seemingly free of footprints. Right then, a woman in a wedding dress strolled in front of the rippling indigo ocean. Was Mihee seeing things? As she stood confused by the bizarre sight, Nami tapped her on the shoulder.

"What are you doing? Let's go."

Mihee smiled and followed her. The sky began to rumble, signaling the rain was about to start again. Just as Mihee was about to pull up the hood of her raincoat, an impatient raindrop fell into her eye. She blinked, and the image of the man lying in the freezer flickered briefly amid her blackened vision. He looked as neat as the sandy beach swept by the waves. Mihee shook her head. She dashed across the deserted road, moving farther and farther away from the scattering crowd.

—

After the two women left, the yawning Heeae finally fell into a light sleep. Ahnna waved her hand a few times in front of Heeae's eyes before heading to the mansion's front door. It felt cold against her forehead. She took a deep breath, and then she quietly, ever so quietly, locked and latched it. She locked everything she could, from the big living-room window to the balcony door, then drew the curtains. The dim house became even darker. Buried in silence, Ahnna felt lonely, like a child left home alone on a weekend afternoon.

She brought the teacup to the sink and poured out the remaining tea. Quite some time had passed since she had vomited, but her headache still lingered. She cupped cold water with her hands several times to rinse her mouth, and pressed on her temples with wet hands. She had been only acting at first. She hadn't intended to throw up, but her agitation made her vomit. Her nostrils buzzed as if a small gong was ringing inside, and emotionless tears beaded and rolled down from her burning eyes. After burying her face in a towel and catching her breath, she furtively headed to the guest room. Beyond the locked door, Yosep was completely wrapped in sleep's net. Only his body remained in the real world, while his breath, as thin as a thread, tethered his body between here and the world of dreams. Ahnna felt a slight urge to plug his throat with her finger. Instead, she shook her head and settled for scratching her flat belly under her cardigan to expel the light itching in her gut.

She took another fresh look around the room. Under the rifles and gleaming swords, taxidermied animals hung as decorations, flaunting the old man's stamina. Some had said that the man had chewed off an obstinate deer tendon with his teeth, and others testified that they had seen the dark blood dried up on his blade, but they were all liars. The taxidermies had been purchased. The only stuffed specimens the old man had killed himself were birds, and those were buried in the darkness of the basement. The old man and Ahnna were the only ones who remembered that those birds had once been alive.

Ever since her childhood, Ahnna had often come with her parents, who had been close friends with the old man, to this mansion. Middle-aged at the time, the man had played the role of a cheerful host who enjoyed entertaining guests, but he was a poor actor even in young Ahnna's eyes. He was cartoonishly chatty and prone to laughter, which only served to make his guests uncomfortable. When the guests ended up enjoying each other's company more than his, the man volunteered to be their servant for his own masochistic pleasure Most guests couldn't stand his behavior and rejected offers to come again, but every summer and winter, Ahnna and her parents made a visit. As if to reassure themselves of their happiness, they called the old man a crackpot and gossiped about Eunyeong, his daughter, who bore a striking resemblance to his personal assistant. Ahnna spent most of the time at the mansion holed up on the second floor, keeping her parents at a distance.

Ahnna and the old man only had their first proper conversation the summer the man adopted a gorgeous parakeet. The man acted like a child who'd snatched the toy everyone wanted to play with. He looked somewhat nervous, caught between joy and fear, between sequestered yet vigorous desires to possess and to flaunt. He fiddled with the cloth covering the golden cage for quite a while before deciding to reveal his treasure to a dumb child. The old man beckoned at Ahnna like he would an animal. When Ahnna approached, he gave a spiel about the beautiful appearance of his parakeet, its orange feathers stamped on the middle of its head covered in dark green feathers, and its melodious chirping. Then, he suddenly snickered and whispered to Ahnna in a lewd, restless voice, like an adolescent girl letting her young sister in on the secret of her birth.

"Did you know? Parakeets die without an *aibo*."

Despite having said that, the old man had never bought a partner for his parakeet. Every year Ahnna visited the mansion, only the bird changed, never the number present in the cage. And the man never beckoned Ahnna over again.

But Ahnna also remembered this:

One year, the old man was raising another mateless female parakeet. It was winter, and the grownups were lounging on the first floor. Ahnna had been dilly-dallying in her room until she was struck by the need to pee. She had thought the second-floor living room would be empty, but the old man was there. He was heating the cage near the fire while warming his hands. He was still there when Ahnna returned from the restroom. Soft noise from downstairs crawled up the walls. The grownups seemed to have begun drinking in broad daylight, wine glasses clinking away. Ahnna's heart grew lonesome. She rubbed her wet hand on her sweater and approached the old man. But when the man opened the door to the birdcage, it stopped her in her tracks.

Like a cold-blooded sniper stealthily choosing his prey, the man carefully snuck a finger into the cage. Though hesitant at first, the bird gently took flight, obediently perching on his finger. While Ahnna stood in awe, the old man smooched the bird, seemingly overjoyed. His light kisses continued like a song; the intimacy made the cowering Ahnna blush. Then, the old man suddenly opened his mouth like a cat and put the small bird's head inside it. Ahnna's entire body stiffened as if she was in the bird's place. Moments later, like in a video rewind, the man casually opened his mouth again and pulled out the bird's head. Its feathers were a little ruffled, but the bird appeared unshaken and pecked at its fluorescent light green feathers with its orange beak. Its eyes were as dark as wild grapes and as dazzling and solid as dried honey-coated peas. The old man lifted his thick thumb and gently caressed the bird's back. Despite the peaceful scene playing out in front of her, what had happened was as if Ahnna had imagined it. A bleak winter afternoon. Looking out the window to bare branches, the old man and the parakeet warmed themselves by the fire. The parakeet groomed itself, unconcerned.

Ahnna had been afraid.

Of the old man for yearning to confine the parakeet at its most beautiful in the museum of eternity. Of herself for understanding how he had felt.

And now, she was becoming more and more like the old man.

The room had fallen dark when Ahnna came back to her senses. She walked to the window and stared out at the thick gray cloud cover before drawing the curtains. The darkness was the only thing that liberated her. She waited until her limbs and face completely disappeared, until everything melted away and left only her eyes behind. Until the objects frightened by the sudden darkness could finally stretch out and flash their sharp edges. Soon, Ahnna took steps again toward Yosep. She sat in the chair next to him.

Yosep slept like an exhausted bird. His broken wings were bound in white bandages. His arms and legs. The things that allowed him to move and dance. Inside Ahnna's skull was not a squishy brain but a music box. If she closed her eyes, she could open the lid and see Yosep dancing inside, whenever and wherever. Her lips would automatically break into a faint smile. Some beauty transcends life. The owner of such beauty would suffer from time to time, but he must endure the pain, for he owns the beauty. It was a cruel thing to say—or was it?—but such was his destiny, so what could be done?

Feeling sentimental, Ahnna gazed at Yosep's face, which was sunken in darkness until she lit the candle on the bedside table. The light fluttered at every breath Ahnna let out and reached for Yosep's face: its flickering red tongue painstakingly tried to kiss his cheeks, only to fail every time. Ahnna couldn't take her eyes off of it. Failure was how his face had been born, after all. His slick brow bones, uplifted nose ridge, and lips were all sedimentation of women's failures over time. His smooth cheeks were the weathered result of countless caresses from women's gazes.

Ahnna remembered Yosep's face before it lost its baby fat. His face had been plump when young, but it had revealed the dazzling future ahead of him like the transparent membrane one might find inside a cold-blooded animal's egg. And Ahnna's predictions had never betrayed her, not even for a moment. That flower had blossomed into an awe-inspiring beauty that mesmerized the public. Like a master sculptor who had brought a sculpture to life from a rock, Ahnna was proud of Yosep's beauty. Though jealousy would set her ablaze from time to time, she could endure it thanks to her belief that a beauty such as his should rightfully be shared with others.

Ahnna loved Yosep's beauty devotedly. Whenever she looked at his face, she could see his bones through his skin. Those bones, more solid and porcelain-like than anyone else's, made Ahnna wonder about its age for some reason.

The shape of his head deserved to be preserved for generations to come. Along with the Happy Prince's sapphire eyes, a green emerald plucked from a lion's heart, and a blood-stained red ruby and a fist-sized white diamond that once sat on top of the mightiest tyrant on earth, Yosep's smooth chin and cheekbones needed to be displayed under subdued indirect lighting, shrouded in the sweet dust of a museum. And one day, they would get shot by bullets, pouring down like rain at the heart of war, and crumble away along with the glittering blue beetles a model of an evolving human. Such sorrow was the pinnacle of Yosep's beauty.

But all of that was to happen after Ahnna died. She couldn't let anyone else have Yosep before then. She didn't want to.

Ah! Ahnna held back the sigh that had nearly escaped her throat. She clenched at the corner of the white sheets, feeling her cheeks warming quickly, only to become cold and damp. Tasting the salty lumps of sadness sliding down her throat, she held Yosep's hand and licked his fingertips.

Ahnna didn't want to lose this body. Here, there were no nasty neighbors watching her through the windows, no husband trembling with anger and asking if she had hired a prostitute, and no doctor scornfully and solemnly announcing that she couldn't bear a child. It was only the two of them. In the pouring rain, they could live for ever. If only Nami hadn't foolishly stabbed Seongwuk.

But paradoxically, his death had granted Ahnna courage. All humans die—she had never understood the fact as acutely as she did now. Just as pickles can't turn back into cucumbers and boiled carrots can't grow in soil, death can't be reversed. Ahnna kissed Yosep's abdomen, which until then she had been appreciating only with her eyes and touching and licking only in her imagination. Then, she pulled down his pants. As far as she knew, there was only one way for two people to achieve eternity. *That man told me that I can't have a child,* she thought. *But even with this moldy, rotting body of mine, I know I can do it if it's with you. Yosep, I'm going to bear a child. I will give birth to a child who is my son, my husband, my father, and my brother. I will give birth to you, to hundreds and thousands of you, and fill up this city. This is for the benefit of humankind. Let's proliferate beauty.*

Ahnna stood up from the chair. She pulled her wet underwear down to her feet and crawled onto Yosep, who was still fast asleep. The springs inside the old mattress creaked beneath her knees. Hot tears rolled down from her closed eyes. She slowly unbuttoned Yosep's shirt and placed her hand on his scrawny chest. His heart was still beating. Its thumps echoed like the hooves of a horse furiously galloping toward death. Like a knife slitting open a fish, her hand slid from his chest down to below his belly button. Ahnna lifted her buttocks. The incongruous harmony of the old floor and the mattress creaking rang inside her ears. She gritted her teeth so as not to make a sound.

Lightning flashed. Startled, Ahnna turned toward the window and glimpsed a shadow over the curtain. Her breath stopped—surely her eyes weren't deceiving her?

"Who is it?" Ahnna muttered quietly.

Were Mihee and Nami back? If they were, they would have gone straight to the front door instead of loitering near the guest-room window. Ahnna got up, went to the window, and peered between the curtains. She spotted a young man roaming near the mansion. She gulped hard at the unfamiliar face; he didn't look like a local. When he waved, two more young men walked into her view. They were chatting away about something, and despite their muffled voices, she could clearly make out Seongwuk's name.

Goosebumps ran down her body. It was like electricity was flowing through every single follicle of every hair on her body and poking her pores like needles. Jittery, she reached behind her neck to brush them off. As she crept out to the living room, she drew deep breaths to calm her heart, which felt as it was about to explode through her eye sockets. Fortunately, Heeae was still asleep. Thanks to the curtains Ahnna had drawn, the men outside didn't seem to have noticed that there were people inside the mansion. She carefully approached the door and pressed her eye against the peephole.

The men had gathered in front of the mansion and were trying to open every window. When that failed, they knocked at the entrance door, ramming their knuckles against the solid iron. Ahnna nearly mistook it for a woodpecker pecking at her skull. One of the men seemed to have noticed something and bent to look through the peephole. Ahnna gulped hard. He was seeing through her. That was how she felt. As if to prove it, the man stared straight at Ahnna, who was trembling with her hand clasped over her mouth, before breaking out into a broad smile.

"Hello," he began. "We're friends of Seongwuk. Is Seongwuk here?"

The small music box in Ahnna's head began to crack.

—

Crow-Tit had said the mansion was near the ocean, but according to the map, they had to drive a good forty minutes into the mountains. Those with a car and those without had a different sense of space. Especially for people like Crow-Tit, who had traveled overseas from a young age. Magpie yet again realized the gap between them, but that didn't mean he could blame Crow-Tit. That was just how he was brought up. There was no point hating him for it. Instead, Magpie would magnanimously comment on it whenever he got drunk. But everyone knew that Magpie actually loathed Crow-Tit more than anyone. They all knew Crow-Tit was bound to betray the rest of them. Before they passed, his cold-hearted parents would bequeath him a goose that laid golden eggs, and he would embrace it with open arms just as he always did—with an embarrassed demeanor and eyes pleading that he had no other choice.

Between the capitalists and the laborers flowed a river deeper than the one dividing the nobles and the commoners. What created the bad blood between them was a feeling of deprivation. The feeling was so intense that the laborers couldn't just accept it as simply how the world worked, and that the problem of inheritance could not be overcome.

Magpie couldn't hide how he felt the way he might hide an icepick in his pocket. He could gracefully imitate those he abhorred, but his comrades knew that Magpie was attracted to certain kinds of criminals. Those who made up their minds to hack the rich to pieces. Those who thieved, kidnapped, and raped their daughters. As long as he didn't own capital, Magpie would always be inferior, a status that entitled him to such actions. Magpie's biggest wish was to see the capitalists' bloodied heads hanging festively in the city square, just like in the primitive days before people turned to screens and sports. What he most often imagined in his head was not the utopia that would welcome him and his comrades at world's end, but the blood that needed to be splattered on the way.

Long Pole was different. He thought that humans had the ability to right wrongs. *We're not animals, we can persuade each other without force,* he would say. He knew that Magpie and Weeble thought he was soft. But he couldn't help it. According to his mother, Long Pole was spineless because he shot up too quickly and the cracks in his bones made him weak. He had height but not guts; that was who Long Pole was.

Long Pole's real name was Seo Sunam, and Weeble's was Ha Cheong-il. People expected the tall and small duo to make them laugh, but the pair knew next to nothing about humor. Long Pole was a shy man of few words. He never gave his opinion. Neither did Weeble, but he wasn't as lily-livered as Long Pole. Long Pole knew that Weeble harbored more words than anyone and sheltered rage as sticky as black tar. Especially about women. *Slutty bitches*, Weeble snarled whenever he saw women sauntering in the grass like antelopes. Long Pole would tremble with anger as if those words were targeting him. He would think, *Why do you hate women so much? Wasn't it women who gave rice balls to the militias during the Gwangju Uprising?* But from time to time, Long Pole felt both an intense sympathy and a furtive pleasure while imagining the despair that the clever Weeble would suffer at the hands of women. Perhaps the equal rights that Weeble dreamed of were as trivial as the freedom to date whatever woman he wanted. But everything begins with trivial matters. To earn another spoon of rice more than others, to be loved. No matter how hard they tried to embellish their motive, that's all there was to it. That was the closest thing to an ideology that weak-willed Long Pole had—if he could call it an ideology, that is.

A wooden sign painted white was fixed on the barbed-wire fence gate. "Private Property" was written on top in black paint, while 出入禁止 ("No Trespassing") was written on the bottom in red Chinese letters. However, the door was held shut with only a loosely coiled chain without locks. Did Crow-Tit leave it open? Long Pole was hesitating when Magpie crept up beside him and quickly undid the chain.

"Are you just gonna stand there?" Magpie asked.

Uhh, Long Pole mumbled. The door opened with a spooky creak.

"Looks like we have no signal here," Magpie muttered as he stepped inside.

"No," Long Pole confirmed, then added, "What's a mansion doing in a place like this, anyway?"

They gazed up at the dense, dark mountain. The darkness was so overwhelming that they almost doubted a mansion would be up there. Once they entered, coming back down again would be yet another grueling endeavor.

Fortunately, faint tire tracks on the ground removed their suspicion. The three men scuttled after them like birds following a trail of breadcrumbs. The gradual slope came to an end and suddenly grew steep, making them lose their breath. The grass squeezed under the tires was forming a path, but not one that looked suitable for a hike.

Not even five minutes had passed when Weeble let out a cry, "Fuck." Embarrassed, he spat. The hanging phlegm didn't fall off at once, making him look rather pathetic. Long Pole had noticed near the iron gate that Weeble's face was sallow. Huffs leaked through Long Pole's teeth, too. Only Magpie was making it up the mountain without heaving; he just flared his nostrils. While Long Pole and Weeble looked like a pair of circus freaks, Magpie looked more or less normal. He possessed a body typical of a revolutionary fighter for Communism—he was supposed to be rightfully strong.

Could it only have been ten minutes? It felt like they had been walking for over half an hour. All three of them were now panting like dogs. Youth should gift the body resplendence, but their bodies crumbled at the slightest pain. They had never been athletic. They preferred not to say as much, but back in their school days, they had all spent time sprawled on the classroom floor, looking up at someone else's calves while clutching their bruised stomachs. Weeble, who was short and round like his nickname, was particularly weak. Keeping up with the others exhausted him. The coolheaded leader that he was, Magpie hiked in silence, paying no attention to Weeble and the salty sweat dripping down his forehead. Only Long Pole slowed down to narrow the distance with Weeble. His body exuded violent heat and resentment towards his leader. *This is why I said we should take a cab from the station—I knew something like this was going to happen.* As Long Pole was about to pout his lips, Magpie hocked and spit out a lump of phlegm. Unlike Weeble's, it emitted a clear snap, like a slap on the cheek, when it landed on a rock.

"Hurry up," he urged.

"Huh? Oh, okay."

Long Pole floundered to catch up with Magpie. His heart raced with the fear that Magpie had read his mind. Lest his thumping heartbeats be heard, Long Pole cowered his huge body. When he glanced back, he saw that Weeble was drooling foamy, sticky, gray saliva. His once-sallow face was now as pale as a sheet. Should he suggest they take a rest? Bent over with his hands resting on his knees, Long Pole contemplated asking as Magpie pointed upwards.

"Is that it?" he asked, to which Long Pole straightened back up again.

A towering mansion overlooked the mountains. Like those of a Greek temple, thick, ash-colored columns glistened on the facade of the two-story building built on the slope. The three men stood in silence, overwhelmed by the mansion's size—it felt as massive as a giant suspension bridge, a transmission tower, or the bones of a carnivorous dinosaur. They were more in shock than awe. Even though they had spitballed grand ideologies over meals and drinks, the young men got cold feet standing before a mere two-story mansion.

"There are places like this . . . in Korea?" Long Pole muttered in a daze, and to no response.

The closer they came to the mansion, the more they could see the details in its overpowering, sophisticated exterior. The imposing columns suspended the entire building midair, and the pointed roofs soared majestically to the sky. Didn't Crow-Tit say a famous architect had designed the place? That would mean the owner could've been a rich young master who had studied abroad in Japan during the colonial period. Or a soldier who shot fellow Koreans, or an industrialist who monopolized capital and exploited laborers. In any case, the owner was an enemy who deserved the three men's hatred, but instead, they had fallen in love with the building at first sight. Even the resentful Magpie, who spat at the ground without a shred of admiration, admitted with sparkling eyes, "He's more bourgeois than I'd imagined." They sparkled just as they had when all of them had gathered in their student club room and eaten disastrous noodles to celebrate Kim Il-sung's birthday. They were the eyes of an innocent child.

Their energy hitting a critical low, the three men arrived in front of the mansion. The windows of the grim building were all covered with curtains, blocking the view inside. They tried ringing the doorbell, but it was broken. They knocked, but no answer. *He has to be here*, Magpie thought, recalling the fresh tire tracks that had led them here. The area spanning from the road to this spot was private property, so it couldn't have been other cars, either. Could he have fallen asleep? Magpie beckoned Long Pole and Weeble over. After sending them off to survey the mansion, he gave a slight nudge to one of the terrace windows just in case. The tightly locked window wouldn't budge. Right at that moment, a flash of light burst before his eyes, followed by a rumbling that resembled a giant beast's growl. Thick, unexpected raindrops fell slowly, one by one.

"Nothing's open," Long Pole said as he emerged from the back of the mansion.

"Where's Weeble?" Magpie asked.

"He's still in the back."

Without a word, Magpie took off in the direction Long Pole was pointing at. Long Pole followed him from behind. Upon entering the backyard, which smelled heavily of soil, they found Weeble hunkered on the ground. *Still?* Magpie didn't bother to hide his exasperation and passed by Weeble, who was grimacing with pain, to stand next to Long Pole. Long Pole had been craning his neck up to stare at the second-floor window.

With a gulp, he called, "Crow-Tit."

Silence fell.

"Hey, Crow-Tit," Long Pole continued. "Shin Seongwuk." But no reply came.

"He's run away," Magpie spat, suddenly convinced. "That

bastard made us come here for nothing. I mean, how do we know if this even is his vacation home, huh? He just gave us the runaround so he could jump ship. That fucker, I knew this would happen. That son of a bitch. That's why I always say that bourgeois bastards need to go . . ."

Magpie's rage made Long Pole flinch. He left the backyard and went around to the side of the mansion. At that moment, he spotted a curtain fluttering inside a room. Could he be seeing things? But despite the lack of wind blowing past the shuttered window, the curtain was surely wavering a little, and the image of a shadow sliding behind it seemed to carve itself onto his retinas. While he hoped it was all in his head, he was certain that the shadow belonged to a woman.

Why did it have to be a woman? Long Pole imagined the worst possible scenario that his friends could commit. If Seongwuk had brought a girlfriend over without telling them, that would cause a headache, even if the girl was also a revolutionary. Even if she wore unironed cotton pants and called them hyeong just as a boy would, the men would imagine the female body hiding underneath her clothes.

Long Pole returned to the entrance to find out who it was. Magpie and Weeble followed him. Long Pole knocked on the door. Still no answer. He tried his luck and bent over to peer through the peephole, but he couldn't see anything. But in an attempt to show the woman possibly inside that he posed no threat, he put on a friendly smile.

"Hello. We're Seongwuk's friends. Is Seongwuk here?" he asked.

"What are you doing?" Magpie asked in disbelief.

Embarrassed, Long Pole replied, "I thought someone might be in there."

"Like who? Did you see a ghost or something?"

Long Pole simply chuckled, while Weeble squealed like a pig next to him.

"Maybe Crow-Tit gave us the wrong date!"

"But he said he'd be here on Saturday just past midnight."

"Yeah, but what I'm saying is, he could have meant Saturday-going-into-Sunday midnight."

Everyone gasped. Considering Crow-Tit's nature, that blunder would totally be in the realm of possibility. The three men sighed, accepting it as fact.

"See, it would've been better if we came with him in the first place." Magpie clicked his tongue. "He didn't say he hid a key somewhere, did he?"

"No." Weeble shook his head, but Magpie pointlessly lifted the doormat and empty pots. The thought of braving the rain back down the mountain without finding any fruit was distressing, but they had no other option.

"What a dimwit."

With Magpie's words as the cue, the three turned around to go down the hill and catch the bus back to the town center. His legs shivering, Long Pole wondered if they even had what it took to be become revolutionary fighters. Real fighters would have broken into the empty house. *We're still green*, he thought. *Or easily scared.*

Weeble, who had been following them at the tail, suddenly halted. Much further ahead, Magpie and Long Pole looked back belatedly.

"What are you standing around for?" Magpie asked.

"There's no need to rush down," Weeble readily replied.

"What do you mean?"

"The last bus of the day has probably already left."

"Already?"

"It's past four," Weeble said, waving around his watch-wrapped wrist.

Magpie sighed. "How long do you think it'll take us to walk back to the station?"

"I dunno. Three, four hours, minimum?"

The rain didn't wait for them any longer. Mottled with raindrops, the earth now turned dark, and the heavy rain drowned out each other's voices. As they gathered in a circle without exchanging a word, Magpie was the one to break the silence.

"Why don't we just go in, then?"

"Can we?" Long Pole asked, astonished. "Wouldn't they have . . . an alarm system or something?"

"We can turn it off once we're inside," Magpie replied, and then muttered to himself, "Gosh, how come it's so cold up here when it's summer?"

He rubbed the skin exposed under his half sleeves, before lowering both arms in determination.

"Let's go," he said. "Let's go up and wait. He'll be here tonight, won't he?"

Magpie led the way, and Weeble followed after him. It seemed like hot steam would rise off Weeble's huffing back at any moment. It didn't take long until his gait noticeably slowed. Long Pole thought about keeping pace with Weeble but decided that ignoring him was more considerate and surpassed his friend. Weeble was really slow. He didn't arrive until Long Pole and Magpie had already reached the mansion and were double-checking the surroundings, including the entrance, terrace windows, and even the tiny kitchen window that would do them no good even if it opened. When they looked back, Weeble was still grunting in the middle of the slope, his hands resting on his knees.

"Fucking pig . . ." Magpie muttered.

Long Pole tried hard to pretend not to have heard him.

"Hey, Long Pole," Magpie called. "Do you think you can jump and reach up there?"

"Where?"

"The gutter over there."

"I think so."

"Maybe if you could grab onto that, we could break into the second floor."

The gutter looked like it would snap off. Long Pole was trying to come up with an excuse not to do it, just when Weeble shrieked, "Guys! Guys, come over here!"

Magpie turned around, annoyance strewn over his face. He grimaced as he slid down the hill. Long Pole followed.

"What's wrong?" asked Magpie. His tone was only a little gruff, but his eyes were fierce, as if he would kill Weeble if it turned out to be nothing serious.

But Weeble was undaunted. He presented proudly, "Look over there."

"Where?"

"No, not there. Here."

His chubby finger pointed at the dark bushes, which were covered by a tree that had been struck by lightning. It looked like a beast with glaring yellow eyes would jump out at any moment from behind the tangled branches and thick leaves. But that was it.

"What about it?"

At Magpie's question, Weeble impatiently walked toward the bushes and removed a few branches, dousing his chest with rain. Was it a sloppy camouflage? Or were the broken branches hiding it? Beyond the bushes was a parked car. Everything was intact except for the broken window on the driver's side.

"A Grandeur," Magpie observed. "Do you think Crow-Tit drove it here?"

"Then it wouldn't be such a fucking wreck, now, would it?"

"Hmm."

Magpie hesitated before grabbing the handle with some force. The door opened wide. He then sat in the driver's seat and mimed turning the steering wheel. The car key was in the ignition, and when he started the car, the gauge showed that the tank was nearly full, too. Thanks to the leaves covering the car, the seats were not completely soggy. Magpie was tempted. The mansion's locked front door had been the last straw.

"Hey, let's go for a drive," he declared boldly.

"Huh?"

"Let's take this downtown and come back."

"Are you sure we can take it?"

Long Pole's frightened voice made something hot surge inside Magpie. Suppressing his anger as much as possible, he replied, "It's been abandoned. We don't need permission to use what's abandoned."

"Do you even have a license?"

"I've driven my father's truck a few times. It's okay, there's no one on the road, anyway."

But Long Pole remained reluctant. Magpie turned to Weeble, but all Weeble did was stare down at the ground, mumbling in a nearly inaudible voice, "I think just taking shelter from the rain would be good enough . . ."

Magpie was so frustrated that he wanted to bash something in. His own chest, or even Weeble's head. But it is not the North Wind but the Sun that takes off the Traveler's cloak. Magpie reminded himself of the story's moral as he reminisced about the town center they had just left. Even though it was a provincial town, it had everything he needed. Eateries selling gukbap and snacks, cheap bars, and hostess salons with names like Honeybee, Renaissance, and Rose. Magpie gulped, his mouth watering.

"Sure, but we're wet and it's cold out—why don't we head down for a bit?" he coaxed the other two. "We could get ramyeon and rent a room to take a nap."

Ramyeon. The mere sound of the word made the shivering men salivate. Their desire to enjoy hot soup quickly intertwined with Magpie's desire to drive an expensive car. Soon enough, Long Pole and Weeble were waving and yelling *"orai, orai"* to signal it was clear to back the car up. After a few trials, Magpie managed to pull the car out of the bushes. With Long Pole in the passenger seat and Weeble in the back, they set off down the mountain.

Twenty minutes later, on her way back from a patrol, Officer Seo Taeyeong spotted a New Grandeur driving the wrong way down the road. The most serious cases in her peaceful precinct involved wild animals coming down from the mountains and digging up vegetable fields. That day, Officer Seo was loading dried peas that a village elder had given her into the back seat before the audacity of the vehicle driving against the traffic made her stop. *Whoa, it's like out of a movie*, she thought, before quickly coming to her senses. Siren blaring, she set off after the car. Following a short chase, Officer Seo arrested the three men at 6 p.m. on the dot. After confirming that the driver didn't have a license and their vehicle was stolen, she brought them to the station. Two hours and forty minutes later, she would be knocked out cold with the butt of a shotgun.

—

"Sir, they're not answering," Taeyeong said.

"No? That's the owner's number, though," Police Chief Lee replied. "Are you sure you dialed the right number?"

Taeyeong squinted at the numbers and admitted, embarrassed, "I think I misdialed. Let me call again."

She waited for a long while, but no one answered.

"They're not picking up?" Lee asked.

As soon as Taeyeong shook her head, Lee sucked his stomach in and bellowed, "You!" He was famous for his foghorn of a voice, and his outburst grabbed everyone's attention. As though it had been an accident, Lee quickly softened his voice.

"Hey, you, the tall one."

"Me?" the tall one murmured after a pause.

"Yes, you. Where did you say you got that car from?"

"Um, it's my friend's . . ."

Lee didn't respond. He simply stared at the tall mophead with his big, bulging eyes. The man, tall like a long pole, stole glances at his friends before he began to stammer.

"The, um, in the m-mountains."

"The mountains?"

"Uh, it was like, abandoned in front of a mansion . . ."

"God, you shitheads. Abandoned? You mean, *parked*, you moron."

Lee abruptly smacked the men's heads with a rolled-up newspaper. Quite a loud thwack resounded, but none of them resisted. Talking back to him would have been irritating, but the police chief found their limp resignation just as annoying. But rather than rage, what welled up in his chest was astonishment. He knew college students to be tenacious; the kind who'd form a scrum to withstand tear-gas bombs and jump two stories to avoid the police, scurrying away with broken legs. That's how youngsters were in his mind. But these young men in front of him right now? They'd been taken in by none other than Taeyeong. He didn't mean to discredit her just because she was a woman, but Taeyeong had a baby face, which made the situation all the more perplexing. Young people, scared of a mere uniform? Maybe people were right when they said a new era of humanity was upon them. Or were these three particularly meek, like herbivores? All kinds of thoughts flooded Lee's mind until Taeyeong's voice intruded.

"Uh, sir?"

"Huh?"

"Should I call the main station?"

"No, I'll call them later. Why don't you go and talk to the car owner or mansion owner or whoever it is?"

"Understood, sir. But I don't think they have a number . . ."

"No. They probably don't have a telephone up there."

Lee glanced up at the clock. It was twenty minutes before eight—clock-out time—and tomorrow was Sunday, Taeyeong's day off. The heavy rain must've made the past few weeks tough for her. Lee himself could give the boys a few more clouts before handing them over to the main station, so there wasn't much else for her to do.

Noticing the bags under Taeyeong's eyes, he said, "Just stop by and let them know what happened. Then you can head straight home."

"Understood." Taeyeong's face lit up as she sprang to her feet and saluted. "On it, sir."

She packed up and headed for the exit. She was tall and scrawny, which made her look undependable and incompetent. Taeyeong, the movie buff. She had supposedly been inspired to become a police officer after watching Jodie Foster in *The Silence of the Lambs*. Lee threw her a pitiful look. He almost told her to have a good day off, but the thought of uttering such niceties made him bashful, so he focused on filling in the report with profiles of the three dumbstruck men. The brats watched with unmistakable contempt as Lee slowly typed in consonants and vowels one by one with his index fingers. At first glance, their gazes appeared defiant, but they lacked the vigor he expected from young men. Lee swallowed a sigh. Suppressing his urge to swat at their heads, who could not necessarily be called "young" except for the heat and stench billowing from their wet bodies, Lee pounded on the keyboard. He was so engrossed that he let go of his last moment with Taeyeong.

Taeyeong took her favorite car, which was quite famous in the small provincial village. The secondhand Sonata 2 was painted, unusually, in purple. Its previous owner had been quite the dandy. After learning that a woman, in a rural village at that, was thinking about driving a car in such a garish color, he had worried about Taeyeong. *Are you sure you're gonna be okay? Standing out will get annoying.* Just as he predicted, the villagers harassed her every time they saw the purple car slowly cruise by. Waving as if their houses had caught fire, they'd flag her down and give her rice cakes, juice, or even just a glass of water. *You should've floated a willow leaf in the water, like in the old tales*, Taeyeong would joke. The elderly would chuckle and grin widely with missing front teeth, a sight that always delighted her.

Driving down a dark road with the headlights on that evening felt like sitting inside a beast's stomach. Or rather, since she was never digested, perhaps it was more like wearing the beast's hide, or becoming the beast itself. She was scared, but at the same time, incredibly empowered. She suddenly felt fully responsible for her future insecurity and exhaustion. Just as with clutching a loaded gun in her hands, even though she had grown accustomed to the sensation, there were still times she found herself handling the whole vehicle chillingly unfamiliar.

But now, Taeyeong only felt euphoria as she drove down the rainy road. The mansion that the mophead and his gang had mentioned was quite a famous spot among the locals, nicknamed "The Deer House." It was said to be owned by an old man who had made his name in the financial world and designed by a world-renowned architect. There were countless rumors as to why the house was built deep in the heart of the mountains and away from civilization. Some said the location stood in symmetry with the old man's childhood home in North Korea across the 38th parallel, while others said the manor was intended for the clandestine hobbies of the rich. Whichever was true, the mansion's mystique continued to live in the villagers' hearts.

Taeyeong was excited at the prospect of going to such a place. As a child, she had been more enamored with Scarlett O'Hara's grand estate brimming with blackberry lilies than her gleaming green dress. A mansion in the mountains seemed like something out of the classic foreign films that used to air on TV during the weekends. Taeyeong was as thrilled as a child who had won the opportunity to tour a movie set. Inside were the secrets of the world, the truth. She was a gatecrasher, a voyeur, but that was fine. If she was lucky, maybe she could slowly descend the staircase, just like Scarlett did at the ball held at Twelve Oaks!

Fueled by her naive imagination, Taeyeong arrived at the entrance to the mountain estate. As the young men had said, the wire-fence gate was wide open, and the lock was simply dangling. She shifted down a gear and unapologetically went up the steep slope. After driving for about ten minutes on the overgrown grass, slippery from the rain, she could see the pointed roof of the mansion. Even though she was visiting as a policewoman on official business and not in a personal capacity, she hadn't contacted the residents in advance. She needed to be polite, Taeyeong thought, which was also her way of apologizing for squeezing herself through the wire fence and roaming the grounds when she was young and expressing her respect for the fantasy world the mansion had cultivated in her young mind.

As she climbed up the dark slope, Taeyeong held a transparent plastic umbrella in one hand and a flashlight in the other. The ten-minute walk uphill left her out of breath, perhaps from the rush, the excitement, or both. The closer she got to the mansion, the more her breathing grew ragged, and by the time she finally made it to the staircase leading up to the doorstep, she had a slight headache from the lack of oxygen. She turned off the flashlight and put her hands on her hips to catch her breath. Shrouded in darkness, the estate seemed abandoned, but she was enthralled by the thought someone could be inside. The mansion's windows were covered with curtains, and as if to prove she was right, a thin light showed between them. With the surroundings immersed in darkness, the light pierced her eyes like a blade. It was so sharp that the vertigo it caused turned her mind pitch dark.

Placing her hands on the railing, she set foot on the steps. When she reached the top, she squared her shoulders and pressed the doorbell with a swollen chest. No one responded. Judging from how loose the button felt, she figured the bell must be broken. Anxiety slithered around her feet like a snake. Nothing could be more miserable than having finally arrived at the castle of her dreams only for a door to shut her out. She reminded herself again that she was an officer in uniform and knocked on the door.

"Police, open up."

No response.

"I'm from the precinct," she said, raising her voice. "Is anyone home?"

Then she heard someone rustling behind the door. An emaciated woman proceeded to open it. Had she been crying? The woman had no fat on her face, making her appear possibly older than her years. She rubbed her cheeks, dehydrated from tears.

"What brings you here?" the woman asked uncertainly.

"Oh, I'm sorry to bother you so late at night. I just wanted to check—was your car stolen?"

"Sorry? A car?"

"Um, we caught a few guys who'd stolen a car, and they said they'd taken it from this mansion. A black Grandeur?"

Right then, Taeyeong saw the woman's pupils grow big

like a cat's at night. Was she terrified? But she could have been mistaken, because the woman soon replied with a coquettish voice: "Oh, yes. That's my son's car. I didn't realize something had happened to it. I dozed off . . ."

"I see." Seized by an impulse, Taeyeong continued, "Would you like to go and check?"

"Yes, yes. Let me just . . . change first."

The woman tried to close the door. *Ah, I didn't get to see the inside properly.* Taeyeong had been stealing looks inside the mansion over the woman's head before she reflexively jutted her foot inside the door. The woman raised her head, meeting Taeyeong's eyes. Only then did the woman seem to have noticed the bad weather outside.

"Would you like to . . . step inside for a moment?" she slurred.

"May I?"

"Yes, my family's here, but . . ."

She mumbled as she turned sideways to make room. Taeyeong removed her shoes and finally entered her dream house. Just like in her imagination, the mansion had a high, majestic ceiling. Crystal chandeliers hung from it, which was made with the same hardwood as the floor. There was also a fireplace, which looked out of use. Taeyeong followed the woman into the living room. The kitchen and the rooms connected to the living room were slightly slanted, gracefully guaranteeing privacy. The woman sat Taeyeong on the couch of honor and disappeared into one of the other rooms to change her clothes. One of the woman's family members, who had been sitting on the couch, headed to the kitchen for some tea. Conscious of her position of authority, Taeyeong took care not to look like she was investigating while she glanced around the house. *Amazing*, she thought. *So people really live in a place like this.* She also observed the two women sitting across from her. Were they the owner's granddaughters? The two, possibly cousins, looked different yet similar. One had a cute look, while the other shot Taeyeong a disagreeable glare as if to study her. Taeyeong smiled when she met eyes with the cute one, and the woman gave a pleasant smile back in response; she seemed to have a bright personality. The smile gave Taeyeong the courage to strike up a conversation.

"Are you family?"

"Yes. The one who opened the door for you is the big auntie, and the one who went to the kitchen is the little auntie. We're cousins."

The young lady seemed sociable and answered readily with a radiant smile. Just her reply lifted Taeyeong's mood.

"Your house is so gorgeous," she continued. "Are you here on vacation with the family?"

"Yes, for the summer . . ."

"This neighborhood doesn't have much to offer, but it's nice and well-kept. I think it's too close to North Korea for people to really know about it. Have you been to the beach?"

"A few times, with a car."

"Isn't the water so clear? It's different from the muddy water in the Yellow Sea. The cliff by the seashore is also lovely. It's not as big as the ones you might find in Gangneung, but the pine grove by the beach is pretty sizable." Taeyeong became embarrassed and trailed off. "Well, I'm sure you already know all this."

"It's such an amazing place."

"Right? Please tell your friends about it so they can visit, too."

The woman smiled and nodded a few times before asking, "By the way, how did you know that the car was stolen?"

"Oh, so what happened was, the person who stole the car didn't have a license. So we asked whose car it was, and at first he said it was his friend's. He was obviously lying, so we pressed him and he confessed that he found it abandoned near here."

"I see. I wonder how he even found this place."

"I know!"

Right then, the little auntie who had gone into the kitchen returned with steaming cups of tea on a tray. "Sorry, we're out of coffee . . ." she said apologetically. "This is mushroom tea. We drink it like water, it tastes pretty good. You might get sick if you drink plain water in the summer, so."

"Oh, thank you."

Taeyeong received a cup with both hands and slowly sipped the hot tea. At first, they all looked high-strung like the city dwellers they were, but maybe because of the dim lighting, or because of the lukewarm welcome from those who would be frightened by a police visit despite being the victims, Taeyeong found herself opening up to them. Even though she was a puny junior policewoman, the elderly often treated her well. But that was because she was the youngest officer reporting to Officers Seo Yonggu and Lee Gyeongho, not because of her own authority.

Trying her best to stay casual, Taeyeong asked, "It's such a wonderful place . . . Do you visit here often?"

"No, not that often . . . We're all busy, so," the little auntie replied.

"Ever since I was young, I've been curious about who lived here. This place looks straight out of a movie, you know."

"Yeah?"

"Yes. In my imagination, it was a castle where nobles lived, or something like a haunted mansion. I've always dreamed of taking a look inside. It's even more stunning than I had imagined."

"Thank you."

"This place is quite old, isn't it? I remember hearing it was built about thirty years ago. Am I right?"

"Something like that."

"But the inside is in such a great shape. I thought it would be a wreck since no one's occupied it for the past few years."

"You know a lot about this mansion."

"My father worked here one winter."

It was an old memory—Taeyeong had only just remembered it. But once the floodgates of memory opened, they couldn't be closed. Not that she wanted them to be. With a slight flush on her face, she let the words slip off her tongue.

"My father would come help with the hunting. I think it was right before the Seollal holidays. He said he was going to hunt for pheasants to put in the New Year's rice-cake soup. I figure he was asked because he knew the local mountains like the back of his hand. He said that there were also girls around that were my unnie's age. Oh, my sister and I have quite the age difference. My father said the girls were so pretty. He'd ask me, 'Hey, do all Seoul girls have skin as fair and beautiful as theirs?'"

The little auntie pulled up her lips into a smile as she refilled Taeyeong's empty cup.

"You have a pretty good memory," she said.

"No, not really, but talking about it brings me back."

Taeyeong took another sip and blinked. Whether she had her eyes open or closed, she could vividly recall that day's snowy mountain, like she had seen it on TV. In her memories, her father seemed more like an actor than her actual father.

Even during the off-farming season, her father was never the type to lounge around at home. The Seollal ancestral ceremony was coming up, but since he had already soaked the peeled chestnuts, and it was the women's job to prepare the food, he welcomed the opportunity to kill time and left home. The men shouldered rifles and were suited up in leather jackets and hats with earflaps. But despite the countless footprints they had left scattered across the snow, all they caught was one scrawny pheasant. It was an inevitable consequence, given that the squad had chattered loudly and had taken brazen steps against her father's advice. But the men, ready to purge their adrenaline, turned hostile towards her father, blaming him for the poor outcome. Then a piercing shriek rang out: *Keee—!* When the men rushed over, they found a panting water deer caught in a trap. *It's not even edible,* one of the men said. He spat between his teeth and fired his gun. The small killing was meaningless but seeing the warm lumps of fresh blood blotching the white snow must have contented them. Shuddering in satisfaction, someone had an idea. *Hey, let's give this to the gimp.* Whatever that slang word meant for them, they laughed their heads off at it. Now in a good mood, two of the men grabbed the deer's front and hind legs and the troop triumphantly carried the useless carcass down the mountains. Back at the mansion, the women were busy boiling some chickens they had bought from the nearby farm. The men pretended not to have noticed the smell of poultry and proceeded to gobble up the tteokguk, which had meat too plentiful to have come from one pheasant. And what about her father? He had cleaned the pheasant and even split firewood for them, but they neglected to offer him a bowl of soup. Tteokguk would be an extra reward, and since they had paid him the money they promised, that was that. Perhaps that was how people did business in Seoul. Instead of complaining, her father had noticed a man limping down the stairs; the man barely ate the soup and joined in the loud laughter and bragging of the other men. *So there really is a gimp,* he thought.

The story Taeyeong's father had told his daughter ended there, but the story he had ranted about to his wife before bed went on for much longer. Despite his attempts to be honest about everything, he knew some things were best left unsaid in front of his young daughter. At the time, Taeyeong had pricked up her ears while pretending to sleep, fascinated by the perversion, but now she blushed when recalling her parents' conversation. *Sure, way back when there was that saying about one jerk-off and two sodomies per three pussies, and men kept boys for their pleasure, but that's . . . all in the past . . . When you're stuck in the mountains in the winter, the nights can be so long. If you're alone in a place where everything is white during the day and black at night, the chill seeps into your bones. If you only have chickens and dogs to warm yourself with, what else can you do but cuddle with them? But he's from Seoul, so why . . . is he such a mess . . .*

Taeyeong gulped down her old memories with the tea. But once those images had begun floating up, they didn't fade away easily. She had to say something. As she was about to speak up, the emaciated woman returned to the living room. She was wearing the same outfit as before but had wrapped a shawl around her shoulders.

"I'm sorry for taking so long," she apologized.

"It's okay," Taeyeong said, waving her hands.

She rose unsteadily from her seat, relieved to be freed from the specter of the old man and the dead deer, yet at the same time saddened to have to leave the house. The woman had taken quite a bit of time, but not enough for Taeyeong to fully appreciate the mansion. Taeyeong smacked her lips reluctantly as she said goodbye to everyone. Only then did the sharp-eyed young woman smile faintly.

Taeyeong and the emaciated woman left the mansion while the rest saw them off. They had to walk a long way since Taeyeong hadn't thought ahead and parked far away. She apologized to the woman, but the woman only nodded and hastened her steps, seemingly unfazed as her pale, thin-

and-blue-veined legs got dirty. But Taeyeong kept looking back regretfully.

"Did you leave something behind?" the woman asked cautiously.

Taeyeong shook her head. "No, it's just, what a gorgeous place."

"Oh, yes. I loved it here when I was a child, too."

"It's like somewhere out of a dream. Not just for me, but for all the kids from this area. There were all kinds of rumors surrounding the mansion. That it was haunted, that there was an air-raid shelter in the basement. All the anticommunist training we had probably did a number on our imaginations. You know, the local kids still hunt for propaganda leaflets from North Korea. Some of us also thought burying dead animals near here would bring them back. That was from a movie, and even the kids thought it was nonsense, so the rumor didn't last long. Oh, but the military base theory was quite popular. Kids thought that space below the columns was for parking a tank in an emergency, and that the backyard hid the Taekwon V robot's secret underground base . . ."

As Taeyeong rambled, she looked back at the mansion and noticed that one of the dark windows on the first floor had lit up. The light seemed to be coming from the room next to the living room, and someone was waving from inside. The heavy rain made it hard to see, but a silhouette was beckoning at Taeyeong and the woman.

Taeyeong sucked in her stomach and shouted, "Looks like someone is calling for you?"

"Sorry?"

"Someone's calling for you. By the window, over there . . ."

The woman's face quickly hardened as if she had seen a ghost.

"Oh . . ." she let out a small groan, before putting on a smile. "Just a moment—can we go back just for a moment?"

"What?"

"I left something behind. Could you . . . come with me for a moment?"

"Oh, sure, I'm not in a hurry."

Taeyeong followed the woman back up the hill. She didn't go inside this time, instead choosing to wait by the stairs in front of the door, but she could hear some squabbling. Were they having an argument? She couldn't tell what was happening, but voices were being raised. Curiosity made her strain her ears to listen, but Taeyeong soon decided to mind her business. She couldn't hear well through the heavy rain, anyway. *Wow, it's raining really hard*, she thought, looking up at the sky through her transparent umbrella. The raindrops were shooting down with enough force to rip through plastic. Like bullets. Like the noise in old Western films that soaked an arid land not with water but blood.

During the boring wait for the woman, her niece, the quiet one, stuck her head out the door.

"Um, officer, could you . . ."

The pouring rain drowned out the last bit of her sentence.

"Sorry?" asked Taeyeong.

"Could you come wait inside for a bit?"

Though she was a bit confused, the thought of entering the mansion again made Taeyeong gladly step over the threshold.

Once she was inside, the woman was nowhere to be seen. The other three women had gathered in front of the entrance. Had they turned on the air conditioning? It felt so cold inside. Taeyeong's teeth chattered, and her body kept recoiling. The little auntie lowered her head and rubbed her cheek with the back of her hand. Oh, was she crying? What was going on?

Just as Taeyeong was going to ask, the quiet niece spoke first.

"Officer, did you see it?"

"What?"

"Please be honest with us. You saw it, didn't you?"

Something was wrong. Taeyeong shook her head. Saw what? Even as she looked at them bewildered, she instinctively reached for the holster at her waist. Right then, like a bird fluttering its wings, a whiff of breeze blew, and—

Even as her consciousness grew dimmer, Taeyeong kept her eyes peeled wide. What she caught in the corner of her distorted vision was a shotgun's butt plate covered in her own blood. A butt plate? Fuck, what was a butt plate doing in a household? A household? Oh, right. This wasn't just any household. This was an outpost, where people stepped on white snow and went hunting. A place where dead animals' blood dripped down to earth. The back of her head became wetter and wetter, and the world spun around her faster and faster. Then her body felt as if it were slowly being submerged under warm bathwater. Her consciousness was growing fainter. Through her blurred vision, Taeyeong saw someone's foot crushing her beeper and thought, *Ah, I should've gotten a cell phone. The StarTAC. I really wanted one.*

Sunday

Park answered any and all phone calls. He was the one who had everything to lose if he didn't. He was sure the same was true everywhere else, but it was especially true in this industry, where many businesses settled things through vague personal connections and spoken promises. Good performers were those who maintained good communication. Even better performers were those who drank well. And Park was someone who had to do better than his boss expected.

But when Park called back, it was already Monday, two days after he'd received that call from an unknown number. For the past two days, he had crept into the Go clubhouse during the day only to leave at night, like he had for the last couple of months. He could have gone to a pool hall or a nightclub, but the idea of seeing a face he recognized made him uneasy. The music they played in teahouses was cheesy, and fumbling around in the darkness of a gloomy theatre was exhausting. What he needed was silence and immersion. The best place for that was the Go clubhouse.

Clothes lines hung between aged buildings in the old downtown area. A worn-out sneaker someone had forgotten to retrieve was swaying in the wind and rain. Park went inside the musty building. When he climbed the stairs to the fourth floor and opened the door to the Go club, the cigarette stench permeating the cement wafted out. He nodded to the owner and handed him a five-thousand-won bill. Their dull game came quickly to an end. The owner didn't say a word to Park, who stared outside the window more often than he stared down at a gameboard. Park lit his cigarette and offered the owner one, too. The owner puffed out the smoke a few times before he went away to a pair playing at the next table. Park leafed through the game records, looked out of the open window at the people moving around in the building across the street, and unfolded a newspaper. When the Sunday afternoon news began on the TV, the owner turned up the volume. Park focused on the reports, but there was no news today, either. Of course there wasn't. No one knew about Yosep unless Park said something about it. But even so—

He was waiting for it.

He waited, in the silence after a gunshot, unaware whether it was a dead bird or just an exhausted one that he wanted to find in the bushes.

Park knew how to talk when needed, but by nature he was prone to grow tired from talking. He had no one to please here in the Go clubhouse, which was all the more reason for him not to speak. But there was one person with whom he conversed: a middle-aged man who everyone else in the clubhouse ignored. Entering the club every day at 1 p.m. sharp, this man was as doleful as a dried-up dishrag. Everyone who came in around that time of day had similar life stories, but he never bothered hiding his defeated spirit, which troubled the other men. In other words, the man existed in the Go clubhouse as a walking mirror. So when he put his hand into his pocket and pulled out a wallet thick with freshly printed bills, the others were shocked, as if they had lost a rock-scissors-paper game against themselves. They were even more shocked when he pulled his young wife's photo out of the wallet.

Since it was too late to show him respect, the men decided to disregard him. That was easy. He had an extremely filthy habit: he always spat out his food after chewing it a few times. The reason why Park had first bothered to speak to him was to ask him why he did that. Because he was anxious, the man answered. His father, his big uncle, his little uncle—all the men in his family had died before fifty. He himself was two years away from turning fifty and predicted that his own cause of death would be stomach cancer. He didn't believe his doctor who had told him he was totally fine.

An obsession with controlling his eating had led to that bizarre habit: he couldn't stand something going down his throat. At the same time, he felt anxious if he didn't put something in his mouth. His nails were ragged from excessive biting, and the tip of his festered fingers always smelled faintly of rot. On the other hand, he was a gentleman who spoke with a graceful native Seoulite accent. He knew how to seamlessly quote Chinese idioms during Go games, which made him seem like an anguished intellectual, despite his appearance. Like a luminous actress playing the role of an impoverished mother, or a TV viewer living in poverty who delusionally thought herself to be a wealthy Pyeongchang-dong madam, he was a man whose body and soul were in conflict.

Once the clock hit 1 p.m., the door opened and the man entered. As usual, he smelled of old saliva and old books from the nearby secondhand bookstore. He sat silently across from Park. His play was typically slow and poised, but that day, it was aggressive. Park made all hostile moves. Then he became gentler, slowing down his offense. During the third game, Park could see that the man was calming down, and after the fifth one, the sun had set. The floor around the man's feet was littered with drool-covered sunflower seeds and shells.

"Shall we?" the man said. Giving a parting glance to the owner, Park stood up and followed the man out of the clubhouse.

The two headed to the man's favorite high-end Chinese restaurant. It had no common dining hall, only rooms suitable for exchanging dirty talk and critical national matters alike. The first time the man had brought Park to the restaurant, he had found them an empty room before anyone showed him to one. He hadn't ordered anything specific, yet as soon as he had sat down in a chair, the staff brought out dishes and placed a bucket next to the man.

"Do you know why the Chinese are healthy even though they consume greasy food?" the man had asked, tucking a napkin around his neck as if he were a little boy from an affluent family. "It's because they all drink hot tea."

So the man commenced the meal and spat his chewed food into the bucket. The only things that made it down his throat were tea and food crumbs stuck between his teeth. Most people would have found the sight disgusting, but Park was more intrigued than anything. And there was no reason to refuse the meal since the payment had also come out of the man's hefty wallet.

For one month, the two had eaten Chinese food every day. They drank soju rice wine and then beer, and then Kaoliang liquor, and then Kaoliang mixed with beer. The man swallowed only tea, and he swished the alcohol in his mouth before spitting it out. Just doing that much quickly turned his face red, proving what a poor a drinker he was. He didn't lose his wits or become chattier—instead, he rubbed his cheeks against Park's chest, just once, like a kitten. That was the first and last time he would act so coquettishly. In the decorous silence, Park and the man ate, drank, and spat.

As the rain cleared that Sunday evening, the main street of the old downtown area remained quiet. It was time for those with families to return home and for young people to flock to districts in the new downtown, like Gangnam. Or maybe he was projecting—Park had forgotten how ordinary people led their lives. He could hear Anita Mui singing from the kitchen; the staff must have left the radio on. The restaurant was unusually empty and dreary that day. Park and the man ate, drank and spat as usual. But by the time they were nearly finished with their grand feast, the man, who had been chewing on the deep-fried pork covered in sweet and sour sauce, suddenly collapsed onto the table.

"What's wrong?" Park asked.

"I'm going to die today."

"Pardon?"

"I'm going to die this evening. I can feel it . . . No, I see it in my future."

Come to think of it, the man's lips had been oddly blackish even before he sat at the table. Park had thought he must've forgotten to wipe them after eating some black bean sauce noodles, but perhaps that wasn't it. The man's back trembled slightly before he began to sob.

"Sir, chin up," Park said. "Succumbing to a disease is a decent enough ending."

The man wept. "You don't understand. You're young and healthy. You can eat anything you want and make love until you're exhausted. But for me, it's all over. Today, tonight, will be my last."

Make love? The expression made Park cringe. The man sounded like one of those girls who get lost in their daydreams.

"That's not true," he managed to say. "I'll die the worst death there is, because I killed a man."

That statement made the man raise his disheveled head. Park continued to speak without much emotion, almost curtly.

"I'm serious. I killed a man. I got a call yesterday, probably about finding the body, but I didn't answer because I was scared. There might be detectives on the streets looking for me as we speak. Who knows, any second now they might burst through the door and handcuff me. My wrists have felt so cold for some time now. It feels like alcohol is flowing through my veins—look. They're changing color, aren't they? They're purple, my hands."

The man stared at Park without saying a word.

"I hate weak things," Park added. "That's why I hate women, laborers, and dark-skinned people. I hate people who groan while lining up in front of the hospital on Monday mornings. I hate people living outside the cities, and I hate old men because they show me my future and children because they show me my past. But a beautiful boy from a rich family, that's different. I don't hate a boy with a future that's the polar opposite of mine. I just despise him. And whenever I saw that kid . . . I'd be filled with such disgust. That's why I committed that awful act. I chose the most cowardly way out because I didn't want to bloody my own hands."

Park couldn't stop talking. He soon began to laugh.

"Do you know anyone whose mere presence makes you feel inferior? Someone who makes you hate yourself just by existing in the same space as you? That was the boy. He clung to me like I was his big brother, but I deceived him. I suggested that he stage a fake suicide attempt. I gave him sleeping pills and charcoal and told him that it would take five hours for it to kill him. I told him that if he drove the car to the reservoir and knocked himself out with the pills, I would go and wake him up in time. Even though I knew that the charcoal worked more quickly in a car. That kid wouldn't have realized he was dying until the moment he died. I deliberately got there late, but for all that trouble, the car was gone, swept away by the flood or something. I just watched the trash float down that muddy water and turned right back."

Though his face was still flushed, the man seemed more sober and straightened himself up. His breaths grew faster and more labored, and suddenly, he grabbed Park's crotch. After glancing down at the man's face, gleaming with joy, Park shook his head.

"I can't."

The man looked up.

"I mean, I physically can't," Park explained. "I've been impotent ever since I met the kid. And I'll stay that way until I see his dead body with my own eyes."

The man was quiet.

"Here."

Park placed a couple of leftover pork pieces on the man's plate, but the man didn't touch them. Instead, he stood up and smoothed his wrinkled suit, murmuring that he was going to excuse himself first. Park could hear the man paying the bill outside. Remaining in his seat, Park let Kaoliang trickle down his throat. It felt like he could spout fire if he blew between his lips. He kept pouring more and more liquor into his stomach, which felt as if it were filled with fuel. His premonition grew stronger, and grins kept escaping him. Yet his mood was neither good nor bad. He whispered to himself, "Yosep is dead." It was so quiet that no one would have heard him. Park tightened his stomach and said a little louder. "Yosep is dead. Yosep is dead!"

But his mood remained neither good nor bad.

Right before he got that call from an unknown number

two days before, Park had talked to his boss on the phone. When the CEO asked if the plan was going well, Park lowered his voice to say that he had been encountering some difficulties. When asked what was taking him so long, he brushed off the question with, "You know how he gets sensitive when it comes to his work." The CEO clicked his tongue but didn't say anything more. Over the past month, a male singer who had built up their talent agency to its current glory had been arrested for drug use, while an actress the CEO doted on had been trashed by the media for having an affair with a married man. Just when things seemed to have calmed down, photos the actress had taken during her secret dates with her lover got leaked, sending the CEO into mayhem. To Park's boss, Yosep was his last hope. Then, what about Park? What was Yosep to him?

Stepping outside the restaurant sobered Park up. He took his cell phone and went into the nearest payphone booth. Someone must have spilled Coke or something, because the booth reeked of a sickly-sweet smell. He flipped through the phonebook to find the number linked to yesterday's missed call. The area code was Gangwon-do; the number belonged to a police station located in Eungrang. Eungrang? Park was confused by the unfamiliar name. During his career as a talent manager, he had been all over the country, but never to a place with that name. Could it be a newly established district? Just then, a nearby stall selling maps caught his attention. He bought a pack of cigarettes and opened up one of the map books while standing in front of the stall.

Eungrang, Eungrang. Checking the location on the map, Park instantly understood what had happened.

The town was a fraction of an inch from the spot where he and Yosep had promised to launch the operation. A seaside village near North Korea. Its regional specialty was squid with rakkyo, or scallions. Squid was famous all across the East Sea, but it was the first time Park had heard of a Korean town growing Japanese scallions. The description informed him that in the past the town had often engaged in trade with Japan's Tottori Prefecture, and its cuisine bore traces of Japanese influence. Even now, ships were sometimes wrecked on the shore, the blurb read, making Park nod to himself. Come to think of it, he had heard the town's name a few times on the news. It also reminded him of his friend who had served on the frontlines nearby.

Latching onto the memory, Park stepped into the massive maze that was Eungrang—where in its innermost corner lived a monster whose face no one had ever seen. With every step he took, he got closer to the ocean. Raging waves. Sandy beach. Birds flying in circles. He reached the center of the maze. There lay the monster, exposing its bare, wet back. He reached and flipped over the damp thing. And there it was—Yosep's face.

Park closed the map and hopped into a cab, which had pulled up just in time. It was 10:50 p.m. when he arrived at Cheongnyangni Station, ten minutes before the last train departed. After quickly buying a ticket, he rushed into the train carriage as a ray of pale fluorescent light pierced his eyes. Slightly dizzy, he wandered the aisle with his eyes half-closed. He arrived at his seat to find it was between three members of a family, who looked up at him uneasily. The seats were turned to face each other, with the mother and son sitting by the window and the daughter next to her mother. Park thought about sitting in a different seat but ended up sitting next to the son, across from the daughter. He wondered, how would he look in the family's eyes? His suit was dapper enough but smelled of alcohol, and he had barely slept for the past two nights, causing his bloodshot eyes to resemble cooked pollack roes. Park smiled at the girl, who had begun to roll and peel a boiled egg even before the train set off.

"Are you the older sister?" he asked.

"Younger."

The girl's aloof response hinted that she was used to being asked the question, which embarrassed Park. He looked away, thinking he should have just minded his own business. He scanned the racks to look for something to read, but not a single newspaper was lying around.

The train departed. The boy and the girl stuffed themselves with boiled eggs and fell asleep in less than five minutes. The woman rested her chin on her hand while staring out of the dark window, exhausted. *We look like family*, he thought, as he closed his eyes. In his sleep, Park became a pair of eyes hanging from the ceiling, looking down on the four people facing each other. On some other earth, one summer at the end of the twentieth century, another Park Seungtae gets on the same late-night train with his wife and two children. Their destination is his hometown by the sea. His aged, impoverished mother serves the children, tired from traveling overnight, freshly cooked rice and soup made with marine fish and seaweed scraped off rocks. After filling himself up and getting some shuteye, Park and his children go to the beach where he used to play as a boy. He watches his barefoot wife and children. The fine sand is stunning, and it bears no history of two young men copulating like beasts.

But the Park Seungtae of this earth was on his way to find a dead person, and unless he was transported to another world, that would remain an immutable fact.

When he opened his eyes again, the woman across from him was dozing off. Her spoiled, sleeping son had rested one of his thin legs on Park's knee. The boy's thigh underneath his blue shorts revealed a muscle as prominent and sharp as a bone. Park rose slightly, picked up the boy's ankle with two fingertips, and dropped it onto the seat. Despite appearing to be asleep, the boy made a "gotcha" face and stretched both his legs out on the empty seat, still warm with Park's body heat. Park clicked his tongue in exasperation. What a spoiled brat. He couldn't stand such small, naughty creatures.

He stopped by the restroom and entered the dining car. Along the windows stood refugees from the world of sleep like himself, keeping a distance from each other and drinking canned beer. Park joined them. He clung to the cold window to see what they were seeing, but he could only see his own reflection in the glass. Sipping his beer, he glared at a single point in the darkness. He thought of the story about a man who grew smaller every day.

When the man sees that the ceiling seems to be getting higher and higher with every waking morning, he thinks he is just imagining things. Only after his clothes become loose and his shoes slip off does he accept the fact that he is shrinking. The man has a lover. He is afraid that she might leave him, but she says it's okay. She says just because he's reduced in size doesn't mean she'll reduce her love. But the man still grows smaller and smaller, and one night, when he shrinks to the size of a thumb, he crawls in between the legs of his sleeping lover and never comes back out. Ten months later, the woman gives birth to a boy.

The story doesn't account for how the woman might have felt. But Park thought she must have been delighted. She would have played with the man as if he were a doll. She would have sewn her lover finger-sized clothes, covered him in napkins, made him rice balls out of individual rice grains, and, in the end, pretended that she was asleep when she knew that he was crawling inside her. Raising the child would have made her the happiest woman alive for the rest of her life.

Park always imagined how nice it would be to be her son. How much would the mother have loved her child, who bore his father inside him? The child who was both her lover and her son? Park's mother had no love for Park. To her, he was worth less than a dog, and he was always thirsty for her love. He had wandered his whole life in search of the water to quench his thirst, but now, even his boss seemed to have forgotten that Park had entered the agency to become a celebrity himself.

That was why he loathed Yosep. Their stories had begun the same way. But Yosep had received around-the-clock care and became a small and beautiful bonsai, whereas Park had twisted into an old, gnarly tree beyond redemption. He was a doll that no one played with. Yosep was a doll worn and broken from countless kisses. That was why he was beautiful. That was why Park wanted to kill him, and in fact, he had been waiting for the news that he had died even before the missed call.

The train stopped to change locomotives. Park jumped off the train along with the other passengers and bought a bowl of warm, salt-laden noodle soup generously seasoned with seaweed flakes. It took him less than three minutes to slurp the noodles down to the last drop. A nauseating sense of fullness soon overwhelmed him, but what troubled him more was that there wasn't enough time left for a cigarette. He returned to his seat and closed his eyes. While repeatedly pushing off the boy's legs that slid down the seat and snuck back up, he dozed off, realizing only after the conductor's voice startled him awake that he had crashed into a deep, short sleep. Dawn colored the sky a hazy shade, and the ocean waves formed ripples close to the tracks. His heart skipped a few beats as he checked his surroundings. The family he had been sitting with had disappeared — they had probably gotten off at one of the midway stops. He awkwardly retrieved his hand from the empty seat and rubbed it on his pants before he got off the train.

A salty breeze blew in. Bracing himself against nausea, Park thought: *Oh, the ocean.* That was his first impression of Eungrang. The station platform was plastered with promotional materials introducing the town as a special tourist zone, but that seemed more like the locals' wishful thinking. Behind the picture of a squid giving a thumbs up with one of its tentacles, the sky looked as gloomy as it had in wartime.

Park skirted between the soldiers returning to their units and left the station. His sleepy eyes were sore by the time he reached the town square. He blinked, standing around vacantly as soldiers passed him by and disappeared into the hangover soup joints that had just begun welcoming morning customers. He didn't feel hungry; the bloated noodles inside his stomach were twisting around like snakes. Suppressing his nausea, he looked up at the old clock tower that stood in the center of the square. 6:30. It was still early. Police stations were open 24/7, but he didn't have it in him just yet to face the corpse. But that didn't mean he wanted to wander around aimlessly, either. After staring at the unlit teahouse sign, he swallowed the acid rising in his throat and, left with no choice, set off to catch a cab. Then suddenly, someone appeared in front of him.

Park's mind went blank. He was used to seeing people wearing stage makeup, but seeing someone seemingly in costume in a strange town distorted his sense of time and space. Completely unfazed by Park's astonishment, the middle-aged woman in a wedding dress fluttered her long, fake eyelashes.

"You're here looking for oppa, right?" she asked.

Park was dumbstruck.

"But you won't find him," the woman said. "You can't."

Her words ignited Park's rage, but before he could act, an older lady, wearing a sun visor inappropriate for the overcast weather, intervened.

"You bitch! Go away, shoo! Shoo!"

She waved her hand at the woman while making the sound of wind between her teeth. It was like she was chasing away a bird rather than a human, and the woman fled like a seagull that still feared people. The woman with the visor stomped her feet a few times. Then, with a seductive smile, she glanced up at Park and linked arms with him.

"Oppa, you nearly ruined the start of your day," she purred.

Park thought about shaking her off, but instead smiled back and said, "Thank you, Auntie."

"If you really want to thank me, come to my place, hmm? I'll give you a discount."

The woman naughtily poked Park in the ribs. Park noticed a few more old women in similar outfits circling the square. They were probably trying to solicit soldiers before they returned to their posts or fishermen who had made it back to land.

Out of curiosity, Park asked, "You ladies are so hardworking. Your girls clocked in already?"

"As if the time of day matters," the woman answered with a laugh. "My girls are the best. I've got a college student, too. I'll get her for you cheap if you want."

"How much?"

When the woman held up her fingers, Park nearly scoffed. Wasn't offering a price so dirt-cheap even more illegal than prostitution itself? He grabbed and gently folded down the old woman's fingers, indicating a price that basically begged for sexually transmitted diseases. He couldn't help but blurt another question.

"Auntie, what about boys—do you have any?"

"Huh?" the woman said, but her crumpled face suggested she must have understood what he meant.

Park smiled with his eyes and said, "I'm just joking. I'm here for business, so maybe next time."

He carefully freed himself from the woman's arm. Then he walked over to a payphone booth and dialed a ten-digit number. Not too long after, a man with a sleepy voice answered.

"Yes, this is Seomyeon Precinct."

"I got a call," Park said.

"Pardon?"

"I got a call from you a few days ago, but I couldn't answer it. On Saturday evening?"

Ah. The man's voice receded after checking Park's cell phone number. A short exchange took place in the background, followed by the rustling of papers. The man then returned to the phone, and in a tired voice explained:

"Oh, yes, so, um, we called you because we found a car. It's a New Grandeur, and, let's see, the plate number is—"

"That's right."

"Excuse me?"

"It is a New Grandeur. That's my car."

Ah. The police officer let out just that one syllable before he continued at an excruciatingly slow pace.

"So, uh, someone stole your car, and that's why we called you."

"Was there no one in it?" Park asked.

"Huh? In it?" the officer asked back, confused. "I mean . . . Obviously not . . . How else would the thief have stolen the car?"

Park remained silent.

The officer hesitated a little before asking, "Er, um, aren't you the mansion's owner?"

"Pardon?"

"They said that's where they found the car. The, uh, the kids who stole it, I mean. They're college students, and that's where they found it."

"Oh . . ." Now Park was the one dragging things out. "Yes, it is my car, but my wife borrowed it. To get together with friends."

"Would it be faster to contact your wife, then?"

"No, I'm in Eungrang right now, too. Should I go to the precinct?"

"Yes, please. Where exactly are you?"

"At the train station."

"Oh, then don't wait for the bus. It's a quick cab ride from there. It'll only cost you the minimum fare."

"Okay, thank you."

After hanging up, Park stood in the booth for a while before heading to the square by the train station. The woman with the visor had joined other ladies in similar outfits, sitting on abandoned dining chairs lined against the square's outer wall, drinking coffee from a vending machine. Her eyes met Park's, but she didn't get up. When Park approached, the sweet smell of sugar brought back the nausea he had barely managed to settle. He swallowed hard and smiled, revealing exactly eight front teeth. But before he could even speak, the woman beat him to the punch.

"No can do."

"Sorry?"

Park frowned, but the woman said nonchalantly, "Our girls won't do that with their behinds."

"Auntie, what kind of a man do you think I am?"

The woman didn't answer and only muttered to herself, "How weird. Why would you prefer something hard over a soft pussy . . ."

This time, Park pulled the woman up and linked arms with her. "Not up to date with Seoulite humor, huh? At this rate, this place will never be a tourist destination. C'mon, Auntie. Give me a cute girl."

The woman didn't answer.

"Or I could ask another auntie."

At that, she glanced at the other women before crumpling her paper cup and rising to her feet. As she continued her disgruntled mumbling, Park followed her through the square where seagulls congregated, and into a breeding ground for sexually transmitted diseases where uncut kiddos popped their cherries.

Park was definitely in the woman's bad books.

Where he was shown to was not a storefront but one of the living quarters. The old woman swung open the door and yelled that they had a customer, and a younger woman twitched and threw off her blanket, which stunk of rice, flesh, and cigarettes. The makeup still on her face hinted that she had spent the whole night awake and was just about to get a bit of rest.

"You've got an hour and a half," the old woman said, locking the door from the outside.

The woman on the blanket seemed flustered at first, but soon calmly lowered her head. Park moved closer to her and gazed at her face under the dim light.

A coastal villager who was neither ugly nor pretty. Still, a woman. The wind and salty air had both raised and ruined her, leaving her with a moderate amount of mystique. The skin beneath her half-faded makeup revealed the passage of time. *God, that old bat got me good.* Park laughed as he recalled the old woman shamelessly bragging that she had a college student.

The woman looked a little embarrassed; she must have noticed something was wrong. Unusual for someone from the coasts, Park thought. He plopped his head on the woman's lap, but out of either shyness or reticence, she remained silent.

"How old are you, noona?" he asked. When the woman hesitated, he quickly added, "It's okay, you can be honest with me. I like older women."

The woman flashed open her fingers and said, "Twenty-five . . ."

Does she think I'm blind? Park snickered, only to realize that the woman's pronunciation was a bit distinctive.

"Where are you from?" he asked.

The woman didn't answer.

"Hmm? I asked where are you from, noona?"

The woman finally replied, "Vietnam . . ."

"Ahh, I see. You're from a warm country, noona. It's nice there, isn't it? No winter."

"Yes . . ."

"How are the women there? Are they all pretty like you?" Park chuckled as he slowly rubbed the woman's buttocks. The woman squirmed with an awkward smile, which made him want to tease her.

"Auntie said you can't do it from behind," he cooed. "Is that true, noona? Hmm? You really can't?"

The woman's face hardened. Park laughed.

"Fucking bitch."

The woman froze.

"I was just joking." Park laughed it off. "I'm here to rest. I'm tired. Could you just stroke my head? Like this."

He grabbed the woman's hand and placed it on his head. Her soft hand moved from the crown down to his cheek. The musty odor and the smell of cheap air freshener gave him a headache, but it was peaceful. Park closed his eyes and imagined what would happen that afternoon.

Under the blazing midday sun, he stands in the square. After waving off the seagulls, he gets in a cab to go to the police station. He hops in the car that some kids have stolen and drives to the mansion where it was supposedly abandoned. It is quiet, suggesting no one is there, but Park knocks on the door and says, *Yosep, it's me.* No response comes. When he presses his ear against the door, he hears gasping breaths. He draws close to the peephole. It is pitch dark inside. But he can tell that an eye, reminiscent of a frightened doe's, is looking back at him.

Park flashed open his eyes. The woman, who had been mechanically moving her hands while watching the muted TV with her mouth agape, looked down at him in surprise.

"Noona, that bastard's alive," Park moaned.

"Sorry?"

"That son of a bitch is alive."

Park burst out laughing. Grimacing from joy swelling too quickly, he buried his face between the woman's legs. Her upper body leaned backwards. As his head slid underneath her slip, Park looked as if he was trying to crawl inside her.

—

Moonlight poured into the window and caressed Mihee's eyelids. She opened her eyes to find the light softly rustling against her cheek like a goldfish's fin. Mihee could see her past memories being projected onto the ceiling. Lying on an old mattress, she slowly drifted back to one Christmas Eve long ago.

Each time Mihee's family moved, Mihee changed her religion. She attended Protestant churches, a Buddhist temple, as well as a Catholic church with a friend. The Buddhist temple was in the mountains and difficult to reach, while the Host from the Catholic church had less taste than even her own skin, quickly boring her. The Protestant churches, however, were fun and well-attended. The era of Holy Spirits and miracles that defined the '70s and '80s was long gone, but churchgoers still gave testimonies about how a reverend's single prayer made a lame man walk on his own two feet. Whenever people ecstatically raised their hands to the sky and looked for their Father, Mihee shuddered. At the time, she had thought what she was feeling was fear, but now she knew: she had been jealous of them. She had wanted to shed her childlike shyness and roar with faith like they did. She wanted to stand in the front row of the Great Tribulation and be martyred as a forever virgin-child.

Christmas Eve. On the night of the festival, the devotees' blood boiled like a bull's before a red flag. After a thunderous hymn, the children's play about the birth of Jesus—the highlight of the festival—commenced. Behind the velour curtains, Mihee stood in the darkness, glaring at her classmate acting out a childbirth on stage. That dumb girl with no friends who was always sniffling in the back of the classroom was now shining as bright as the moon, and not just because of the stage lighting. After the play was over, Mihee watched the girl's mom hug her daughter, whose face was glowing with smug arrogance. It was then that Mihee decided, *It's going to be me next time. I'm definitely going to play the Virgin Mary.*

But she never got the chance to hold a fake baby in her arms. Instead, she would hold not one but two corpses with dark hair sticky with blood. Death scattered its spores everywhere. The virus spread like mold and penetrated through the projection of her daydreams on the ceiling. Invisible bugs fell from between the cracks. They grazed her skin like raindrops and penetrated like bullets. *I'm so itchy.* Mihee couldn't stand the sensation and scratched away at her skin. Skin flakes and blood gathered underneath her nails. Traces of blood, like brushstrokes, stretched across her chest, abdomen, and back. Her body burned with fever, and her vision went pitch dark. In the vertigo that made her feel like collapsing even when she was already lying on her back, what floated into Mihee's mind was the scene from a few hours ago.

"She's not breathing," Heeae said, her eyes watery as she massaged the police officer's chest. "You said you were just gonna knock her out."

"It was a mistake. A mistake," Ahnna muttered, forcing herself to stay calm. After a round of vomiting and passing out, her face was as pale as dough.

To Mihee, their argument sounded as if it was coming from from far away, from underwater. The dead body before her eyes felt like a block of wood. Like a scholar contemplating what fire was when her own feet were on fire, she asked herself a fundamental question: what had brought them to this point?

They couldn't blame it on hunger. They couldn't have freshly cooked meals every day, but they hadn't gone starving; they frequented the supermarket to buy groceries. Was the isolation the problem, then? Or was it the pouring rain that deprived them of a single ray of sunlight? But this wasn't a jail but a small heaven. A heaven inside a snow globe where glittering sand fluttered around. There was only one way to find the answer to this question. Going back to the beginning.

Thinking it over, Mihee reached the conclusion that seeing Yosep in the first place was the problem. As she sat in between broken household items watching TV, the moment she saw Yosep appear on screen, she was overcome. Then and there, she was convinced that only the boy—with his long, lustrous hair, deep-set, heavily made-up eyes, glittering earrings, glossy faux-leather pants, and soft hands that carefully wiped the sweat trickling down his forehead—held the power to help her not face reality.

But was that really the case? Don't roses wither when plucked, and sparkling jewels turn to pebbles when held in the hand? Mihee recalled the story of Thomas. To Thomas, who only accepted that Jesus had been resurrected after touching His wounds, Jesus said that blessed were those who had not seen and yet had believed. In other words, He fucked Thomas over, didn't He? If He really cared about Thomas, He should have let him be so that he wouldn't have had to touch Him. He should have left him disbelieving. According to the Bible, Thomas made a huge fuss about the dead coming back to life. But in fact, upon feeling His cold skin, Thomas must have realized deep down in his heart, deeper than ever, that Jesus was also human. Because physical touch is stronger than faith. And in Thomas's mind, Jesus must have been stripped of His status as the Son of God. Regardless of what he said, that would have been how Thomas truly felt. Because that was how Mihee herself felt when she touched Yosep for the first time.

Mihee finally understood her mother's true intentions. She hadn't chosen to be unhappy, but rather, she had chosen not to touch happiness, ever. Everyone needed a star in their hearts, an unreachable flower on the cliff to watch for the rest of their lives. That was why her mother had got on the nerves of the fathers. On their best days, out of all days. Whenever they found a job or bought a rose or cake for her, her mother became excited before she could stop herself, and it angered her to feel happy in that situation, where she had been sitting around all day in a dark, sunless room where the wallpapers were grimy and the linoleum was scorched and stuck on the floor. And eventually, it led her to raise hell. Because that pathetic reality mustn't be her star. If that cold lump of ice were really her star, she would loathe herself for devoting all her delusions and love to it.

Heeae no longer breathed into the dead police officer's mouth. Instead, she kneeled in front of the body.

"She's not breathing," she muttered to herself as if she had lost her mind. "She's not breathing." Heeae slowly began to muss up her own hair. "We killed a police officer. A *police officer*. The person who came to tell us to pick up Yohan's car. We can't even hide it. They'll know. Other police officers know that she's here. They'll come and ask us where she went, right? Even if we pretend that we don't know what they're talking about, they'll notice something's off and trample and ransack this place, right? They'll take Yohan, won't they? I haven't done anything yet. I couldn't even touch my boy. I couldn't touch his cheeks, couldn't kiss him, couldn't tell him that I'm his mom, that I love him, and now it's all over. It's over, and it shouldn't have ended this way."

"Stop it," Ahnna warned in a low voice, but Heeae's frantic cries grew louder and louder.

"Someone is going to come soon. To take my Yohan. They're gonna steal him from us. We have to hide him before that happens. Yes, that's right—we should take him somewhere."

"Are you out of your mind?" Ahnna snapped. "Where could we possibly go?"

Meeting her gaze, Heeae dropped her head helplessly. But when she raised her head again, her face gleamed with strange delight.

"North Korea," she declared flatly. "Yes, we'll go to North Korea. I'll take him. After all, I'm his mom. I'll take care of him for the rest of my life, I can do that much. That's what a mom does, isn't it?"

Sounding completely worn out, Ahnna asked, "Are you kidding me?"

But Heeae, unable to handle the ideas pouring out of her brain, rattled on. "Why can't I? Lim Su-kyung managed to go by herself, and she was just a college girl. If not, Japan could work, too. We could take a boat, a dugout canoe abandoned on the beach. It's a quick trip across the Genkai Sea. I have a relative living in Niigata. He sent all his children to North Korea and lives there alone. We'll go there, inherit and farm his land. Yes, we'll grow rice. We come from a family of farmers to begin with, so we'll just go back to how we used to be. That would be better for Yohan, too. This, here, this place is bad for him. People ruined my boy. I just want to reverse everything. I just want to go back to the beginning, when it was just me and Yohan."

Ahnna gritted her teeth and asked, "Who are you to decide if Yosep can go or not?"

"This all started because of me, didn't it?"

Ahnna clammed up.

Heeae continued, "You said it yourself, Ahnna. That Yohan wanted to meet me. That this was about reuniting a boy with his mother he so desperately missed. That's why I began all this, all because you said so. That's why I cleaned up after that insane old man, to bring Yohan here."

"Lee Heeae."

"Oh, no, don't get me wrong. I'm telling you all this because I'm grateful. Yes, thank you, Ahnna. But it's just that the time has come. The time to go back. Thank you, really." There, Heeae turned to the other two women. "Nami, Mihee, thank you to you, too. You enjoyed him enough, right? You cherished him so much, didn't you? Did you kiss him? Did you suck those thin silver strings of saliva after getting the kiss you wanted? Did you gulp them down? Did you get to touch and lick his flesh enough while you pretended to clean him? No, it's okay. I know about it all. You're young, I understand. I'm not blaming you for doing those things. If you didn't have such motivation, you wouldn't have been able to do anything. Those thoughts of yours are what made you bring Yohan to me. So thank you. I'm truly, truly grateful. Thank you so much. I'd like to thank you as Yohan's mother. Now I'll take him with me. Now I'll take care of him."

"Hey, Lee Heeae."

Ahnna's irritable voice silenced Heeae.

"Did you just say we did all this because of you?" Ahnna scoffed. "You stupid bitch. You really believe that?"

Either from agitation or fear, her entire body trembled as words began to pour out of her.

"Mother? Did you say, *mother*? How brazen of you to mention it. How could a mother ever act like you?"

Heeae tried to refute her. "What did I ever—"

"*What did I ever?* Hey, I told you before that we're living in convenient times, right? That people with money can find out anything?" Ahnna twisted her lips into a smile. "Heeae. I never realized Yeongki oppa was so generous with his money. I think you could've easily bought a couple of apartment units with the amount he paid you. With that much money involved, wouldn't you say your boy was sold, rather than taken? What did you do with all that money, huh?"

"I . . . I've done nothing wrong. It's all because he—"

"He? Who is this *he*?"

Heeae fell silent.

"Who is this man? Huh? Tell me. Or can you not? Because there's more than one?" Ahnna sneered and continued. "Gosh, no wonder Yeongki oppa made all that effort to change the boy's name and bring him to the States. There was no way that a mother such as yourself could've raised him properly. What would he learn from a mother who switches up men almost every day?"

Heeae was at a loss for words.

"Heeae, let me ask you one thing. Didn't you feel anything when those men beat the shit out of your son? Or do you just not care when you're crazy over a man, even when your kid is scared shitless?"

Heeae's silence only made Ahnna more agitated.

"As if I don't know you. It's not like you couldn't meet Yosep because of your promise to Yeongki oppa, am I wrong? You couldn't because you were fucking embarrassed of yourself. Yet, I brought you in on this because of our old friendship, and now what? You're gonna go to North Korea? To Japan? You crazy fucking bitch. You think you can take good care of him over there when you couldn't do shit for him here? You really think you can make him happy? And, what was it that you called him? Yohan?"

Ha! Ahnna's scorn made a giant droplet of spit shoot out of her mouth.

"Let's get this straight. Yohan is no more," she declared.

Heeae didn't respond.

"Your son Yohan is dead, okay? The moment you sold him off for money, he was as good as dead. That right there is Yosep. No, not even Yosep. He's just a clean slate born right here. He rose from the ground, he fell from the sky. He never had a mother, and he never will. He died the day you deserted him, and it's me who brought him back to life."

When Heeae remained silent, Ahnna pressed, "He's mine, that boy. Every single strand of his hair, even down to his eyebrows. It's all mine. I'm going to use every piece of him like I would a pig, from top to bottom. He's all mine, down to his last piece of bone."

"Crazy bitch," Heeae finally cried, trembling. "How could you? You, you—"

She jumped on Ahnna and pulled out a few locks of her long hair. Ahnna had been putting in a great effort to grow it out for a year. She let out a small shriek at the sight of her hair in Heeae's hands.

"You fucking—"

Ahnna's eyes flashed before she reached for Heeae's hair. Her ruthless grip yanked Heeae's neck back. Heeae screamed as a fistful of hair fluttered in the air like dog hair. Then, she instinctively waved her fist, which landed on Ahnna's right eye with a *thwack*. Ahnna staggered for a second, and then charged at Heeae like a bull. She fought as fiercely as a boxer who had only one minute left in a championship match.

Heeae was the first to let go. Her mouth was bleeding. Swinging her last counterpunch with her teeth clenched, Ahnna yelled, "Grab that bitch quick, now!"

The howl echoing through the living room jolted Mihee and Nami, and, before they realized it, they had grabbed Heeae's arms. Ahnna tied her arms with the cable ties that they had planned to use when kidnapping Yosep. She stared at Mihee, her eyes blazing. As Mihee blankly stared back at her, Ahnna shoved the younger woman.

"Let go now," she shrieked. "I said, let go!"

Mihee screamed in pain. She had no idea how Ahnna's scrawny body was able to summon such power, but even the slightest graze bruised her arm blue. Ahnna was unmoved when Mihee fell to the ground. She grabbed Heeae by the hair and dragged her, semi-conscious, to the pillar between the living room and the kitchen. After tying her limp body against the post, Ahnna forcefully ripped a towel and gagged her. Red blood seeped into the white cloth. Succumbing to the pain, Heeae no longer put up a fight. The other two women remained compliant. What had unfolded before their eyes could have happened at any point, but what shocked them was that Ahnna was the perpetrator. She had committed the violence so swiftly, as if it was second nature to her. At that moment, Mihee remembered her mother, sniffling while scooching among their broken household goods. Had Ahnna been beaten like this, too? The thought made Mihee shiver uncontrollably. Although she had grown accustomed to the cold while living in the mansion, she had never felt such a chill.

Ahnna, who had been standing with her back to Mihee, turned around.

"Do you have a mirror?" she asked suddenly.

Mihee couldn't answer. The impact from Heeae's blow must have been pretty severe since Ahnna's right eye was now purple and swollen. As if she had anticipated Mihee's lack of response, Ahnna didn't bother asking again. Instead, she wobbled into the bathroom.

Silence swelled like a balloon, until Ahnna's piercing

sobs popped it. They began as hiccups but soon grew louder into wails. Her wet voice bounced off the tiled walls and floor and surged into the living room. Her howls that resembled those of wailing ghosts caused the floor and the ceiling to squeak. It was as though the entire mansion had become a massive cradle, rocking with the sound of Ahnna's moans. And then, her weeping suddenly stopped.

"Go check on her," Nami said, poking at Mihee's side.

As if she was a robot commanded with the press of a button, Mihee made her way to the bathroom. Standing by the open door, she could see the mirror and Ahnna's back, leaning against the sink. Ahnna's shoulders were trembling from trying to catch her breath. Her seemingly calmer state gave Mihee the courage to step into the bathroom. Just at that moment, Ahnna jerked her head up. She must not have spotted Mihee behind her, because she met eyes with her reflection in the mirror and clutched her hair in one hand, trying out different ways to tie it back. She began to tilt her face, which was now quickly swelling up, and observed it from various angles. At the sight, Mihee couldn't help but wonder:

Is she in love with her own face?

Or is she in love with the drama of the situation?

Soon, Ahnna placed her hand on her cheek and began to stroke it softly, muttering to herself in a low voice. Her touch was gentle, as if she were caressing a lover. Mihee mistook the display as Ahnna confessing her love to herself, but no. Her voice, growing louder, was saying the exact opposite.

"It's hopeless. Ah, it's all done for. Look at me. My face,

what happened to my face? I can't show Yosep this. No, I can't. But look at this. Ah, the bruise, it's swelling. It's getting bigger. Ah, what do I do? Why did it have to be on my right side? That's my better side. I have to show my right side to hide my hooked nose. See, the left side's . . . Huh? What's all this? When did I get . . . all these . . . wrinkles? What? What's going on? I'm not an ajumma yet. Wait, ajumma? Huh? When, how did this happen?"

Ahnna's hand went into the sink and rummaged through a pouch. Standing at a distance, Mihee caught a whiff of something: a milky powder smell. Ahnna was puffing out the smell while patting powder on her face. At first, her gestures were slow and careful. She started from the cheekbone to the side of her face. But as her hand passed near her eyes and lips, the motion grew faster and faster. And the intensity with which she applied the powder grew stronger and stronger, as if she couldn't control herself.

"Oh, no. I see the wrinkles. No. I have to put on more. It can't fall off like this. Oh. Oh. Oh."

Muttering, Ahnna kept patting her face without avoiding her split lips or bruised eyelids. Blood smeared onto the cushion puff. The reddish liquid spread across her foundation, pale and thick as a theatre actress's. Mihee thought that she shouldn't look, that she should turn away now, but her feet . . . Her feet wouldn't budge. The two women were caught inside the same mirror; as Ahnna dabbed powder on her face, Mihee stood behind her, transfixed. And then, inside that very mirror, the two women's eyes finally met, and—

"Mihee."

Ahnna's voice, as clear and bright as a gemstone, called out.

Ahnna had turned around before Mihee even realized it, looking straight at her. Revealing her bluish-white teeth that looked almost bleached, Ahnna whispered:

"Mihee, come here for a second."

Why? Mihee would have asked if things were normal. Only if. But at that moment, Mihee felt herself being dragged toward Ahnna, unable to resist, as if Ahnna's fishing rod had hooked her skin. She took one step, and then another. The closer her reluctant steps brought her to Ahnna, the stronger the scent of the powder grew. Its aroma stung her nose. Just when Ahnna's smooth skin—so smooth that it almost looked thick—drew close enough to touch Mihee's eyeballs, Ahnna reached her hand out. *I'm gonna get slapped!* Mihee instinctively closed her eyes, but the touch that landed on her cheek was soft.

Mihee opened her eyes. Right before her eyes, Ahnna, wearing a peaceful expression, was patting Mihee's face with the powder, which was slightly too bright for Ahnna's own skin tone.

"Mihee, I've never done this kind of thing for you before, have I?" she asked.

What was she up to? Confused and scared, Mihee managed to shake her head.

"Aw, how smooth," Ahnna marveled. "Mihee, your skin looks so smooth up close."

"No, it's not that smooth," Mihee said, attempting to be modest.

"What do you mean? It is. It's so smooth. You don't go to skin-care shops, do you? So how is this possible? Is it because you're still young?"

Mihee had no words to say.

"I see. It's because you're still young," Ahnna concluded.

Mihee swallowed hard. Even though her neck felt stiff, she couldn't turn her head. Ahnna's cheekbones gleamed right in front of her eyes. Those very cheekbones, prominent as if only a layer of leather covered the bone, were emitting heat after taking a hit. The warmth flushed even Mihee's face. Upon her face poured down Ahnna's girlish voice, high-pitched like a small bird fluttering up into the sky, mingled with droplets and heated breath.

"You know . . . I never thought you were pretty before, Mihee . . . No, don't get me wrong. You know, it's just a matter of taste . . . I don't think Hwang Shin-hye is that pretty, either. They praise her beauty, say she looks so perfect, it's as if she was drawn with a computer. But, you know, she looks kinda boring to me. Do you remember? When we went to the ski resort together for that music show . . . Hwang Shin-hye was the special emcee. That day, when I got you her autograph . . . Yeah. Even when I got to see her right before my eyes, it was as good as thrusting her in front of a blind person. No matter how long or close I got to look at her, I thought of nothing . . ."

The sound of Ahnna pressing the powder puff onto Mihee's face became louder.

"And the same went for you, Mihee."

Much louder. Ahnna's voice also grew more booming.

"That's how you were, too . . . So when did you . . ."

Ahnna's hand halted. Specks of powder floated in the air like dust.

"You know, I have a favor to ask," she said.

Trying her best to stay calm, Mihee asked, "What is it?"

With her thumb and index finger, Ahnna gently stroked Mihee's hair.

"Cut it," she demanded.

"Sorry?"

"It's unfair, don't you think? How only you get to be young and pretty. If you can't do something with your face, cut your hair at least. I've lost all my hair, and now when I tie it back, it looks more like a goat's dropping than a ponytail. Don't you think it's weird for you to let your long hair down like this?"

It was bizarre logic. When Mihee didn't reply, Ahnna blinked her eyes accusingly.

"Why aren't you answering? You don't want to?"

Mihee remained silent.

"You don't." Ahnna let out a light sigh and muttered, "Then, die."

Mihee felt a sharp twinge at the nape of her neck. She pressed her hand against the spot out of reflex. She wasn't imagining things when she thought her head was getting lighter. Neither was she imagining her bare feet tingling, nor sheets of her hair falling upon them. The pair of scissors that had been used for Yosep's haircut had moved from the water glass to Ahnna's hand. When Ahnna tried to yank at her remaining hair, Mihee let out a squeal.

"Die! Just die!" Ahnna shrieked, brandishing the scissors.

Soon, footsteps loud enough to break the floor sounded, and Nami stomped in. She somehow twisted Ahnna's arms behind her back and yelled.

"Mihee! Run! Quickly!"

Like when Mihee had come to the bathroom, only after Nami's words did her feet come off the floor. Mihee quickly climbed up the stairs without looking back. Her legs shook so badly that she nearly crawled to her room before locking the door behind her. Her heart pounded as if she was standing in front of the speakers at a concert hall. Those heartbeats alone made her chest ache as if her lungs had collapsed.

All that happened last night. Mihee couldn't tell how long it had been since then.

Mihee heard a knock. The door opened before she could reply. It was Nami, her face pale.

"Ahnna's okay now," she said. "She was probably just worked up."

When Mihee didn't respond, Nami urged, "Come with me. We need to move the body."

"I'm not doing it. Get that ajumma to help you," Mihee spat.

"You think she would?" Nami sighed and continued in a coaxing tone, "We can't leave the body like that. It'll start to rot. Why don't we move it first, hmm? We should do something about it, right?"

Do something, like what? Mihee wanted to retort, but she

had no energy left to do so. Besides, Nami hadn't done anything wrong. In the end, she meekly rose and went downstairs.

The two handled the police officer's body as they had done with the other body a few nights before. After sweating buckets while making the trip from the living room to the basement cellar, Mihee was parched. Nami must have felt the same way; she looked for water as soon as they returned to the living room. Then Ahnna, who had been simply sitting there like a doll, served up cold tea.

"Thank you." Mihee hesitantly took a cup.

While quenching her thirst, she stole a glance at Ahnna. Her temper extinguished, she looked calm, but a shadow was cast over her face. She looked more tired and frighteningly older than Mihee had imagined. And not just because of her age, the lighting, or the bruise on her face. The sight made pity suddenly well up inside Mihee.

Not to offend Ahnna's feelings, she asked carefully, "What about Yosep?"

It was Nami who answered instead. "He's asleep."

Mihee stared at the closed door to Yosep's room. She then turned her gaze in the other direction, at the spot in the mansion her mind had kept coming back to. Slumped against the white pillar on the way to the kitchen was Heeae, still tied up. Was she asleep? She wasn't moving. If it weren't for the sound of her breathing, Mihee would have thought that she was dead. She felt bad. As a human with a heart. But before she could say anything, Ahnna began to speak.

"She must be thirsty." After a pause, she continued, "I suppose we could ungag her, at least."

That was a good enough signal for Mihee. She quickly approached Heeae. Muzzled by a towel, Heeae was limp, her head hung low to her left. Her fine-boned neck looked like it was about to break. Mihee knelt down, took the towel out of Heeae's mouth, and tapped on her shoulder. When Heeae managed to lift her eyelids, Mihee looked into her eyes.

"Are you okay?" she asked.

Heeae didn't reply. Her blank gaze conveyed only severe physical exhaustion. Her cheeks were stiff and she drooled saliva that she couldn't swallow. The skin around her mouth was festered and raw with slobber, and her dry mouth smelled faintly of bad breath. Only after a long while did she manage to form a few hoarse words.

"Water. Water, please . . ."

Mihee got up and brought a cup of cold tea to Heeae's lips. Even as she let nearly half of the liquid spill down her chin, Heeae hurriedly sipped the tea, cherishing it. Watching her drink, Mihee came to understand more than ever that all humans die. And that she didn't have long until she would meet her own demise. She felt her complicated thoughts emptying all at once. Her arms and legs ached, but those belonged to the realm of the body. As far as her mind went, it was as though her ice-cold brain was floating in crystalline cerebral fluid. She felt a sharp sense of clarity.

After quenching her thirst, Heeae breathed heavily. Mihee's guilt lessened as she watched Heeae's eyes regain their strength. She stood up and brought a pair of scissors from the kitchen. As she was cutting the cable ties one by one Ahnna said, "I thought about what Heeae said."

A short silence fell before she continued.

"I know I just went a little overboard, but she did make a good point. The police could arrive at any minute. We can't keep Yosep in a place like this. There's a chance that they might think that he took part in this nasty incident . . . Right? One of us has to take him with us. And keep everything that has happened here a secret."

"Who's gonna do that?" Mihee asked.

"Well, I suppose we have to discuss that . . ."

There was a hint of wishful thinking in Ahnna's voice; she seemed hopeful it'd be her. But then someone interjected with a small *ahem*. Mihee and Nami turned to where the voice came from and found Heeae sitting there.

"In any case . . . it shouldn't be someone who killed a person," Heeae muttered, rubbing at her swollen wrists. Mihee was worried that Ahnna might grab Heeae's hair again, but Ahnna only nodded with a wry smile.

"Yes, that'd be a problem. I'm really sorry about what happened. Even though it was a mistake, it still doesn't change the fact that I killed someone."

The unexpectedly quick concession flabbergasted the rest of the women.

"I just, I did it because I care about Yosep," Ahnna added. "I'm sure you all do, but I wanted to protect him, that's all."

She then buried her face in her palms and began to cry silently. *Should I console her?* Mihee wondered, but didn't dare move. Instead, Nami approached Ahnna and gently wrapped her arm around her shoulder. Ahnna looked up at her and smiled, before shooting up from her seat.

"What's wrong?" Nami asked, slightly unnerved by Ahnna's oddly bright expression.

"Just, you know. I thought we could have a drink before we talk things over," Ahnna said.

"Right now?"

"Yes, yes. This could be the last time we get the chance, it's making me emotional . . . No, it's okay, you don't need to help me. Just take a seat."

Ahnna brushed Nami off and went into the kitchen alone. After a cacophony of cabinet doors opening and glasses clinking, she brought out a tray. On it sat tiny shot glasses containing cognac, one for each woman. When Nami reached over to take one, Ahnna shook her head.

"No—since this will be our last drink together, let me hand you each a glass."

She distributed the glasses, from the left, one by one.

When the liquor warmed up in their hands, Ahnna began to speak.

"So, we're disbanding soon. Great work, everyone."

No one responded.

"Unfortunately, this is how things turned out, but we did our best, didn't we?"

Still no response.

"Yes. This is our last hurrah," she proclaimed. "We'll probably never see each other again, we four. But we were once comrades with the same goal. I told you the secret I could never tell anyone else. My love for Yosep. I trust that you feel the same. A lot has happened, but we made it this far, didn't we? Really, I don't regret a single thing. Even if

I could turn back time, I would still ask you to come to this mansion."

The other three remained silent. Ahnna paid no heed and continued her speech.

"Yes, it was really fun. Spending this past month with Yosep has been so, so much fun. I never knew that looking after and loving another human being could feel so nice. I'll never be this happy again. I hope you found the time we spent here just as meaningful. I'm sorry that things got a bit complicated and you got here later than planned."

Ahnna met Heeae's eyes and lowered her head slightly. Heeae averted her gaze. Ahnna cleared her throat a couple of times before raising her voice.

"Now then, let's end this whole thing as beautifully as we started it. Raise your glasses, everyone."

Geonbae. Ahnna muttered her cheers and held her glass in the air before downing the liquor all at once. Nami followed suit. Mihee wasn't planning to drink but ended up gulping down the alcohol with them.

It felt as if her eyeballs had spun around. The high alcohol content made her cough then her throat burned, and a leaden bell dinged in her skull before a faint aftertaste made it up to her nose. Mihee slapped her throat to swallow her saliva. Her eyes watered, but she didn't dislike the sensation. In just a moment, the pleasant tipsiness that would make this shitty situation bearable would take hold of her. As she waited for that moment to come, Mihee took a seat on the couch. Or rather, she tried, but slipped and fell.

God, what is wrong with me? Embarrassed, Mihee flailed

her arms around. She managed to just pull herself up to the edge of the couch, but her head kept spinning. She reached for the table to drink the remaining cold tea. The cup fell, even though her hand hadn't even touched it. She saw it rolling across the floor but couldn't will herself to grab it. Was the liquor too strong? Did she down it too quickly? Was this all happening because it had been too long since she'd last had a drink? Through her blurred vision, Mihee could see Ahnna chattering away, but her voice echoed as if they were in a cave. Mihee's face felt wet, so she rubbed at it and found that her nose was running. She was just so unbearably sleepy. As her senses grew weaker and weaker, Mihee held onto Ahnna's voice. After struggling to make out her mumbling, she could finally catch, "I'm sorry, I'm sorry."

Ahnna was muttering, justifying herself. "I'll save him. Save him from this place. It all went south, but him, at least he could stay pure for ever and ever . . ."

—

Mihee opened her eyes to find herself on the floor. How long had she been out? The dark mansion was shrouded in a faint bluish light. She was used to head-splitting hangovers, but the sensation of her scalp buzzing as if bruised was new. She felt her head and found that the right side was indeed swollen. Even after she took her hand away, a searing pain remained. She must have hit her head when she fell. Only after she got up did she realize she had slept on top of her own vomit. Considering how dry it was, it must have been quite a long time since she had fainted. Racking her rather uncooperative brain, she tried to figure out what had happened. Was there something wrong with the alcohol? Was everyone okay?

Staggering, Mihee grabbed at the backrest of the couch to help herself up. Something caught her foot, so she looked down and found Nami sleeping on the floor. Instead of bending over to wake her up, Mihee gave a swift kick to Nami's side.

"Nami," she called. "Nami, wake up."

Nami let out a low groan and blinked her eyes. Her dazed look seemed to suggest that she was as much in the dark about what had happened as Mihee was. Rubbing at the dried saliva on her cheek, Nami sat up, only to throw up what she had eaten. Mihee patted her back hastily and asked Nami, wiping her face, "Do you remember what happened?"

"No," Nami replied. "I had the drink . . . and just fell asleep, I think. What about the others?"

Only then did Mihee look around the living room. Despite her pulsing headache, she let out a scream upon realizing Heeae and Ahnna weren't there. Nami merely gawked at Yosep's door. Mihee's gaze followed after hers.

The door, which they had always made sure was closed, was ajar. Mihee stood in front of it as if she were getting sucked inside. To her disbelief, the slightest push from the tip of her finger opened it. Amid the dizzying vertigo, she saw Heeae sitting on the red carpet. With one hand on the bed and her head resting on it, Heeae looked as if she had fallen asleep while nursing. But she would never wake up from her slumber. Her other hand limp on the floor, the wound on that wrist, and the red dots scattered across the white wall like a decoration served as proof. As did the blood streaming toward the door, soaking the carpet.

The next thing Mihee noticed was a big hole in the floor. Even without peering down into it, both Mihee and Nami could tell it led to the basement. Ahnna would have left the mansion through this hole. How in the world did she know that it existed? When they had first arrived at the mansion and asked where to put Yosep, Ahnna had pointed to this room. Back then, they had been too exhausted to question her, so they simply followed her instructions. But Mihee had been thinking it was strange to pick this room when it was so close to the living room. Could this have been Ahnna's plan all along? To one day flee the mansion with Yosep, leaving everyone else behind?

But no matter how long she had planned her escape, it was obvious that it had only been partially successful. The evidence was on the bed. Mihee couldn't muster the courage to get near it. She merely stood close to the door, her whole body stiff. Nami lightly shoved her as she partly wrapped her arm around Mihee's shoulder and stepped on the blood-soaked carpet. Her feet turned red, like she had stepped on grapes, or as if they belonged to a pigeon. She seemed calm on the outside, but her hands were shaking as she lifted the sheet. Once the thin sheet was drawn away, the truth revealed itself. The two women discovered why Heeae had died, and why Ahnna had run away on her own.

Once upon a time, there were two women who claimed

that a child was theirs. To determine the truth, the wise king ordered that the child be split in two and for each woman to receive one half. One woman agreed, while the other changed her statement and wept that the child wasn't hers. *The baby's birth mother would never harm her child,* the king said, granting the baby to the sobbing woman. But you know, wouldn't some mothers rather rip their children apart with their own hands than lose them forever to someone else?

Staring at the blade stuck in Yosep's chest, Mihee imagined that was what had happened. The knife looked like a part of him. Leaving behind a life riddled with pain, Yosep looked more peaceful than ever. His face was clean, with nothing left in it. Those thin eyelashes would never again tremble. Those freckles would never again multiply under the sunlight. Those wet lips would never again sing.

Nami slowly knelt beside the bed. She gathered her hands covered in vomit and blood, lowered her head, and closed her eyes. Mihee thought she was smiling faintly, but when Nami opened her eyes, her face was devoid of expression. She grabbed Yosep's hand, which had slid out from under the sheet. After briefly hesitating, she kissed it and placed it back on his chest. Then she pulled the sheet over him, just as they had found him.

"It's over," Nami said and got up.

She was still faltering from her drowsiness but continued to walk toward the kitchen. Mihee thought Nami was going to wash her face. But a moment later, she came back out with the dead police officer's gun. Mihee's mouth hung open as Nami stood in front of her, with a shy smile that Mihee had never seen on her before.

"I was gonna kill myself," Nami began. "But I want to stay with Yosep a bit longer."

Mihee couldn't speak.

"How long do you think it'll take before he rots? I'd like to stay with him for as long as possible."

Nami's oddly innocent smile took Mihee aback.

"How could you?" she snapped.

"How could I what?"

"How could you be so . . . thoughtless . . ."

"Haven't I told you? Yosep and I are meant to be together, it's fate. Everything other than Yosep is just in my way."

Not that fate bullshit again. Listening to Nami's relentless nonsense made Mihee scoff.

Nami smiled and added, "I have a favor to ask."

"What?"

"I want to be with Yosep. For as long as humanly possible. So, could you please help me stop people from entering?"

"And how would I do that? With what means?"

"You could become my hostage."

"Your hostage?"

"I won't tie you up too tightly. You can just pretend that I'm holding you hostage. Then the police can't easily come in, since they'll think that I might harm you."

Mihee nodded. Even if she left, it's not like she had anything better to do.

"Then let me ask you for a favor in return," she said.

"What is it?"

"Give me the last bullet."

Nami seemed to understand what Mihee meant. She didn't ask any more questions and simply nodded. Upon the conclusion of the short contract, bitter laughter began to escape Mihee. At least that was how it started, but the laughter lasted a long while and didn't stop until tears were streaming down her face.

While Nami made a mask out of an empty sack, Mihee assembled a fake bind from a rope, with loose knots. The two worked together to set up a barricade, pushing a couch in front of the door and piling a few more chairs brought down from the second floor against it. They didn't stock up on food or fill water bottles. They both knew that it would be over soon enough. They weren't sad about that, exactly. Mihee couldn't speak for Nami, but she knew she was tired of waiting.

They cleaned the old hunting tools that had been hanging on the wall. Lining up the six shotguns that had only been used as decoration made their hearts race. Their retreat cut short, they felt like they had become rebels. Except they didn't know what and whom their fight was for, nor who they were fighting against.

The two women ate rice balls made from leftover rice. Sleep came over them once the sun set. Since the wait was lasting longer than they'd expected, they decided to take turns to be on lookout in the living room. When Mihee suggested that Nami rest first, Nami got up and headed to the guest room. After the door closed, faint murmurs trickled along the walls. To not overhear the whispers of a woman in love, Mihee turned on the radio. A Japanese man was mumbling over a tranquil piano. Even though she knew she wouldn't be able to decipher him, she paid close attention to his voice amid all the noise. After dozing off, she woke up to find the broadcast had ended, leaving only the static of the radio. When she turned off the power, everything went quiet. But something felt different.

Mihee got up and opened the terrace window. She carefully extended her hand, but nothing fell from the sky. Had it been a month? With the rain gone, the early morning sky was as beautiful as if she were seeing it for the first time. She glanced at an especially big and bright star. She kept her eyes on it until she couldn't see it anymore. The sky's bluish light soon became tinged with light gray, which brought in a few drops of rain again.

Time went on. Up the hill, a shadow stopped in front of the police officer's parked car. Nami came out to the living room and stuck her head outside the window. Then she fired a shot in the air. The shadow let out a short scream and rolled on the ground a few times before rushing down the hill.

"They'll be here soon," Nami said, lowering her gun.

As she said it, sirens wailed throughout the valley. Small lights multiplied, like when the squid-fishing boats were approaching land from far out to sea. *Pop*, a sound burst. Nami and Mihee moved away from the window and leaned against the wall. The loud noise ripped through their eardrums. They could hear a man's muffled voice through a loudspeaker.

"Police! You are surrounded."

"Here I go," Nami whispered, pulling the mask over her head.

At Nami's gunpoint, Mihee moved towards the window with her arms tied behind her back. She stood under light that felt like a ray of sun. She wasn't scared, but her body stiffened like an animal caught in headlights. When Nami pointed the gun at her head, Mihee nearly broke into laughter. As she clenched her teeth and forced a gloomy expression onto her face, she thought about the process by which a body decays under wet soil and becomes nourishment. Imagining green sprouts springing up from her remains, for the first time in her life Mihee felt useful. *Not too long now*, she thought. The fact that soon she would no longer have to endure being alive cheered her up. It delighted her.

After firing a few more shots, Nami returned to hiding behind the window. The rain had finally let up. The two had eaten nothing since the small rice balls the night before, but neither was hungry. Rather, sustaining themselves on nothing but water had made their minds much more lucid. The faint, lingering smell of gunpowder, the sound of raindrops hitting the ground, the murmurs of the police, the sticky heat billowing from their bodies, the scent of wet soil, the wriggling of the worms hiding underground, the flapping of the birds in the faraway sky, the drifting of heavy clouds—

all of that they could perceive. They could clearly sense that they were alive.

At 8:10 a.m., Nami fired the revolver she had borrowed from the dead police officer at another officer who tried to come up the entrance steps. It was a blank round. Lightly hurt from the gas pressure of the percussion, the officer shrieked and dropped to the ground before retreating. It was quiet for a while after that, until a young officer approached with hands in the air and attempted to strike up a conversation. He rambled at the two women with an unsolicited story about his hard life and asked how old Nami was, if she had family, and what had made her do all this. Nami ignored him, except when the officer pleaded that she should at least tell them what she wanted so that they could give it. To that, she merely answered: she just didn't want to leave here. Mihee knew that by "here," Nami meant Yosep's side, but the police understood it as Nami claiming ownership of the house she had illegally taken over. Later, when the public discovered that Heeae had worked as a housekeeper for the mansion's owner and Mihee and Nami were only middle-school grads, and a Gangnam cafe part-timer and an orphan, respectively, their crime was interpreted by some as a disturbance caused by a couple of female gangsters, and by others as a political action. No one listened to Nami's confession, where she claimed everything had stemmed from love.

At 11:45 a.m., Nami fired a live bullet at the police approaching the window again. The bullet grazed an officer's calf, ripping through his pants, and left a burn mark. The police retreated again. Nami stuck her upper body out of the window and fired three warning shots in a row. It was a gesture to show off how many bullets they had, but they only had one left that they could use. Leaning against the wall, Nami sat wordlessly. Mihee thought now would be the right time to ask.

"How many bullets do we have left?"

Even though Nami should have known it was a rhetorical question, she kindly replied, "One."

"Then it's over."

Nami handed Mihee the revolver without saying anything more. Mihee grinned and sprang to her feet. Seeing a silhouette holding a gun flashed across the window, the police mistook Mihee for Nami and held up the loudspeaker again.

"What do you want?" they shouted.

The question made Mihee think. *What I want is* . . .

She dramatically marched to the front of the window. She could see the vast sky and windy mountain ridges. The clouds cleared away, and the sharp sunlight of noon pierced through her. Gazing at the dumbfounded looks on the policemen's faces under the sun, Mihee thought to herself: *As if there even is such a thing, you dumbasses.*

Mihee flashed her teeth in a wide grin. She aimed the gun at herself.

Birds flew from the highest branches. Raindrops dangling from the leaves splattered down. With Mihee's body falling to the ground as the signal, the police commenced their tactical solution. They fired water cannons, and the wooden mansion—the ancient, beautiful, and exotic mansion that had seemingly been dropped from the sky—began to fall apart. The windows were smashed, and the fierce streams of water soaked the two women's heads and shoulders. Nami thought that the splitting and spouting water looked like the fingers of a giant. She was envious of her parents for having died on the same day at the same time. But any moment now, someone was going to pull her out and bite off her head. She was going to follow Yosep into the forever kingdom. But—

. . . . . .
. . . . . .
. . . . . .
. . . . . .

Fuck, why am I not there?

When the police squad broke down the door, they were met with Nami on her knees, soaking wet with both arms spread wide open, and Mihee taking weak breaths. A few officers quickly transported Mihee to the nearest hospital, while the others subdued Nami. They suspected she might resist, but she didn't scream even when her arms were twisted behind her back. The well-trained police force swiftly searched the mansion. They couldn't find anything suspicious amid the furniture covered in white sheets or inside the dust-filled rooms. They wondered: *What was this woman doing here? Why did she hold out against us, and what was she protecting with her gun?*

As their curiosity deepened, the squad's newest recruit

spotted a door near the living room. Somehow, no one had noticed it as they were combing through all the bathrooms, closets, and even a secret storage space below the kitchen floor. The door was there for all to see, so how come no one else had thought to open it? The recruit grew suspicious and grabbed the doorknob, and Nami, who'd remained docile until that point, started shrieking as if she had lost her mind. It has to be there. There must be something in that room. With conviction and determination, the police kicked down the locked door despite Nami's hysterical screaming. And that was when they saw it.

The room was covered in blood. In that little bloody-red agora, surrounded by four walls covered with taxidermied animals as gorgeous as the nobles' heads hung by angry mobs in the olden days, a dead woman was leaning against a bed as if to block off intruders. Some present at the scene say they saw a decapitated head on a silver plate, while some alleged they saw a naked corpse with a hole in its rib cage. Others claim to have seen a corpse with its chest split open, with a grayed, desiccated heart wrapped in cotton sitting right next to it. However, when one brave police officer walked up to the bed and lifted the bedsheet, he found an exquisitely decorated mannequin. "What the—?" everyone cried in disbelief. "All this panic because of this mere fake?"

Despite their brief confusion, they soon learned—and would later publicly disclose—that Nami was hallucinating due to the magic mushrooms the women had eaten and drunk as tea. Parts of what Nami rambled about to the police **about contained some truth. Thanks to her statement, the** police released dogs to hunt down the missing accomplice. After searching deep within the mountains for two days, they eventually found Ahnna in an underground tunnel, slowly dying from hypothermia, which concluded the case for the time being.

As I later learned, Ahnna's plan all along had been to kill her co-conspirators and flee to North Korea. But the series of unforeseen fights and murders, which transpired before the rat poison she had laced their food with could take effect, had pushed her to escape as soon as possible. It wasn't hard for her to deceive the boy, who was suffering from amnesia, that she was his mother and persuade him to run away with her. But her accomplices hadn't died as planned, even after she had slipped the rat poison and sleeping pills into their drinks. As it turns out, rodenticides these days are chronic and are mostly benign for humans, but an upper-class lady like Ahnna had no reason to know this and had made a vain attempt based on outdated information. On her part, staging a stabbed mannequin to buy her some time had been the right choice. If it hadn't been for the dummy, Heeae likely would not have taken her own life, and Ahnna's former collaborators would have scoured the entire mountain looking for her. Her efforts still went down the drain, though, because after she'd dozed off in the tunnel, the boy had vanished without a trace.

Thanks to her swift hospital admission, Mihee narrowly survived surgery and earned a new life. However, her lovely face had been destroyed, rendered unrecognizable. People lamented her lost beauty, but Mihee didn't really mind that.

Instead, what anguished her was her good fortune at having been excluded from the high fatality rate of handgun suicide. Two months later, in the middle of the night, she would finally rest in peace after sneaking out of the ward and jumping off the hospital roof. Her suicide resulted in the demotion of the police officer who was assigned to guard her, which started another cycle of misery as the aggrieved officer—who ended up retiring and starting his own business after his cousin pressed him to turn his crisis into opportunity—eventually went bankrupt and killed himself along with the rest of his family. But I don't think we can blame Mihee for that. After all, the dead can't foresee the future. And even if no one punished her, her life was already miserable enough.

I realize you probably find the series of events detailed so far highly peculiar. But what I find truly strange is Yosep's existence itself. I'd also like your opinion on the matter.

Do you think such a beautiful boy actually existed? In reality? They say love is mighty, but do you really believe it could be so strong it wouldn't shatter even after a month of cleaning feces?

I started having these doubts when I discovered something strange about what had happened at the reservoir on the day Yosep was kidnapped. Retracing their steps, I parked my car on the roadside and went down to the reservoir just like they had. Even as a fast walker, it took me over thirty minutes to get through the bushes. Back then, they would have had to locate Yosep's car, and since they had relied on a single flashlight, it surely would have taken them at least twice the time. I've heard it takes as little as ten minutes to kill yourself by burning charcoal in a car. Weird, right? They claimed they'd managed to break the window to rescue Yosep, still breathing.

To resolve this inconsistency, I made several assumptions. Maybe Yosep didn't light the charcoal properly. Or maybe there was a leak even after he had tried to seal off the car. As my imagination unfurled, I finally arrived at a chilling possibility.

Maybe Yosep had already been dead to begin with. To forget the shock, the women could have self-induced a collective hallucination, indescribable with mere mushrooms and such, and to revive in their minds, superimposed a soul of their liking onto his dead body. You might be wondering, are you suggesting that they fell in love with a corpse? In fact, I believe that corpses are easier to tolerate than living humans. Because the dead don't change. It's also not impossible to preserve a decaying corpse. Remember how Ahnna kept wiping Yosep's body with alcohol rather than water? She kept doing it just so she could keep touching him, but I think this unintentionally prevented the bacteria from propagating and mummified his remains. It's not complete nonsense. There are a few cases in Korea as well where neatly preserved bodies were discovered after their caretakers' deaths or arrests. There might be someone out there enjoying a silent tryst with their dead lover. Human minds are like rooms behind thick, closed curtains. What happens inside them remains forever a mystery.

But the women swore that Yosep was alive then. Even

though they'd forgotten about the passage of time during their mildly hallucinatory retreat into the mansion, they insisted that they really had stroked Yosep's head, spoon-fed him soup, and changed and washed his dirty sheets. I always strive for the truth, and after much contemplation, I concluded that what they said must be true. Well, it's the only plausible conclusion. If they're wrong, that would mean that the corpse that lay next to Ahnna—who had fallen asleep trembling in the cold—must have walked out of the underground tunnel on its own and disappeared.

Nami and Ahnna, the two survivors, were brought to trial. Though Yosep had vanished without a trace, two dead bodies remained in the basement freezer, earning the two women prison sentences. Given the defendants' complicated circumstances and their feeble minds, people expected a prolonged trial, but the court made a surprisingly swift ruling. Nami was sentenced to life, while Ahnna was to serve fifteen years. Her mental illness helped her receive a reduced sentence. After fulfilling one-third of it she was released on a special pardon and left the country under wraps, never to return. But this happened many years after our story takes place; no one knows what the women thought when their sentences were handed down that Christmas Eve at the turn of the twenty-first century. Maybe they calmly accepted reality or fell into insurmountable despair, but no matter what their circumstances, time flew by, and a new year began. When that year ended, another year came. The gate to the new millennium flung wide open to cheers and fireworks at the Bosingak pavilion, ushering in a bright and hopeful future and cementing the previous century as the past, which only necrophiles would reminisce about.

Now, you must be wondering where I learned all of this. A woman sent me letters that told the story. She didn't write a single word about discovering her pregnancy through a pre-imprisonment physical examination or about raising a child behind bars for eighteen months. She never asked or became curious about how her daughter was doing in the outside world, if she had a good appetite, got along with her foster family, or had started to talk. Instead, she tirelessly wrote about a boy and the things that had happened between them. The woman had a certain conviction. A conviction that the recipient of these letters, no matter how melancholy or angry, would never tear them, burn them, or flush them down the toilet, but instead enshrine them in her halls of memory for ever. I detested that confidence of hers and tried several times to destroy the letters, only to fail, and the woman got exactly what she wanted. Miserably so, per my mother's wish.

Yes, that's right. I'm the only child of Yosep, your beloved.

I understand you may find it hard to believe. I also don't know how I escaped the attention of the despicable news media. It's probably because no one wanted to believe me. Or maybe they thought it was unnecessarily cruel to reveal the deceased was a rape victim. Sometimes, I wonder: wouldn't Father have woken up at least once during the intercourse that presumably happened dozens of times? Considering the circumstances, it's an undeniable fact that Father copulated with all the women in the mansion, including my mother—please don't get mad. Stay with me here. I'm not trying to blame Father like those pathetic men who obsess over women's virginity. Incapacitated, and with no other forms of entertainment available, maybe he secretly awaited the women's visits, even if he might have mistaken them for succubi.

But even if he was bored out of his mind, I find it strange that he had intercourse with women who were so messed up. Not only emotionally but physically as well. Biology aside, how could he possibly look at those women and feel love? Aren't men more hopeless with their bodies than women, who are more proficient at feigning pleasure in bed? Besides, men like Father who experienced trauma during boyhood tend to be almost impotent, don't they? Gloomy boys exposed too early to the world of grown-ups are often put off by the scent of a woman's flesh.

Then, last night, while watching a video clip from Father's golden days in preparation for today, I found the answer to my questions.

The video was a recording from his one and only concert. In it, Father seemed a little anxious but lively, just like the women who must have forgotten him by now. Father did his best to dance and smile, but in all honesty, the production was disorganized and tedious enough to put me to sleep. The stage, which screamed of cutting corners, wasn't even worth getting mad over, and Father's outfit was so shabby it looked like he was wearing rags. With the volume down, my thoughts darted in every direction. I stared at my own reflection on the dark screen, until I spotted a woman coming up on the stage. I rewound the video to find out what was going on. There was a contest where the prize was a photo with Father, and the woman was the lucky winner. I straightened and turned up the volume.

Was she even twenty at the time? The woman, who couldn't look Father in the eye and continued to weep from the moment she emerged from the audience, wasn't exactly a stunning beauty. Rather, she was plain, like someone you would run into on the train every morning but never remember her face. However, as she stood on the stage with tears streaming down her cheeks, she exuded a certain power that drew people's attention. In other words, she made everyone look at her by not looking at Father.

The emcee tried to engage with her several times, but the woman merely wept. Sweating, the emcee tried to keep things light with some jokes. There were murmurs from the crowd. The camera panned to Father's face. His hair was glistening with light sweat. His cheeks were flushed and his eyelids were wet. Father smiled awkwardly at the woman, who refused to look at him, and, tightly pressing his lips, faced the audience.

Then countless lights greeted him.

Myriads of dots, as captivating as stars and as sticky and disgusting as frogspawn.

The moment I saw Father's face—tinged with pity, loneliness, slight affection, and a peculiar sadness for mortal beings—I realized that, unlike those women, his body had meant nothing to him. Father had resigned himself to distributing his meaningless, bound-to-decay body to wretched women who could only satisfy their hunger with his flesh and their thirst with his blood. After this epiphany, I felt at peace, as if enveloped in a massive body of light. My father was a saint. A Holy Boy, who resolved to love no one yet loved everyone.

It's such a pity that he's left no blood legacy behind him. Yes, I am his daughter, genetically speaking. But I don't mean on a superficial level, I'm talking about something more substantial. I'm only my mother's daughter. No, I'm closer to my mother's clone, to be precise. You can see it for yourself. I'm standing right before your eyes. Ugly, right? I don't look anything like Father, do I? Sometimes, women around my mother's age gawk at me as they pass me on the street. In those moments, I grimace and think to myself: This person knows. Even if she doesn't remember who she's seeing, she's undoubtedly seeing someone in me. Of course, that someone is my mother. It's not exactly a good thing, since my mother was ugly. Ugly to the point where you'd think, Who would risk having a child with such a woman? No wonder she tried to abduct her mate.

My mother passed away last year. She had cancer, and by the time it was discovered it was too late. The last letter she sent me recounted near-death experiences she seemingly copied from her mysticism books. Rivers, or flower gardens; it varies from person to person, but the places people travel to in a near-death experience make them feel relieved and at peace—as if surrounded by pure light, she wrote. Beneath the accounts, she confessed she'd been to a similar place herself one night. Somewhere by a river, with the sound of water flowing and soft sunlight grazing the grass. Next to my mother, watching the light melting between her fingers, was Yosep, in all his pristine beauty. Mother put fresh green grapes into Yosep's mouth. As she shoved the eyeball-sized grapes one by one in his mouth, she saw a teardrop running down Yosep's cheek. When she woke from her dream, she wrote:

Yosep, we have finally met.

But what good is it if you don't love me even there?

Since I was born into this world, I must be bound for that field full of flowers. When I think about that, I'm incredibly relieved and find it fortunate that I was born only as my mother's daughter. Because if Father's child were to die, my mother would certainly lose herself in grief.

Author's Note

1

One winter, I saw a diamond bird
I had never seen anything so beautiful and wanted to have it at all costs
I slit my stomach open and offered it a black, lustrous, red jewel
I opened my chest to make a white, sturdy birdcage
My happiness spread like fire

One morning, I opened my eyes
The diamond bird had melted away
People laughed at me
You're fooled
There was never a diamond bird
And you were holding onto an ice bird, someone said
But the birdcage remains here and reminds me of the shape of the bird
As a pickled cucumber remembers the summer sunlight
As a sliced carrot remembers a rabbit's stomach

Fondling the empty cage, I say
For such a beautiful thing I could do anything

—

That water turning into trickling urine is a secret to the bird
That the bird had never entered the birdcage is a secret to myself

2

This novel was first published in a series from April to June 2021 on the webzine *Weekly Munhakdongne*. The title is after Yumiko Kurahashi's *Holy Girl* (聖少女/Seishōjo). The first murder scene has a reworded quote from Ryūnosuke Akutagawa's *The Spider's Thread* (蜘蛛の糸/Kumo no ito). For the conversation of Taeyeong's parents, I have referred to "A Study on the Gay Sexuality in the 1940s in Korean Society" by Bak Gwan-su.

I would like to express my deep gratitude to Editor Jeong Eunjin for always looking after my work. Thank you to the Munhakdongne editorial department and Ms. Oh Eun-gyo for your recommendation.

Thank you for reading this book.

Fall 2021
Lee Heejoo

—

After watching the police all day, Hwang thought there were no more spectacles left to look at. But when he took another look, he saw a grown man sitting in a parked Grandeur, weeping over the steering wheel. Hwang didn't hide his curiosity. Watching the man intently, he thought, *What a pity, that guy looks swell. A girl must have dumped him, huh?* As he stared at the car for a while, he noticed something was off. The window on the driver's side was shattered. Was that why the man was crying? What a fucking nutjob. Hwang smacked his lips and dragged on his slippers. *Gotta tell Hyejin. When is that girl coming out, though?* He squatted on a wheel stopper and bit into the cigarette filter, sing-songing. *When are you gonna come out, Hyejin? When? Your oppa's gonna die waiting. Come on out already, Hyejin-ahh.*

Not too far away.
 Ok was walking along an empty beach after everyone had left, all by herself.
 The waves were licking the shells as white as bones. The ocean itself didn't rot but corroded everything. The lonely ocean. The ocean that eats into everything. The salty wind

tickled her face like dried saliva. Ok gently scratched her cheek as she walked on the sand hardened by rain. The sun above the sea glittered, emanating soft light that resembled shattered glass, but the waves arriving at the beach, exhausted travelers that they were, lost their tempers and splashed white foam.

Ok walked from one end of the beach to the other. As she paced back and forth, she spotted a rock she hadn't seen before. When she approached, she found a pale boy who had drifted ashore like a dead mermaid. She waved away the tiny bugs that had gathered around him, and pulled away the sticky seaweed entangled with his arms and legs. Then she pressed her ear against his bony chest. Thump, thump, thump. Just like a conch shell harboring the sound of the sea, the boy's heart reverberated with the low and distant sound of a drum.

The ocean waves soaked Ok's dress blue.

Under the moonlight, she caressed the boy's face and whispered:

Oppa, you are finally here.

Translator's Note

Do you have a Holy Boy of your own?

I can talk about mine for days on end—how I first saw him one summer in a Los Angeles stadium brimming with thousands, how an inexplicable thrill shot up my spine when the crowd broke into a fan chant during the climax of the song, and how, even to this day, he never fails to amaze me with his talent, effort, grace, kindness, and, above all, his beauty. I also confess that as much as I want everyone to celebrate him with me, I sometimes daydream of one day becoming his Mary Magdalene, cradling him in my arms alone when the rest of the world deserts him.

I believe—and can even prove—that my devotion to my Holy Boy is what led me to translate an idol-kidnapping novel by one of the very few Korean authors who so unflinchingly explores the essence of love. After all, isn't that what all fateful encounters do? Irreversibly alter and determine the course of your life?

If you, too, have your own miraculous, awe-inspiring Holy Boy, you may easily spot little pieces of yourself in the four women who drive this novel. The follow-up to her award-winning debut novel *Phantom Pain*, *Holy Boy*'s unvarnished depiction of female fans' fierce and unapologetic love for their male idols solidified Lee Heejoo's fame in South Korea. Though on the surface it might strike readers as just another tale of twisted adoration, it is crucial to understand the historical events referenced in the book to fully appreciate its depth.

In one of the book's early scenes, Mihee and a man on the road discuss the Bee Gees' song "Holiday" and a newsbreaking hostage situation. They are in fact referring to a famous 1988 jailbreak incident in which Ji Kang Hun and three fellow inmates escaped from prison and took a family hostage. Denouncing the unfair justice system that subjected him to a long sentence for his petty crime, Ji proclaimed on live television, "There's one law for the rich and another for the poor." During his final standoff with the police, he requested a cassette tape of "Holiday," a tune that subsequently played on every television in the country. He was shot by the police and later died at a hospital.

Even though Ji was a convicted criminal, his words continue to resonate across contemporary Korean history. Particularly in the late 1990s, the decade in which the novel is set, the IMF currency crisis devastated the national economy and eroded public trust in capitalism and the legal system. The four women in *Holy Boy*, like Ji's four-member crew, take matters into their own hands and act on their socially unacceptable yet deeply human desires.

The novel's hostage situation also draws upon the 1972 Asama-Sansō incident. In Japan, five United Red Army

(URA) members took a lodgekeeper's wife hostage, leading to a ten-day standoff with the police. The incident prompted deeper investigation into the group, which revealed the brutal purge of their own ranks in the name of ideological integrity, which inspired the overarching question of *Holy Boy*: when human beings are completely consumed by something—be it ideology, beauty, or love—where does that lead them?

After immersing ourselves in the novel's most dizzying twists and turns, it is only in its final section that we are reminded that this entire story may be nothing but the imagination of a woman who dubiously claims to be Yosep's daughter. The mansion in the mountains where the kidnapping takes place is also described as resembling a film set, suggesting that the whole narrative is merely a "fiction." In our fantasies, our Holy Boys (and Girls, respectively) can become anything, and even offer themselves as our daily bread; these delusions are what sustain our reality and make it more bearable.

Since that summer day in the Los Angeles stadium, whenever I face a challenge that flusters me—struggling to write a Translator's Note for the first time in my life, for instance—I imagine my Holy Boy taking a break between his grueling dance practices or dozing off in a van on his way to a photo shoot. Those quiet, vulnerable moments he can never share with his fans are what eventually build up who he is on the stage. Imagining those utterly human sides of him often gives me the strength to keep going and the hope to achieve something greater than myself. Here's my heartfelt thanks to my Holy Boy and to all other Holy Boys and Girls out there, who allow us to live more freely in our fantasies and more courageously in our realities.

Joheun Lee
June 2025, Shanghai